Seeders

Seeders

Christopher McMaster

Southern Skies Publications

ISBN: 978-1-99-116014-0 (paperback)
        978-1-99-116015-7 (Epub)

www.southernskiespublications.com

First Printing, 2022

For Claudia and Natasha, who put up with a dad talking about the stars and watched sci-fi on the television with him without too much complaint

CONTENTS

Planting

The flier lifted smoothly off the runway and ascended, as if a destination were the last thing on its mind. The island of Pounamu had a mountain range running down its spine, far enough north in latitude and high enough in elevation to have snow on the peaks. Story had it the island was a gift. Or a bribe. From what he'd heard of the man, Peter didn't think either was necessary, or necessarily true. The name was a give-away. *Te Wai Pounamu*, the waters of greenstone, was a large island with a mountain range running down its spine, just like the South Island of New Zealand. The island's main city grew smaller in the distance.

"*Ootautahi,*" Peter said quietly.

He pursed his lips as he made the first sound, 'ohr'. Practiced the second sound by pressing his tongue to the roof of his mouth and pulling it back, then sharply touching his palette again before breathing out. He liked how his tongue danced around his mouth as he said the word.

"Ohr-toe-tah-hee," he repeated.

This name was what Jens' birthplace was called in the Māori language, the original inhabitants of that place. It was also called Christchurch in the colonizer's tongue. Peter loved languages, and he preferred the melody of the original to the harsher English name.

The question wasn't whether the island was a gift or a bribe. Peter wondered if the man was homesick, or just sentimental. And Peter knew it could also be neither. Naming new places after old is what we do when we move. We bring old names with us. York—New York. Hampshire—New Hampshire. Maine. London. Lisbon. Moscow. There were dozens of towns and cities named after those places scattered across North America, brought by generations of immigrants. And the Pacific migration: Rarotonga. Ruatorea. Whanganui. Hawaii. Those names traced ancient routes across the largest ocean on Earth. Maybe that's all he was doing—continuing a naming tradition, taking it across space, regardless of what the original inhabitants called those places, originals who were long gone. At least physically. After studying the ruins of that ancient civilization for the last few years, he felt there should be more acknowledgement of the old names. But his was a minority view. To the new settlers this was their planet, regardless of who or what was here before them.

He gazed out the window with his thoughts. Peter could see the resemblance between islands. He asked the flight program to take him higher and the computer obeyed. Peter gazed down on the leeward side of the island, drier than the land below him, plains levelling to the sea. Large estates carved their signatures into the land, rectangles of fertile crops dissected by irrigation canals. The settlers' attempt at social ecology, a relationship between the environment and the people in it. From this distance it didn't look any different than the domination practiced on old Earth before climate disasters changed all that. Large stretches of land making up farms below. Rectangles seen from flier windows. Then again, there was much more land here, much more space, unpopulated for centuries. And he had been here long enough to know that looks can be deceiving, and that life on the ground was much different. Peter knew that there was no doubt a myriad of plant species working together in the rectangle, as well as a collective of settlers. Polyculture in the fields—different varieties working together, attracting insects for pollination, protecting crops from others, feeding into the soil what another takes or needs. Same for the settlers, Peter mused, coming from all over Earth, and the colonies, and collectively building a new world.

Peter instructed the flier to return to its pre-programmed course along the greener, windward side of the island. After another hour of flight, he saw the peninsula jutting out and curving in, like a protective arm shielding the shore. It was a beautiful natural harbor. The flier vibrated as the landing pontoons lowered. The sea grew closer as it descended, skimming above the water until gently touching down. Peter leaned forward as the craft slowed, unbuckled his strap and collected his bag as it maneuvered to the jetty.

Once the machine was satisfied it was secure, the entry hatch opened. Peter stepped out and onto the wooden jetty. The door closed behind him and the flier powered down, not needed until his flight back. He walked past a large power boat on the left, and an old-fashioned sailing boat on the right. He stopped to admire the craft. He had seen many at sea and in the harbors. On this ocean world it was a popular pastime, as well as mode of transport for those in no hurry.

"There's nowhere else to go," was a common retort. *"Why hurry?"*

They had a point. Peter smiled as he read the name painted on the bow. *Cirrus.* Maybe the old man was sentimental after all, naming his yacht after the ship where it all started, a space freighter as elegant in design as a shoe box. This *Cirrus* was much shapelier. He rapped the side with his knuckles and smiled. Made out of wood. He looked forward to the promised sail.

Peter walked up the jetty, stepped onto a gravel footpath and up stone stairs to the house. He knocked on the door and waited. An old-fashioned custom, but everything seemed old-fashioned in this place. The wooden veranda that surrounded the house was something out of another century, but somehow fitted the surroundings. Green forest surrounded the property. Peter turned his back to the door and looked out at the blue ocean stretching to the horizon. Ocean everywhere, starting out as turquoise near the shore and becoming a darker blue as the waters deepened. A water world. What a find. The only planet in the known galaxy, aside from Earth, able to support life.

The door opened and Peter turned around. There he was, the man himself. He looked shorter than in the movies, even average height. His hair was greying, white at the temples. His sunburnt face told of a life outdoors. Slim. Fit. Who wouldn't be fit in this environment? Peter knew he was the same age as his own father, but he didn't look as old. He stared at Peter with clear blue eyes as a moment, then two, passed.

"Dr Taylor," he finally said, offering a hand. "Please come in."

"Ambassador Jensen," Peter replied. "It is an honor."

"Please, call me Jens," he said. "Ambassador ... I haven't been called that in a long time. Fran," he called into the house. "Our guest is here."

Peter followed Jens through the door and into an open plan living area. A woman slightly younger than Jens, and who held her age even better, approached wiping her hands on an apron.

"Captain Lu," Peter said, bowing.

"Enough with the titles," she said. "Merely captain of the kitchen now—"

"Of the house," Jens interrupted.

"Never mind that," she said. "Welcome."

Peter took her outstretched hand. She held it firmly. "Thank you for coming. He doesn't get many visitors up here," she said before letting go.

"Thank you, thank you both, for allowing me to come," he said. "And call me Peter." He admired the interior of their home. "You have a wonderful place."

"Thank you," Fran said. "We started it as soon as we returned. We brought back plans and milling equipment."

"I set up a milling cooperative down the coast," Jens added.

"As I was saying," Fran continued. "We built it together. By hand. It was a very grounding experience. Literally."

Jens smiled at the memory. "Well, Peter, sit down and relax. I hope beer is okay."

Peter followed Jens and sat down on a chair that seemed to swallow him. He ran an appreciative hand over the surface.

"It feels like real leather," he said.

"It is," Jens answered. "Real. From a tannery on Xin Taibei. About four hundred kilometers that way." Jens indicated out the window, in a south west direction across an empty sea.

"Cattle have taken wonderfully to the climate. It's a very niche market, but has its following." He smiled as Peter shifted in his seat.

"Comfortable?"

"I've never sat on real leather," Peter admitted.

"You get used to it," Jens said. "I thought you might see more of that. Earth slipping back into bad habits."

"She has. Some," Peter said. "Not that one though."

"Would you like to sit elsewhere?" Jens asked.

"No," Peter lied. "I'm fine."

A small dark-haired child approached Peter with a plate filled with misshapen candies. Peter could see faint remnants of both Fran and Jens in the child's face. The girl lifted the plate towards him.

"Oh," he said. "No thank you."

"She is sharing with you," Jens said, inclining his head.

Peter smiled at the girl. "Actually, I changed my mind. I think this is just what I want." He reached over to the plate and picked up an orange-colored candy. Her eyes followed the treat from plate to fingers and lingered expectantly. Peter placed it in his mouth.

"*Xiexie*," he said around it, almost exhausting his Mandarin vocabulary. "Thank you! This is so good."

"Well done, Jiao," Jens said as she carried the plate back the kitchen.

"Grandchild?" Peter asked.

"She is usually very shy," Jens said. "She must like you."

"I'm honored," Peter said. "And thank you again for agreeing to speak with me about the Ruan."

Jens looked up sharply and shook his head. "Not here," he said.

Fran brought two tall glasses of beer and stood between the two men. She looked down at them as she held the glasses. "You can see our guest is uncomfortable on that disgusting chair," she said to Jens. "Nobody likes that chair, Peter, even Jens. He only had it made for his friend Poara who visits sometimes. He lives in the Western Hemisphere."

"Poara Maniapoto? The Chemist?" Peter asked. "Who designed GLR?"

"He'd say he was only part of the team," Jens said.

"Why don't you two sit on the veranda and enjoy these?" Fran said. "And quit teasing Peter. Nobody likes to sit on that grotesque piece of furniture."

"Poara likes it!" Jens protested.

"Has he actually told you that? I didn't think so," Fran said. "Follow me, Peter." She carried the glasses outside without waiting for a reply and pushed the door open with her foot. The two men exchanged glances, stood and followed. Fran set the beer on a small table between two chairs that faced out to sea.

Jens picked up his glass and took a sip. "Finest on Pemako," he said. "At least it's my favorite. Really hoppy. Brewed on the west coast."

"As soon as you stow your gear, we'll have some lunch. Then we can take her out," he said, looking at the jetty below. "You'll see some amazing coastline, and we'll talk out there. Do you get sea sick?"

"I don't know," Peter answered. "I've never sailed before."

Jens bit his lip. "Crash course then," he said. "There's some tincture on board if you start to feel queasy. Fran swears by it. There's a really nice anchorage just around the north cape we can stop at, and the winds will be perfect for guiding us back home tomorrow."

"She's a beautiful boat. Was she built here?" Peter asked.

"On Pounamu? No. But the wood is from the mountains behind us," Jens said. "It's a species of hard wood that can grow to up to a hundred meters. I contracted a ship builder on Jongnag, really skilled builder—"

"I know Jongnag," Peter said. "I spent several months at the remains there."

"And you didn't sail?" Jens asked. "Everybody seems to have a boat there."

"Not doctoral students with deadlines and meager scholarships, I'm afraid," he answered.

The door opened and a small face peeked out. "*Wucan*," Jiao said before disappearing back inside.

"Lunch is ready," Jens translated. He gulped the last of his beer. "We'd better not keep the ladies waiting."

They followed Jiao into the dining area. She climbed onto

a chair at the table filled with plates of grilled vegetables. Peter and Jens joined her. The little girl sat smiling at the guest.

"*Maorongrong de lian*!" she giggled.

"In English, dear," Jens said.

"Hairy face!" she said.

Peter laughed and pulled at his beard with his fingers. Jiao glanced at her grandfather, who nodded, and she reached out her hand. Peter leaned in and let her grab a fist full. She let go and giggled again.

"Not at the table," Fran said as she set down a bowl of rice. She smiled at Jiao as she spooned some rice onto the girl's plate.

"*Xiexie*," she said. Her grandmother looked at her.

"We'll speak English because Peter doesn't know very much Mandarin," Fran told her.

"She's quite the linguist," Peter said.

"Jens is trying to teach her some Spanish, but I think it is just confusing her," Fran said.

"She's picking it up nicely," Jens protested.

"I understand you are a linguist, Peter. And congratulations on your degree," Fran said, moving away from what Peter took to be an ongoing disagreement.

"A xeno-linguist, actually," Peter said. "I study the language of the Originals," he said, glancing at Jens and receiving a look that conveyed permission to continue. "From the little traces we have found. The remains leave nothing as large as what was found on the ship—" Peter glanced at Jens and steered his explanation back to ground. "But the ruins here have produced some promising traces. Digital recordings we can decipher."

Fran indicated the food on the table and Peter filled his plate. "They were an advanced civilization so didn't carve their writing into stone, which would have been very helpful. At least if they did, we haven't found any. But the finds at Jongnag added some key samples. My whole study was based on those. Well, a very little portion of those."

"And you worked with Patricia?" Fran asked.

"Patricia?" Peter's look of confusion caused Jens to laugh.

"Dr Lin," he said.

"Patricia," Peter repeated. "I've worked with her for four years and never knew that was her given name. I thought it was—"

"Lu Er," Jens said. "Very few people know she is also called Patricia. I'd recommend not using it until she invites you."

"I won't," Peter said.

"It must have been wonderful working with her," Fran said.

"It was ... wonderful," Peter said, deciding that was the most diplomatic word to use. Frustrating, infuriating, humiliating, exhilarating, exacting—all were candidates, depending on circumstance and time. But ultimately, he had to agree with Fran.

"So, you can speak their language?" Jens asked.

"Oh, I don't think anybody can do that. Yet. There's some clever folks trying to collate everything we know into a translation program, but that's still in development." He looked at Jiao and winked. "This one could probably do it," he said, watching her lick soya sauce from her fingers. She tried to wink back, squeezing both her eyes shut.

"My study was only focused on grammar," Peter said. "Very narrowly focused. A doctorate is much more of a research apprenticeship than anything else. It doesn't really matter what it is about, as long as you learn the trade. There are some pretty obscure research topics out there, though. Silly, even."

"Patricia wouldn't spend her time on anything silly, or around anybody who did," Jens said.

"That is very true," Peter said.

Fran stood and started to collect empty plates. "Sit down," she told Peter as he tried to rise and help. "Do you two want another beer?" she asked.

"Not before we sail, thanks," Jens answered.

"Which is why I set up the coffee machine," Fran said.

"Let me show you where you can stash what you won't be bringing," Jens said. "Or, a better idea—Jiao, can you show Peter where he will stay when we get back?"

Jiao smiled and jumped off her seat. She grabbed Peter's hand and pulled him down the hall.

"Are you going to be alright?" Fran asked, once Peter and Jiao were out of the room.

"I'll be fine," Jens said. "He just wants to talk."

"It's more than that, and you know it," she said. "You don't have to talk about anything you don't want to."

"I know," Jens said. "And I won't."

Fran brought in a cup of coffee, set it in front of Jens and placed a hand on his shoulder. "It's a lovely day for a sail," she said.

"Every day is a lovely day for a sail," he answered on cue.

2

"By running the line through the cleat and back to the boat we can release from the deck," Jens told Peter. "Just keep the line on the deck cleat in this 's', see? That's 'stand by'. It stops us from leaving before we're ready, and won't slip out of your hand." He looked at Peter's face and knew most of what he was saying was lost.

"When I say, 'release', all you do is take the line off the cleat and pull the other end of it," he said.

"Okay," Peter answered.

"Which line are you going to pull?" Jens asked.

Peter pointed.

"That's right," Jens said. "Stand by."

Peter looked at the lines on the deck.

"That's the 's' thing," Jens said. "Just undo it until ... that's it. Hold it there until I call."

Jens went back to the cockpit and readied the stern line. "Release!" he called, pulling his line in. He slowly reversed the yacht off the jetty, turned the tiller and shifted the engine to forward. Jens checked that Peter was pulling the right line before he turned and waved to Fran and Jiao on the bank. Setting the helm to autopilot on the desired course, he quickly coiled the mooring line and joined Peter on deck. Jens picked up the line Peter had dropped by the cleat and started coiling it.

"I can show you how to tidy these up later," he said. "Let's get these sails up. You can sweat, and I'll work the winch."

Peter stared back blankly.

"Exactly," Jens said. "There's no rush, the wind won't arrive for another forty-three minutes. I'll show you."

"That's rather precise," Peter said. "Forty-three minutes?"

"Well, close enough," Jens said. "It's an easterly that's quite regular this time of year. Beautiful for running up or down the coast." Jens started unclipping the cover to the main sail and returned to the mast. "Just pull the halyard—that line there—and when it gets hard, pull it away from the mast and feed the slack to me. That's the sweating part. I'll finish it off with the winch. Ready?"

Peter nodded.

"Hoist the sail!" Jens ordered with a grin.

Peter pulled the halyard and the main sail rose up the mast. He breathed harder the higher, and heavier, it became, until he was forced to pull outward as Jens instructed. Jens wrapped the tail around the winch, pulled a handle out of his back pocket, inserted it into the top of the winch and cranked the remainder of the sail until it ran taut all the way to the top. He tidied the excess line and left it in a neat coil on the deck.

"Great," he said. "Well done. Let's go to the cockpit and get this gib out. Grab the handle on your way."

Jens made his way to the stern and handed Peter another line as he stepped down.

"If you pull on this it will unfurl the head sail," he said. "Go on," Jens added when Peter responded with a blank look. "Hand over hand. I'll tell you when to stop."

Peter tentatively tugged on the line, pulling faster as Jens made a rolling motion with his hand. The headsail wound itself out until it formed a full triangle.

"Perfect," Jens said as he fixed the clutch in place. "We'll adjust these once the wind arrives, but that'll do for now."

"I thought all you had to do was press a button," Peter said.

"That's right," Jens agreed. "Sit back, press a button to raise a sail. Program a course and let the computer adjust your sails. Pour a wine and catch some sun," he said as he coiled the line. "Nah! I wanted to go as basic as I could, just a sturdy old keeler."

"No foils?" Peter asked.

"Absolutely not," Jens said.

"That must make everything a bit slower," Peter said.

"Why hurry—"

"—when there's nowhere else to go," Peter finished.

"Exactly." Jens scanned the horizon. "I would have preferred an older engine, but even if I found one and got it running, sourcing the fuel would have been impossible."

"A diesel?" Peter asked. "Weren't those originally designed to run on vegetable oil?"

"Kind of, I think," Jens admitted. "You got me there. It could have been done. She's got a standard fusion converter below. It'll last a lot longer than me or this boat, and never break down. There's a comforting degree of reassurance in a dependable motor."

Jens searched the horizon again. He tapped Peter's shoulder and pointed. "There's our wind," he said.

"Where?" Peter asked.

"See the sea on the horizon? It looks a bit ruffled?"

Peter leaned forward and nodded.

"I'd say a few minutes out. When she hits, just open this clutch here and release slowly until I say to stop. Then close the clutch, okay?" Jens asked.

Peter nodded, waiting at his station. The ripples on the surface grew closer until a breeze started to play in Peter's beard. Jens released a stay line and let the wind push the main sail out. He nodded to Peter, who eased out the head sail.

"Good," Jens said, securing his clutch. Peter did likewise. He lowered the clamp into place and grabbed the gunnel as the wind caught the sails and the yacht heeled to leeward. Water splashed against the hull as the ship gained speed. Jens caught Peter smiling.

"Now you're sailing," he said. "Do you want to take the helm?"

"No," Peter answered.

"Go on," Jens said. "Take the tiller in your hand, that's right." Jens reached over and switched off the auto pilot. "Keep your eye on the sails, and when you see they start to luff—flap a little—adjust your course until they're taut again. Take the tiller to the left, we go right. Take it to the right, we go left."

Peter stared ahead at the sails, brow furrowed.

"Just relax," Jens said. "See how the compass says 030? Keep us at that and we'll be fine." Jens disappeared into the cabin and returned with two mugs of water. He handed one to Peter, who gingerly took it while grasping the helm.

"Relax," Jens said. "She'll practically steer herself." He took a drink from his mug. "Do you know why you're here?" Jens asked. "Probably the only reason?"

Peter looked at Jens and the yacht began to veer to port. Jens put his hand over Peter's and helped him guide the yacht back on course. He thought of several likely answers, but dismissed each as possibly wrong. As far as he knew, Jens hardly—if ever—spoke of his experience with the Ruan, and to be honest, Peter was surprised when he consented to meet. He shook his head.

"I got a call from Patricia," Jens said. "She told me you wanted to talk with me, and that I was going to listen to what you had to say. As you know, when she says she wants you to do something, it's not very easy to say no."

"I don't even think that is possible," Peter said.

"Maybe not," Jens agreed. "But she is a very dear friend. And here you are. What is it you want to talk about?"

3

Peter focused on the sails, trying to maintain course. "I want to ask you about the GLR run," he said.

"That's what I thought," Jens said.

"But not just ... Patricia—Dr Lin—thought I should I run something by you. Ask your advice, or ... she said, 'run it by you and see what you think.' Did she talk to you about anything when she called?"

"No," Jens said. "Just that I was to meet you."

"Okay," Peter said. "I thought I knew how to start, but now I don't."

"There's plenty of time," Jens said. "Want me to take the helm so you can relax?"

"Yeah," Peter said. Jens reached over and took the tiller as Peter slid over to the other side of the cockpit.

"That run changed everything," Peter started.

"It did," Jens agreed. "You know what it started as, don't you?"

"As a mission to bring God's Living Room to Earth," Peter said.

"It was a drug run, Dr Taylor. Forget all the myths and legends. It wasn't a 'mission'. The motivating factor was profit. For most. They knew they had a product that was going to sell big. They wanted to cash in, and then cash out, in style. With mansions and fliers." Jens smiled at Peter. "It was a good product, though. Have you taken it?"

"Of course," Peter answered. *Who hadn't?* Peter thought. *It opened doors, it tore through walls, it expanded whatever notion you had or thought was 'real'—*

"Yeah," Jens said. "I can see you have." He pointed at the sea with his free hand. "This, however, was a total accident."

"Which also changed everything," Peter said.

"That it did."

"We know from the records we've found, especially those from the ship that attacked you, that their entire species was dying," Peter said.

"Patricia wouldn't get off that ship," Jens said. "She was obsessed with the find."

"Her research has helped us find out so much."

"You know she was originally a colonist on her way to *Sukhavati*, don't you?" Jens said. "She was facing spending the rest of her life under a dome on a lifeless planet."

"But she never made it—"

"Nobody made it," Jens said. "Look around you—those colonists have their own islands now."

"And Dr Lin gave up even that, to study the Ruan," Peter said. He watched as Jens peered beyond the sails at the sea in front. "She found it difficult to believe an entire species could die out, especially one capable of space travel."

"But they did. Whatever killed them, killed almost every

mammal on the planet," Jens said. "It was bad, and they couldn't figure out how to stop it."

"True." Peter nodded. "But they didn't just give up. Just like we wouldn't give up. We would try everything."

"Like they did, right?" Jens worked his jaw muscles. "They sent out berserkers to locate any technology that might help, to find it and take it and bring it back. If you saw what they did, you wouldn't think they were like us at all."

"I meant—"

"All they had to do was fucking ask." Jens said each word slowly.

"I'm sorry—"

"Instead, they tried to just take it, no matter who was in the way."

They were desperate, Peter almost said, but he knew that it would sound like an excuse. Jens was not the man to offer excuses to, especially after what he had experienced.

"They were desperate," Jens said. "Who wouldn't be in that situation? They cast these maniacs out into deep space, just sprayed them out like machine gun fire, hoping to hit something. That crew was in cryo-sleep for—how many years? Two thousand?"

"That's pretty close."

"I imagine to them it was just a sleep. At least the ones who woke up. Launch on your mission to save the world, wake up when technology was detected. Two were just desiccated skeletons. You'd think that would have slowed them down, made them realize they were probably too late. But it seemed to make them even more desperate. It saved the *Cirrus*, anyway."

"How so?"

"Two-thousand-year-old technology can sometimes break down. They launched a flier to board and take over the ship. But their engine failed as they decelerated. If they boarded, the crew of the *Cirrus* wouldn't have stood a chance. We wouldn't have known what hit us. Like on the *Ryk*."

Jens leaned forward and pressed the auto-pilot to maintain course. He took his hands off the helm and climbed into the cabin, returning moments later with two beers.

"Shouldn't drink and drive, I know," he said, handing one to Peter. "But all of a sudden I need one."

Jens took a sip, admired the label, and took another. He gestured aft with the bottle. "She's an old-fashioned design, but like the engine, the back-ups are all very modern. She'll guide us to a pre-programed sheltered spot up the coast, lower the sails, lay anchor and send a trip report home. If we wanted. She won't cook us dinner though, but I've got that covered. Or rather Fran does. She made a dish."

Jens stared at the waves rippling against the hull of the ship. "They knew it was a medical supply freighter," he finally said. "The *Ryk*. That's why they went for it. They knew what each freighter carried."

"They had very sophisticated computer technology," Peter said.

"But they couldn't Step," Jens said. "Put themselves to sleep and spent hundreds of years flying through space." Jens aimed his bottle at Peter. "They must have thought they hit the jackpot when they figured out what the Donut was. Fold space and Step from one star system to another. Step right back home and save their people, no matter who they had to kill."

Peter knew their names, the eight astrogators in the Donut Hole who were slaughtered as they programmed the coordinates for the Step to *Sukhavati*. And just like the other computer systems in the convoy, the Ruan hacked the AI and plotted a Step to their home planet. It was all in the history books.

"That's where you saw them?"

"No," Jens said. "I didn't see anything. Herschel did, somehow. He pointed."

And you shot, Peter thought. *And stabbed. And saved the two remaining astrogators, and probably a couple thousand colonists and crew on the other freighters. Killing the last two members of a dying species.*

"It's a pheromone released by their bodies, that affects our physiology—our ability to see them," Peter said. "We think it originates in the plant life here. For some reason it didn't affect Mr Folkes."

"He thinks it was because of the GLR still in his system," Jens said.

"Dr Lin thought so too. She tried that," Peter said.

"I know," Jens said. "It took over four years for us to get back to Earth. She had a lot of time to study. She tried a lot of things."

"She still is," Peter said.

"And she is no doubt finding lots of things."

"Well, that is why I'm here," Peter admitted. "To talk with you about what we found."

"Like I said, I'm a xeno-linguist," Peter started. "I study their language. I was nearing the end of my program when I came across a discrepancy that had somehow been missed by, well, everybody. I wanted to concentrate more on it at the time, but Dr Lin insisted that I focus on my thesis as I was so close to completion."

"Which you completed," Jens said.

"Exactly." Peter looked for a place to set his empty beer bottle, following Jens' eyes to a sack hanging from the stern stanchion. He placed it inside and wiped his hands on his pants.

"From the recordings we have we've learned that their language was tonal, so something this subtle could be overlooked quite easily. But as I had to listen to certain tracks so many times, I started to notice a slight difference in how a word was used. The Ruan you met—"

"I met?"

"Sorry—that's not what I meant," Peter said. "Those Ruan were called—"

"Seekers," Jens interrupted again. "They were known as Seekers."

"Yes," Peter said quickly. "I thought that was who was being talked about in the recordings. But now I don't. In fact, I'm certain of it, which is why I'm here. The word is almost the same, it's even spelled the same way in their language. The only way you can tell that it is a different word is by the tone of the speaker. Well, tone is probably the wrong word to use, it's a word that humans use to describe human speech.

I think *feeling* is a better way to describe it—the *feeling* it is said with."

"Slow down," Jens said.

"Right, sorry."

"And quit apologizing," Jens said. "Take your time. Tell me what you found."

Peter breathed in deeply through his nose and exhaled through his mouth. "I was concentrating at the time on cultural values found in the language samples," he said. "Any indication of what might have been important to the Originals. As I had to concentrate on the feeling of the speech, I found the discrepancy in an important word."

"Which word?" Jens asked.

"Seekers," Peter said, trying to gauge Jens' reaction.

"Go on," was all he said.

"The Seekers were trained soldiers," Peter said. "More than that. They were trained in many things. But they had a single-minded focus: seek out any technology that could be used to combat the plague that was killing their people, acquire that technology, and return. Scientist warriors. No compromise. Succeed at any cost."

"That sounds about right," Jens said.

"When Seekers are spoken of, if you tune in, you can feel it. The word has a force of its own. All I can use are human terms, like strength. Determination. Fear. It is a word like a spear. Thrusting. But there's also a hope when it's used. These guys were a hope. That's how it got missed by other researchers, I think." Peter checked his pockets and looked around the cockpit. "Do you have something to write with?"

Jens reached into a pocket and withdrew a small notebook.

"I can maybe explain better like this. In the Latin alphabet Seekers looks like this, see?" Peter wrote the word down. "But all we're looking at here is one letter, the 'k,'" Peter said, circling the letter. "It must be a confusing script to learn, because the letters must look so similar to anyone not familiar. Lots of sticks with circles and lines. Look at the 'k'. It's really just a stick with a little 'v' stuck on it." Peter drew a line with a 'v' next to it. He closed his eyes and turned his head to the side.

"I'm starting to feel a little sick," he said.

"Look at the horizon for a while," Jens said. "You can feel nauseous if you look down for too long. Do you want me to heave to? Stop the boat? Or there's tincture—it's a micro dose of GLR people swear by."

"No," Peter said. "I'll try to finish."

He lifted the notebook and drew another line, turning the 'v' around and attaching it to make new letter. "What does that look like?" he asked.

"A bit like a 'd'," Jens answered.

"That's right," Peter said. "In our alphabet, at least. It makes an entirely new word. Seek becomes—"

"Seed," Jens said.

"Totally different word, totally different meaning," Peter said.

"In English," Jens said.

"Which is why it's just an example," Peter said. "What I heard was a type of oral writing. It just helped point us in the right direction."

"Us?" Jens asked. "You and Patricia?"

"That's right," Peter said. "And a colleague, Michael Hollis. We met at grad school and he's been involved since the find. He's a mathematician—"

"Your letter, the 'k'. Or 'd'," Jens said.

"When you listen to the recordings the word 'Seekers' is used. Listening to it, after what we know about what happened, I think what was happening was a bit of confirmation bias. You know, when we hear or filter what we hear to fit what we already believe. We all heard the word 'Seekers' and immediately thought of who you encountered. But the more I listened, the more I started to believe that two different things were being talked about. Two similar, yet entirely different things."

"Does that make sense?" Jens asked.

"Yes, it does," Peter said. "It has to do with purpose. Like I said, the language is tonal, but tones based on feelings. Layers of feelings. One feeling when the two words are spoken is *hope*. Seekers were a hope, regardless of how desperate it was. I thought the difference I was hearing, though, created a whole new word, a different kind of hope, and that I was actually hearing two different words. Not Seekers, but *Seeders*."

Peter stopped and smiled. Jens continued to look at him, withholding expression.

"I relistened to everything we had with this new ear," Peter continued. "And I noticed how the phraseology was slightly different in certain passages. It changed everything we thought we were looking at, or at least what we were looking for. I think the Ruan sent out two different types of crews. The pandemic was infecting their entire population, even spreading to larger mammals. Maybe it came from there, who knows. In some of the recordings the tone or *feeling* for hope is … it's hard to describe. Losing hope. Knowing they were nearing an end they couldn't stop. So, hope again, they sent out ships, with crew that were not yet infected. One type of crew was like the one that attacked the GLR convoy. They were *Seekers*. No doubt about it. And other *Seeker* ships were sent out too. We don't know how many.

"But there were other crews sent, and they were different from the *Seekers*. Very different. They were a last-ditch effort to seed another world. Those crew were *Seeders*."

"From the sound of it, they're also just ideas," Jens said. "Theory."

"No, not theory, and they're not just ideas," Peter said. "We found proof."

"None that I've ever heard about," Jens said.

"That's because we haven't told anybody about it," Peter said.

"What proof?"

"In the recordings we found at Jongnag," Peter said. "Dr Lin has kept it secret. She doesn't want anybody else to use it. Especially Consortia interests. Even though she knows we'll have to work with them, she doesn't trust them."

"Not in the slightest," Jens agreed.

"But the recording confirmed everything I thought about the words," Peter said. "And a lot more."

Jens raised his eyebrows. Peter continued.

"Just like the Seekers they sent out, the Ruan put this other type of crew into cryo-sleep and launched them into space.

They sent out *Seeders*. Uninfected, or at least not showing any signs of infection. They use a word for that I haven't been able to translate. 'Uninfected' doesn't quite capture—"

"Anyway," Jens interrupted.

"They put them into cryo-sleep and sent them out," Peter said. "Just like that. Off the planet, away from certain death, on a large ship in the direction of a nearby star. Like the Seekers, the ship was self-guided, equipped with sensors that would revive the crew when they found what they were looking for. Only rather than waking up to technology, like the Seekers, they would be woken when a new home was detected, a planet that could support life. A planet they would seed."

"Good luck with that," Jens said. "There aren't any."

"They had hope there was," Peter said. "Just like Earth did when it sent out ships."

"Exactly," Jens said.

And yet here we are, sailing across a beautiful blue ocean, ten thousand light years from Earth, Peter wanted to say. *Those planets exist, they're just very rare gems!*

"You're right," he said instead. "There's nothing but dead rocks and gas giants in front of them."

Jens leaned forward and turned off the auto-pilot. Taking the tiller in his hand he adjusted course to sail closer to the wind. The speed of the yacht decreased as the sails spilled their wind.

"There's the anchorage," Jens said, pointing. "A really beautiful little bay. Take that line and we'll close the gib."

Peter grabbed the line and together they furled the sail. Jens steered closer into the wind and centered the main sail.

Motioning Peter forward, together they climbed on deck and lowered the empty sail. Returning to the cockpit, he started the engine and steered into the sheltered bay. Slowing the yacht, Jens checked the depth again, and pressed a button to release the anchor clamps. The weight sank to the sandy bottom.

"We'll anchor the easy way," he said to Peter. "I'd send you up there but I want you to keep your fingers." Jens reversed the boat until the anchor bit, turned off the engine and folded away the tiller.

He stood with his back to Peter and surveyed the bay. The water was calm and clear. The anchor chain could be seen leading down from the boat, ending in the seabed. Darker patches of seaweed swayed gently in underwater currents. The shore was mostly rock except for one inviting sweep of golden sand. The land behind sloped upwards into lush forest.

Peter couldn't see that Jens' eyes were closed, but he heard the man breathe in deeply. "I love it here," Jens said turning. He sat and stared at Peter for a long moment.

"You know where they are," he finally said.

"Yes. Well, where they will be," Peter answered. "Michael calls it 'easy math', but it took him months to compute. They would have passed the nearest exo-planet, the star they originally aimed for, but would have found a hot, lifeless rock. It's orbiting a star I can point out to you tonight. When the ship's computer deemed it uninhabitable, they would have slingshot past it towards another, and around that one when their sensors detected more lifeless rocks, but mostly gas giants. And then they would have accelerated towards another star. Their ships were fast, but it would still take generations to even to reach the first star. But that kind of technology ... from what I can gather from the data, it's very impressive. The course though, that's all direction and velocity."

"Easy math," Jens said, still looking towards the shore.

"For a guy like Michael," Peter said. "Their course would be predictable, which means it could be plotted. Even this many years later."

Jens didn't respond. Instead, he stood and stepped towards the cabin.

"Dr Lin has a message for you," Peter said to Jens' back. "She wanted me to tell you something."

"Go on," he said.

"She said to tell you what this means ..." Peter said. "She said I had to use her words. She said, 'Quit carrying your guilt. You did what you had to do, but you didn't kill the last ones'." Peter waited for Jens to turn, but he didn't.

"I'll get some dinner started," Jens said as he climbed down into the cabin.

4

Jens didn't carry guilt. Patricia was wrong about that. He may have, when he was much younger and when she knew him then. But that was for other actions at other times and on a planet he left behind. He used to wake screaming then. And after what happened in the Donut Hole, he would wake up with Fran Lu standing above him, or shaking him, worried about her captain. But he didn't feel guilt, not about the Ruan. Once the dust had settled, and he had taken command of the convoy sent back to Earth to tell them the news of the discovery of an inhabitable planet, he had learned to sleep more soundly. It took some time. He had Fran Lu to help, to make sure he kept up appearances, was the captain the crew expected, and that he himself aspired to be. Seeing that fragile side of him was part of what had turned her admiration into love.

On the long trip back, he had a crew to train, and, before long, a family to raise. In the ten years it took to get to Earth, and then return to Pemako, he thought less and less about that day in the Hole. Patricia tried to quiz him about it a couple of times but eventually stopped bringing it up. Jens found himself smiling as he remembered an interaction.

"I need to know everything," Patricia said.

"No, you don't," Jens answered.

Jens had flown a tender over to the docking bay containing the Seeker ship. It was after First Step on the journey back to Earth. She did join the crew of the *General Xing* for Step, one of the few orders she actually obeyed. Jens insisted that she was not to be on board the alien craft during the procedure. During Step, she joined the ships contingent, strapped in their chairs, just as confined and uncomfortable as they as space and time were folded. As soon as the Donut was established in an orbit around the targeted star for recharge she wanted to return to the ancient ship. Jens made her wait until the freighter was detached and in convoy to a safe distance from the solar radiation. Two months travelling away from the Donut, Flip and Decel, then two months back. She spent as much of the time as possible secluded in the Ruan ship. He worried about her isolation more than she did. She didn't even seem to notice, appearing to the others in the convoy to prefer the company of dead aliens to that of living humans.

"I cannot have holes in my research," she insisted. "You saw them."

"No, I didn't," Jens said. "Herschel did. Talk to him about it."

"*Do you think you are being funny?*" she demanded, lapsing into Mandarin, which she did whenever Jens annoyed her. "*He is on Pemako, and he hid from me when I tried to speak with him.*"

"*What do you think that's telling you?*"

"*Don't be so difficult!*" she shouted.

"I brought you some roast cavy," Jens said. "You work too much and need to eat."

"Don't change the subject and try to distract me with guinea pig," she said, but Jens could tell she was pleased he brought a meal.

"I prefer the term 'space pig," he said. "I re-hydrated a couple for a picnic."

Patricia hrmmphed, but Jens could see a small smile.

"I'll try, okay?" he offered. "But don't pressure me."

So, he set a table, or what she thought was the table, in what she thought was the galley of the strange craft. And they spoke about the aliens over a dinner, just as he would soon be doing with Peter. After a while he didn't even mind exploring the Ruan ship they carried back with them, or at least that's what he wanted her to think. She couldn't fail to notice that he rarely went near the two Seeker corpses kept on ice, and as he opened up more during ensuing visits, she gradually brought him closer to them.

"The sounder hit them," he said, gazing down at one's chest. Its clothing had been removed and skin cleaned. Jens could only see blood in his memory. Dr Lin had taken care to clean all traces off the corpse. The knife wounds remained, some dark slits, others longer gashes revealing muscle and even bone underneath. Jens wanted to close his eyes, to not see what he had done. He had turned into a berserker himself that day. But he kept gazing down.

"I must have struck him two, three times," he added. "Those pulses would have a killed a human at that range.

I mean, they knocked him down, but he was still alive. Moving.”

She placed a hand on Jens' shoulder. He wasn't sure if it was for comfort, or to keep him from moving away.

“The pulses caused damage, but were not fatal,” she added. “Their skeletal structure is like ours, but their bones are more flexible. And more strongly knit. Like bamboo can bend and flex in strong winds. Their bones were incredibly resilient. Their muscle tone provided additional protection.”

Jens let his eyes travel the length of the long body. Patricia had covered the flesh in a fine layer of powder, ensuring visibility. The creature's sinewy arms ended in long dexterous fingers, slightly curled in death and resembling claws. Flat chest, hardened abdomen, muscular legs. He stared at the narrow, beak like face.

She guided him to the other corpse. It lay within another cryo-pod that Dr Lin had set to a low temperature. It too was covered in a fine layer of powder. Like the other, it also bore the cuts of Jens' attack, as well as the stitches of her autopsy.

“The sounder pulses caused fatal damage to this one's internal organs,” she said.

“It followed me into the resting quarters,” Jens said. “I fired point blank. I emptied an entire magazine.”

“One of its hearts ruptured. I don't know if that was enough to kill it,” she said. “Other pulses collapsed part of its single large lung. Severe hematoma causing pooling of blood in the abdomen. Bruising to the right leg. This one was practically already dead before you stabbed it.”

Jens thought more about the astrogators he saved, Suzie Reynolds and Lena McGee. Lena had never recovered. Teal, the captain and medic of the *Cirrus*, kept up a regimen of micro doses of GLR, the new wonder drug. It was more than a sedative, administered as it was. It took the patient's mind to a place beyond bliss, a place Teal hoped would allow recovery from the trauma they had experienced. But for Lena it wasn't enough. She had never resurfaced from her trauma-induced coma. She looked peaceful in her rest, as if she were merely asleep. And then one day she simply ceased. All monitors went blank, all vital signs stopped. It was as if she simply decided to get up from God's Living Room and step over to whatever follows.

Suzie re-joined the living, but was never the same. She remained on the island settled by the crew of the Cook Islander freighter, *Avarua*, cared for and loved in the best way they knew. The last time Jens visited she seemed to have no memory of their past, despite how close they had been. He liked to think he saw a brief glimmer of recognition, but understood if she needed to erase every moment prior to the attack on the Hole.

"She's fine," Herschel lied on Jens' last visit. "She has a nice house next door to Pani and me. The kids do things for her, like weed her garden. Not that she asks."

"Does she ever speak about what happened?"

"No," Herschel said. "But she smiles more now. And she touches people's shoulders when they greet her. I think it's to make sure they're really there."

"What is it?" Jens asked. "You seem like you're not telling me something."

"She's just..." Herschel tried, "I don't know. She's not the same Suzie from the *Cirrus*. Serious, focused, intent... She just seems to be slowly retreating, withdrawing. Maybe it's just something she needs to do right now. So, we give her space. Pani's keeping a close eye on her."

Did Herschel feel guilty about what happened in the Hole? Jens wondered, but the old friends didn't speak about what had happened in the months before the convoy returned to Earth. And they never had in the years since. Maybe that was common among veterans—moving past an experience, leaving it somewhere behind so they could move forward.

The moment returned, fresh in Jens' mind. Herschel rushed into the control room as a distraction, slipped on the blood-coated floor and crashed into the central AI computer. But he pointed as he fell, and that was enough. Jens followed right behind, firing his sounder, a spray of pulses until the gun was empty. He hit the unseen target. Then Herschel was hurled against a wall and Jens fled to the resting quarters, followed by the Ruan. Maybe if Herschel had seen his friend killing the creatures, how he killed them, he would be looking at him differently.

Returning to the control room, the blood on the floor seemed to move, a blurry motion, and Jens instinctively jumped to finish it off, withdrawing his knife and bringing it down again and again. No, Jens didn't carry guilt for killing them, even if they were the last of dying species. They had killed his friends, and in a way killed Suzie. She didn't just avoid the past, she seemed to forget, to erase it from her memory, including the relationship she had had with Jens when they crewed together on the *Cirrus*, living as lovers for a brief time before the incident in the Hole.

Jens let Patricia do whatever she wanted to the Ruan, even dissect one of the creatures on the way back to Earth, and put her medical knowledge to a different use. The first xeno-biologist. One of many new titles she would give herself. Xeno-linguist. Xeno-technician. Xeno-phile. She was originally destined to spend the rest of her life on a colony she never even wanted to go to, on the run or exiled, like himself, for reasons he never wanted to know. She similarly never asked about his reasons.

But the Ruan changed all that, for both of them. Patricia became the renowned Dr Lin, expert on an alien species. And Jens became Ambassador. Deliver the news of the new planet back to Earth. A simple request, except for the ten years the round trip it would take. If they were allowed to return, and not thrown into prison for stealing consortium property. Finder's rights. The planet of Pemako rightly belonged to the largest Consortium in east Asia, as it possessed a majority stake in the original convoy to *Sukhavati*.

Only right doesn't always mean just.

"Make it public domain," Alverez, captain of the *Calderón*, argued.

The other captains in the meeting looked from Alverez to Wu Pen, captain of the *Sunrise Blossom*, and the official representative of the consortium. He folded his hands on his lap, saying nothing. The other captains returned their gaze to Alverez.

"Pemako doesn't have to be like Earth," Alverez said. "We don't need Consortia hierarchy and their corruption. It's a new world. Let's make it one."

Jens took a sip from his wine. It was one of the last bottles of Alverez's store. It made each taste all the sweeter. At that time, they were still counting down their return in years. As chair of the fortnightly captain's meetings Jens knew he had to say something. What Alverez was talking about would be seen as worse than mutiny by the Consortium executives. Alverez could have been put in the brig, stripped of his command and his ship confiscated for his suggestion.

"Go on," Jens said instead.

The captains exhaled. A less attentive leader would not have noticed, but Jens could sense the group relax. Wu Pen was harder to read. The captain of the *Sunrise* sat like a statue. But he knew Jens well, and the almost imperceptible tilt of his head told Jens that Alverez wasn't the only captain harboring such views.

"If we hand over the coordinates to the planet, we all know what will happen," Alverez said. "They'll either rape it and mine it, like they're forbidden to do on Earth, or they'll hand out access to a favored few. You all know this."

Teal nodded. Jens watched Fran Lu out of the corner of his eye. He saw a smile form on his wife's face. Three captains so far, with Wu Pen sitting somewhere on the fence.

"I know where the crew of the *Xing* stand," Fran said. "They volunteered to crew in this convoy to share what we found, to tell the families they left on Earth, and take them back to Pemako."

Wu Pen said his first words. "This is a decision for the captains, not for crew."

"Of course it's a decision for the crews!" Fran shot back. Jens was getting used to her growing confidence, since handing over command of the *General Xing* to his First Mate. He tried not to smile at his wife. He still needed to appear impartial, if only to watch it play out.

"They have sacrificed too much to be left out of the consultation," she said.

"As you were saying, Alverez," Jens said.

"We know they will take Pemako as their own," Alverez said. "They will divide up shares with a few select Consortia, like the one that owns the *Calderón*. I say, fuck them!"

"Fuck them!" Teal agreed. "I'm not in this for them."

"You're in it for the drug, we know," Wu Pen said.

"Damn right I am," Teal said. "It will rip minds open. It will free the masses. I have no intention of handing that power over to the Consortia."

"Or your profit," Wu Pen added.

"You know this isn't about money," she said. "We don't need that anymore."

"If the Consortia don't confiscate your cargo and file you away somewhere in a secret prison," Wu Pen said.

Silence settled over the room. Jens broke it. "Alverez?" he asked.

"Just like what they did with fusion," he started, "we put it in the public domain. If everybody has the coordinates, then every Consortium with a Donut will take the Step."

"They'll tear each other apart," Teal said, unable to hide her approval of such a scenario.

"Which they don't want, any of them," Alverez said. "And a war between the Consortia won't help us either. We don't have to cut them out. We offer a share. But on our terms. Or the terms of the Collective."

"What 'Collective'?" Fran Lu asked.

"The one that will spring to life as soon as we get back with our news," Alverez said. "It'll burst forth just like with the *Waking Up*. This will wake them up, that's for sure. And just like then, the ground will shake and the executives will quake."

"We don't need poetry now," Wu Pen said. "We need a plan."

We. There it was. Jens sat back. The meeting no longer needed a chair.

"The *Waking Up* was about saving the Earth and stopping ecocide," he said, joining in the discussion. "What makes you think the same thing will happen now?"

"This is about saving another planet," Alverez said. "And it's about saving a dream, the one they'll remember when we tell them about Pemako. Humanity's dream about life in the stars, a second home, a planet with life! They won't let that be taken away. Those lifeless rocks we call colonies are one thing. This is different."

"Damn right," Teal said. "Public domain. I like it. But what's to stop them from silencing our transmission?"

"We transmit simultaneously to all stations, all networks, all mediums," Fran Lu said. "An info-bomb."

"That won't be enough," Wu Pen said. "Somebody will need to be planet-side, to win some support in the right circles. Consortia politics is like a pack of wolves. Or monkeys. There's always those wanting to take down the alpha male. Or alpha executive."

They all knew the only person with the standing to do that was Wu Pen himself. Jens felt even more respect for the man.

On reaching Earth, Wu Pen took a flier to the surface and met the representatives of his Consortium. He promptly disappeared into a secret prison for betraying the trust of his employers. Jens bought him back, at probably the highest ransom ever paid—a thirty percent share of a planet. But Wu Pen must have whispered in the right ears before he was whisked away, because the offer was accepted. The Consortia and the oligarchs could fight amongst themselves to divvy that up.

But by then their first cards were played. The people came out just as Alverez said, and in timeless fashion, the powers that be were frightened of democracy. Faced with world-wide protests and boycotts, and the development of the Peoples' Collectives, the Consortia handed over concessions as fast as Jens could think of them. Donuts, freighters, equipment for building a new world. Teal even won legalization and distribution rights for GLR, not just on Earth, but on the colonies.

The final trump card, however, was what Dr Lin had to show. Not only an alien species, but new technologies that would revolutionize space travel.

5

"Did you enjoy the sail?" Fran asked. "Peter?"

Peter started, brought back to the family table from a memory still at sea. He set down his fork. "Yes, I did," he said. "I listened for the *puruha*. Jens said there might be a few late migrators." It was his favorite sound on the whole of Pemako, the great Cetacea emptying their lungs in an explosion of warm air.

"They're often around this time of year," Fran said. "You can hear the spout for kilometers. Did you hear any?"

"I couldn't believe how loud it was," Peter said. "One came close to us, studying us through its massive black eye."

"Imagine," Fran said. "Having an entire ocean world to yourselves for so long. And then we show up. I think they know we mean them no harm."

"It was beautiful," Peter said. "And so big! It made our boat feel so tiny." He smiled at Jaio. He balled his hand into a fist, unwound his middle, ring and little fingers, put his hand over his mouth and blew out. "Peeeewwww!"

She giggled, put her small fist over her mouth and copied the sound.

"I'm sure they're the smartest creature on the planet, and that includes us," Fran said.

"You're probably right about that," Peter agreed. He pictured the creatures, silvery blue skin glistening in the sunlight, their backs arching slowly out of the water, seeming to never end, until tails that made their boats look like toys pointed upwards and slipped beneath the waves. He put his fist to his mouth, winked at Jaio, and blew again.

"Peter's returning to Earth," Jens said. "He's going to present his research to a Consortium and ask for backing."

"That sounds exciting," Fran said.

Exciting wasn't exactly the word Jens used, when he finally consented to talk about it. He called Peter down into the cabin after half an hour, and served the delicious meal Fran had prepared, washed down by local beer. Once the table was cleared and dishes washed, Jens brought out a bottle of rum and a brownish liquid in an unmarked bottle. He poured two generous amounts of rum into glasses, then an equal amount of the mix.

"As captain, I have to stick to tradition and provide your ration," Jens said. "I wouldn't want to have to put down a mutiny."

"What did you put in it?" Peter asked.

"A bit of water, a bit of sugar, some nutmeg," Jens answered. "Exact measures are a trade secret."

"Well," Peter said, taking the glass and touching it to Jens'. "Thank you, Captain." He took a sip and smiled.

Jens sat down opposite Peter and gazed at his glass. "What

the Seeders were sent to do," he said. "That sounds worse than finding a needle in haystack."

"Not with the technology we copied from their ship," Peter said. "They were way more advanced in some ways. All we have to do is get within three hundred million kilometers. If there's a ship there, it'll be detected."

"That's not a lot of kilometers," Jens said.

"It's like the distance to the sun and back," Peter said. "That's a workable radius."

"And we've managed to build these sensors? I haven't heard anything about them."

"The technology is there."

"Which means it doesn't exist yet," Jens said.

"It will, with enough money. Which is why I need to go back to Earth."

"And this ship would be going rather fast," Jens said, still working the problem. "If you even detected it, what would you do? Catch up, attach your ship, and start to Decel? That would take a very long time. Not to mention the g-force."

"What's the hurry?" Peter asked.

"No," Jens said. His glass was half-empty and sinking. "I get it now. There is no hurry if you do it in your sleep." He reached for the bottle of rum and topped up his glass. Reaching over the table, he did the same to Peter's. "Just hibernate in a cryo-pod until you're there."

"It's what we do to reach the Donuts now," Peter said. "And most choose to sleep through the Step as well. Just wake up and see a new sun."

"Donuts took us months to reach," Jens said. "And months to re-charge after Step."

"They still do. Only you don't have to wait around."

"Just sleep."

"Exactly," Peter said.

"Have you ever experienced a Step?" Jens asked.

"Awake? Hell no!"

"I was awake every time," Jens said, feeling his age. The old man lamenting the soft youth of the day. But if the choice was given, to sleep, or to take the mind elsewhere ... No. That nearly killed them all.

"Teal had a ceremony before each Step," Jens said. "A surreal sort of communion. Once everything was handed over to the Donut Holes, each crew member got a kiss and a tab of GLR."

"But not you?" Peter asked.

"Not as a newbie," Jens said. "The rule was that you had to experience at least one Step wide awake. I had to sit there and watch the countdown, and then experience my body being dissolved and stretched across hundreds of light years as the Donut created the worm hole. It felt like I wanted to vomit, but couldn't, because my throat and my stomach were in different parts of the room. Or different parts of space. At the second Step I was on another ship. It operated under another type of discipline."

Peter knew the story but didn't interrupt. He sipped his second rum and let Jens talk. The GLR run was the stuff of legend. Jens on the *Cirrus*, being seduced into the ring, and by his captain, Sandra Teal. Jens and the crew of the

Sunrise Blossom, learning how to fight and lead. Collecting the ingredients needed to manufacture the drug under the guise of a settler transport convoy to a far-flung colony they never did reach.

Then the Ruan hijacked their Donut.

During the first Step returning to Earth, the Donut Holes, new astrogators, barely trained and untested, miscalculated and came out of the worm hole almost catastrophically close to a star. Almost. And Jens almost sacrificed his ship to push the Donut safely away. Three crew had died. Teal might not have liked Jens' order to maintain a *conscious* watch during the remaining Steps, but she didn't argue. There wasn't a great deal of argument about his leadership after that. Third Step the astrogators placed the Donut a safe distance from the target star, and months were spent pushing the disc close enough to harvest the solar photons and recharge, while the freighters sheltered from the radiation a safe distance away— preferably behind an inner planet. Then another step to Sol.

"That time would have been wasted if we slept," Jens said. "Crew trained and studied. We prepared for our return. We started families. That's when Fran Lu and I decided to marry. Our oldest, Ling, was there when we reached Earth. You met her daughter this morning. And she had a sister and a brother by the time we got back to Pemako."

The return voyage to Pemako consisted of five Donuts, each carrying twenty-four freighters, and Jens found himself the admiral of the largest interstellar fleet in human history. One hundred and twenty ships in total, and most of those with two thousand settlers turning a rectangular lead-lined box into a self-sustaining home for the four-year trip to their destination. One hundred and twenty thousand souls —mostly chosen by lottery, as agreed at negotiations—and others associated with the crew that had volunteered to return to Earth. And, of course, the Consortia percentage of berths. During the time in transit, they learned what they needed to know in order to build a new civilization, from farming to flying, and from med tech to machinery. Ten years after leaving Pemako, Jens returned with the first batch of settlers. Over the ensuing years many, many more were to follow.

By the time of their return the two thousand settlers that had originally stayed on the planet had a capital city, complete with landing strip. Smaller towns had sprung up. Plantations dotted several islands. To those arriving, it still looked empty and inviting. And it was. Empty and inviting enough for Jens and his family to build a house on a sheltered bay on an island reminding them of home.

"You should use the time," Jens said. "Keep learning and preparing."

"I intend to," Peter said. "But it won't take nearly as long."

Twelve months? Jens wondered. Newer, larger, more efficient Donuts, that can Step ten thousand lightyears on one charge. It was amazing how quickly technology advanced when there was a good reason. Usually, it was war. This time, it was hope. Alongside help from some alien technology.

"You seem to have it all figured out," Jens said. "I'm at a loss as to what you want from me."

Peter finished his rum and placed a hand over the glass when Jens offered a refill.

"Dr Lin said that it was important that you ... that you knew," Peter said. "And that, well, you thought it worth doing."

"You've come for my blessing?" Jens laughed.

"We think they're out there," Peter said. "And we think we have to at least try to find them. There may be thousands—"

"That's what you said," Jens interrupted. "Thousands of sleeping Ruan with a lot of expensive technology. Nobody's intentions are pure, Peter. There's a huge profit to be made. Who are your backers?"

"That's what I'm going to Earth to get," Peter admitted.

"At least you dream big," Jens said.

"So, what do you think about it?" Peter asked.

Jens started to pour himself another rum but stopped. He set the bottle down and put the cap on it.

"If they're out there like you say, then go and get them," Jens said. "Just don't be naïve about motives—yours, Patricia's, or anybody else's."

"Can I have that in writing?" Peter asked. "A letter of endorsement?"

"I think you over-estimate my influence, but sure, I'll give you that."

Peter shifted uneasily. "There is something else I'd like to ask you," he said.

Jens leaned back and waited, making the younger man squirm in the silence.

"It's ... well ..." Peter stammered. "I'm going to Sapporo."

Jens closed his eyes. It made sense. Peter needed backing for his project. If he could get it all in one place, everything would move faster, and quicker. Focus on a Consortium that was not one of the major players, but was hungry to become one. And Peter was here, with Jens, before he started negotiations. Peter didn't just want one letter. He came for another, more private type of note.

"I mean … before you left Earth," Peter started. "Before you got work on the *Cirrus* and left the planet …"

"I worked on a refuse collection scow, harvesting plastic waste in the Pacific," Jens said. "Or what little was left in the oceans."

"On the *Ana Marie*," Peter said.

Jens sipped his rum. *The xeno-linguist had done his homework. But what else did he think he knew?* Jens wondered.

"I mean, this is ancient history—"

"I'm not that old," Jens said.

"No … I didn't mean that." Peter felt like he was back in the leather chair, being teased, or tested, by his host. "It took a bit of digging to find out, especially from here, but the *Ana Marie* was owned by a subsidiary of the HakKor Consortium. Based in Sapporo."

Impressive, Jens admitted to himself. He wasn't happy about this ghost revisiting. "And?" he asked.

6

Peter swallowed. He had a copy of the report on his tablet, but he wasn't prepared to tell Jens that he did. He felt guilty having it, like he had read his sister's diary, privy to secrets another person didn't want shared. Or worse. Like he was trying to blackmail the man across from him, prying into a personal space he had no invitation to enter. It wasn't quite a complete report, merely a summary of an investigation. It took a lot of searching through old data bases. If he were more suspicious in nature, he would have thought it was deliberately buried. He never found the full report, or any following investigations. It was a mere forty-five kilobytes, but that was enough. It still had plenty of boring parts. It also had data somebody might want to bury.

Peter reread the document again on the flight to *Te Wai Pounamu*.

"Summary of Independent Investigation into the Man Overboard Fatality on Board the Bougainville Registered Refuse Collection Scow *Ana Marie* in the Central Pacific Ocean," read the title. "Prepared by the Japanese Maritime Transport Safety Bureau, 4 Chome-5 Kōmachi, Chiyoda

City, Tokyo 104-0086." All very official, almost as dry as an academic paper. Except, that is, for the transcripts at the end.

"Purpose of Investigation," it stated. "This incident is investigated in accordance with the IMO Resolution MSC 455(74), the Code of the International Standards and Recommended Practices for a Safety Investigation into a Marine Casualty or Marine Incident (Casualty Investigation Code). The purpose of this investigation conducted by the Japanese Maritime Transport Safety Bureau is to determine the circumstances and the causes of the incident with the aim of improving the safety of life at sea and avoiding similar incidents in the future.

"The conclusions and recommendations drawn in this report aim to identify the different factors contributing to the incident. They are not intended to apportion blame or liability towards any particular organization or person except so far as necessary to achieve the said purpose. All information gained in this report has been forwarded to police authorities in the vessel's home port (Gladstone, Queensland, Commonwealth of Australia)."

"Blah, blah, blah," Peter muttered as the sea passed below him.

"Meteorological Information," the next heading read. Peter skimmed the names, glancing at the acronyms. "Observations include subjective satellite-based Dvorak technique intensity estimates from the Tropical Analysis and Forecast Branch (TAFB) and the Satellite Analysis Branch (SAB), and objective Advanced Dvorak Technique (ADT) estimates and Satellite Consensus (SATCON) estimates from the Institute for Meteorological Studies of the Northern Mariana Observatory.

"Around 1100 OTZ, 2 October, an Imperial Ocean Service (IOS) observation site on Saipan, reported sustained winds of 62 knots (114 mph) and a gust of 74 knots (137 mph). The highest measured storm surge was 2.6 meters above normal tide levels at an IOS gauge near San Vicente on Saipan. Tropical Cyclone advisories were issued on all stations at 1700 OTZ on 2 October."

"Big storm a-brewing," Peter said softly.

The passenger in the next seat glanced over. "Sorry," Peter said. "Just thinking out loud."

"Victim's Details," came next. Jens' captain. Here Peter paid closer attention. "Henare (Henry) Manuel, aged 42, was an Aotearoa/New Zealand national. Mr Manuel was a registered skipper and had been in charge of the vessel for the previous five years. Crew members described Mr Manuel as a competent and exacting skipper. He demanded high standards from his crew, although some crew have indicated that he could show impatience or anger at tasks not completed to his high standards.

"Mr Manuel suffered from a persistent alimentary canal ailment that could make him experience periods of painful cramping. However, he was cleared during his most recent seafarers' medical examination and ruled fit for service.

"When last seen by crew on deck he was wearing red wet weather jacket and black wet weather pants. It was reported that he was not wearing a personal floatation device nor tether line."

"Last seen by Jens," Peter said. He looked at the man sitting next to him and shrugged before turning back to the screen.

And the investigation summary, the record of that night: "*Ana Marie* is a Refuse Collection Scow of twenty-two meters length. Her area of operations was the North Pacific Ocean, to the Japanese territory of Guam in the North, Marshall Islands in the east, and Fijian Islands to the south. The *Ana Marie* is part of the fleet representing the world-wide efforts at sea initiated by the Great Clean-Up. She makes up one of six ships belonging to Pacific Clean-up Solutions (PaCSol), a subsidiary of the Hokkaido/Korea, or HakKor, Consortium. The *Ana Marie* was the only PaCSol vessel operational at the time of the incident (the remaining five being mechanically impaired or in dry dock).

"As sea-borne refuse grew increasingly scarce during the present phase of the Great Clean-Up, her retrieval operations were extended to involve the seas north of the Mariana Islands. Her incursion into these waters was the cause of one altercation between the *Ana Marie* and the Refuse Collection Scow *Hindrance,* which took place one week prior to the disappearance of Mr Manuel. According to *Ana Marie* log entries, crew of the *Hindrance* shot down a drone belonging to the *Ana Marie* (this action was not witnessed by any crew of the *Ana Marie,* and is denied by the skipper of the *Hindrance*). The two vessels drew close to each other and a shouting match ensued between Mr Manuel and the skipper of the *Hindrance*. Both vessels then departed. This incident is added to this report to emphasize the competitive nature of the industry, as vessels sought the remains of this valuable resource, and to indicate the level of pressure skippers, including Mr Manuel, are under to acquire their quota and fulfil orders.

"At the time of the incident, the *Ana Marie* was in the Central Pacific 300 nautical miles north east of Guam near the Northern Mariana Islands (18°21'04.3"N 147°58'46.9"E). The mission of the ship on its current voyage was the fulfilment of a contract for the Australian Space Administration for rare plastics to recycle into radio isotope laced fuel for ship reactors. The *Ana Marie* was, at the time of the incident, running behind schedule and two weeks late for delivery of that rare, valuable, and diminishing resource.

"During the night of October 3, the skipper of the *Ana Marie* went missing. The scow was making way in heavy weather, on a course bearing of 060 degrees, to what he believed was a potential field of refuse. Seas were reported as very rough and winds at gale force. Mr Manuel was last seen on deck the previous evening by the vessel's First Mate, Andrew Jensen, who was Officer of the Watch during those hours. Mr Manuel was reported to have issued orders to First Mate Jensen before leaving the deck in the direction of his quarters.

"At 0600 the skipper of the Refuse Collection Scow *Ana Marie*, Henare (Henry) Manuel, was reported by the First Mate as missing when he failed to answer calls to his quarters. After discovering his absence, a search of the ship was conducted and Mr Manuel could not be located. It was noted that the clothing he was last seen wearing was also missing, and he was presumed to have fallen overboard. The First Mate immediately initiated Man Overboard (MoB) safety procedures in accordance with the Maritime Operators Safety Plan of the vessel. Current location was logged, a Mayday distress call sent, the vessel turned and search initiated.

"Taking charge of the vessel, First Mate Andrew Jensen reversed course and instituted a Drifted Track Line search pattern, taking into account conditions of the previous hours. This search continued during the daylight hours. At nightfall, and given the worsening of weather conditions, First Mate Jensen was advised by Rescue Coordination Center, Guam, to cease search operations. Jensen then skippered the *Ana Marie* to the deep-water port of Apra Harbor in the Japanese Territory of Guam."

But it was the "Excerpts of Interview Transcripts (transcribed audio recordings)" that Peter found fascinating. "Interviews conducted by Constable Yuji Tamoro, Piti Prefecture," they began.

Excerpt from Interview 1: Able Seaman Samuel Rodgers

Tamoro: Mr Rodgers, how long have you served on board the *Ana Marie*?

Rodgers: Almost six months. Just more than four, I think.

Tamoro: What were the conditions of the night that Mr Manuel went missing?

Rodgers: They were rough. The scow was near flying off the swell. She's designed to ride the waves, which is great in big swells, but not in what we were in that night. I was down below. It wasn't my watch. I had to tie myself down to stop from flying off my bunk.

Tamoro: So, to clarify, you were not on watch, nor on deck, during the night the incident took place?

Rodgers: I just said that, didn't I?

Tamoro: Did you hear anything from your quarters during the night?

Rodgers: I heard a lot of crashing about. I mean, the scow was up and down. The storm really tossed her about (*Mr Rodgers slapping his hands together to illustrate*). It's bad being below, but it's [*expletive*] being up there in those conditions. It's a real [*expletive*]. Especially at night.

Tamoro: Did you hear any human sounds?

Rodgers: I heard a shout. Or more like shouting.

Tamoro: And you could differentiate these human sounds to the sounds of the storm? Of the waves, the slapping, the gear moving about?

Rodgers: It was pretty much right above me.

Tamoro: And could you identify the voices?

Rodgers: It sounded like Skipper and Jensen.

Tamoro: Sounded like?

Rodgers: It had to be. I mean, Jens was officer of the watch.

Tamoro: Was Mr Jensen on watch alone?

Rodgers: No. Chrisp was with him.

Tamoro: And you are certain the voice was not from Chrisp?

Rodgers: When you hear Skipper shout, you know who it is.

Tamoro: And you would hear Mr Manuel shout frequently?

Rodgers: Only at those that deserved it. You heard him shout at Jens *quite* a lot.

Tamoro: Can you describe the relationship between Mr Manuel and Mr Jensen?

Rodgers: Now you're asking the right questions. Jens and Skipper were always clashing. Jens was a know-it-all. Thought he knew how to do things better. I don't even think he wanted to be out there. They argued that day about turning back. God only knows why Skipper made him First Mate.

Tamoro: The meteorological records show evidence of a storm of gale force 10. Did First Mate Jensen want to turn back because of that?

Rodgers: I don't know. All I know is that they argued, again. Jens thinking he knew better.

Tamoro: And yet the scow didn't turn back, and Mr Manuel was lost at sea.

Rodgers: All Skipper wanted was loyalty, and Jens never showed it. Now Skipper is dead. You're a cop, right? Why is that guy not behind bars? He killed Skipper. There's no way Skipper could have fallen overboard. If you knew him, you'd know that too. It was like his feet were glued to the [*expletive*] deck. No way a storm could shake him loose. Why aren't you arresting that [*expletive*] Jensen?

Tamoro: The purpose of this investigation is not to ascertain blame, nor make accusations. It is merely to collect data for further examination. All information will be forwarded to both Maritime and Police authorities. One last question: The communications log shows that Mr Manuel was under a great deal of pressure from PaCSol headquarters to fill the hull as soon as possible and return to home port with a delivery. My question is ... Do you think that, um, his disappearance was deliberate? An act of self—

Rodgers: No way. That's the stupidest thing I've heard yet. You know who did this. Why don't you arrest him?

Excerpt from Interview 2: Able Seaman Walter Chrisp

Tamoro: You were on watch during the time that Mr Manuel is presumed to have fallen overboard?

Chrisp: That's right. We pulled night watch. Jens and me.

Tamoro: Did you hear or see Mr Manuel at all during the night of your watch?

Chrisp: No, I wasn't on deck.

Tamoro: No? I thought you said you were on watch.

Chrisp: I was. But Jens sent me below, to the engine room.

Tamoro: Is that common practice?

Chrisp: Nothing was common practice about that night. Skipper insisted on pressing on north, despite a [*expletive*] of a storm bearing down on us. Jens tried to talk him out of it. Maybe if it came from somebody else, somebody like Rodgers who lived up Skipper's [*expletive*], he might have listened. But because it was Jens talking sense, Skipper couldn't hear.

Tamoro: Is it unusual to not be on deck during your watch?

Chrisp: Not on a night like that. Being on deck would have been ridiculous. Jens sent me down, saying the same thing, that it was a hazard, an … 'unnecessary risk', is how he phrased it. So, he sent me down to monitor the engine, which was running hard out just to keep us heading forward. He's a good officer. He stayed on deck because he was Officer of the Watch. He didn't want to, but Skipper ordered a watch, so he kept it.

Tamoro: Did Mr Jensen disagree often with Mr Manuel?

Chrisp: Skipper had it in for him, that was pretty obvious. I think Jens sometimes encouraged that too.

Tamoro: Encouraged?

Chrisp: It's like this. If Skipper was shouting at Jens, ranting or raving at him, it meant he wasn't taking it out on me. Or any other crew. That's the kind of officer Jens was. He ran cover for us.

Tamoro: There are several books in Mr Jensen's quarters—

Chrisp: So, you've rummaged through our stuff?

Tamoro: As part of this investigation, it is our duty to examine the vessel thoroughly. There are several historical books, notably about a ship called the *Bounty*.

Chrisp: Jens was a bit of history buff. He read a lot.

Tamoro: And did he speak about his readings?

Chrisp: 'Course he did. Watches are long and you gotta talk about something.

Tamoro: The story of the *Bounty* is one of a mutiny, correct?

Chrisp: It's in the title. Why are you asking me that?

Tamoro: Did Mr Jensen ever speak about mutiny?

Chrisp: When he was talking about the *Bounty*. Which he did a lot, because that was what he was reading.

Tamoro: And about the *Ana Marie*? Did he speak of mutiny?

Chrisp: (*Laughs and shakes his head in the negative*).

Tamoro: What did Mr Jensen speak about, when he spoke of the *Bounty*?

Chrisp: The First Mate. He thought Christian was a good one, but weak. He said First Mates were often put in very difficult situations, especially if the captain was a first-class [*expletive*].

Tamoro: And in what way did Mr Jensen think that Mr Christian was weak? You need to explain, as I am not overly familiar with the story of the *Bounty*.

Chrisp: Bligh, the captain of the *Bounty*, was an outright tyrant. Jens thought he was also a bit unhinged. Christian bore the brunt of Bligh's outburst and punishments—

Tamoro: To protect his crewmates?

Chrisp: Yeah, that's what Jens thought. But eventually Christian and the crew snapped, so they mutinied and kicked the captain off the ship.

Tamoro: That does not sound weak.

Chrisp: Yeah, right? But they hunted down the mutineers, because Bligh lived. Christian let him live, along with his followers. And Bligh returned to hunt them down. First lesson of mutiny, Jens says, kill the captain.

Tamoro: Mr Jensen said you should kill the ship's captain?

Chrisp: [*expletive*]! No! That's not what I'm saying! He was talking about a [*expletive*] book! If you saw how hard Jens looked for Skipper that next day, there's no way you could think he could do that. I'm not saying the two were buddies. But Jens immediately took command when we couldn't find Skipper on board, issued orders without missing a beat. He turned the scow around, man. Anybody else wouldn't have dared, 'cause it could have capsized the scow. It damn near did, too, but Jens was always one step ahead, knowing what was coming and what to do before it happened. When a swell like that hits you broadside, you tumble and sink. It's [*expletive*] dangerous. If Jens didn't care about Skipper, he wouldn't have even risked a search. He only called off the search when your people ordered him to!

Tamoro: Some historians claim that, as you mention Jensen saying, Fletcher Christian was indeed weak, that he, um, 'lacked a back bone', if I have the English correct. Some claim he was manipulated by the crew, that his Captain was not only supportive of his career, but was a friend. Captain Bligh made Mr Christian his First Mate, just as Mr Manuel made Mr Jensen First Mate. Some even maintain that Christian suffered mental health issues. Can you describe the mental condition of First Mate Andrew Jensen?

Chrisp: I thought you weren't familiar with the story.

Tamoro: Can you answer the question?

Chrisp: Of course I can. Jens was upright. He wasn't manipulated by anyone. And he always knew what he was doing. Are we done here?

Tamoro: Thank you, Mr Chrisp, yes. It is not my role to assign responsibility to the incident, merely to investigate. One more question. In your opinion, do you think it possible for Mr Manuel to have killed himself?

Chrisp: (Laughter) Not at all. He was far too stubborn for that.

Excerpt from Interview 3: Able Seaman Benjamin Stuart

Tamoro: What can you tell me of the night Mr Manuel went missing?

Stuart: Nothing much. It was a hell of a sea. After my

watch I went below to my bunk and fell asleep about as fast as my head hit the pillow.

Tamoro: And you heard nothing during the night?

Stuart: Like I said, I was out. I didn't hear anything until Jens was waking me up to start looking for Skipper.

Tamoro: Do you have anything to add? About the decision to carry on? The relationship between Mr Manuel and Mr Jensen?

Stuart: No. It's not my place to get involved with officers.

Tamoro: Did you see anything that may have led you to believe that Mr Manuel would have deliberately fallen overboard?

Stuart: If you knew Skipper, you would know that he would rather throw all of us overboard before he ever considered himself.

Tamoro: Thank you. I need to explore all possibilities in this investigation. Is there anything you can add will help with the investigation into the incident?

Stuart: I don't have anything to add.

Excerpt from Interview 4: First Mate Andrew Jensen

Tamoro: Mr Jensen, you were the last to see Mr Manuel alive, is that correct?

Jensen: As far as I know, yes, I was.

Tamoro: Why was Mr Manuel on deck during your watch?

Jensen: I don't know. Perhaps to check the vessel one last time before he turned in.

Tamoro: And what did he see?

Jensen: He saw line strewn across the deck. He was very upset about it, and he let me know—

Tamoro: By shouting at you?

Jensen: That's exactly how he let me know.

Tamoro: And what did you do, in response?

Jensen: I tidied all the line.

Tamoro: What was Mr Manuel wearing at the time?

Jensen: He was wearing his wet weather gear. Red jacket and black pants.

Tamoro: And personal floatation device or tether line?

Jensen: Skipper never wore those. At all.

Tamoro: Were you wearing a personal floatation device and tether?

Jensen: Of course I was. All the crew, at least when they were on my watch, wore them.

Tamoro: Your watch, Able Seaman Chrisp. Where was he at the time Mr Manuel was on deck?

Jensen: He was in the engine room. I ordered him down to keep an eye on the engines, and get him out of the storm.

Tamoro: You raised the alarm of Mr Manuel's absence six hours later. Why the delay?

Jensen: I don't understand what you mean by delay. I was kept very busy by the storm, and when my watch ended and I handed over the deck, I was exhausted. So, I caught a couple hours sleep.

Tamoro: And Mr Manuel was not on the next watch?

Jensen: The skipper doesn't take a watch. A skipper has to be above that, to keep a clear overview of the ship at all times. I went to Skipper's cabin to wake him for breakfast and coffee. He didn't answer, so I entered his cabin and found it empty. I checked the head, and other parts of the scow. When I couldn't find him anywhere, I ordered all hands to search. When they, too, couldn't find Skipper, I initiated MoB safety procedures.

Tamoro: Do you think it possible Mr Manuel deliberately fell overboard?

Jensen: I have no idea. Maybe. He was pretty stressed about the contract.

Tamoro: Your actions during the emergency were logged in meticulous detail. Your search was very professional.

Jensen: Thank you. MoB is a very serious situation.

Tamoro: The logs show that you held a MoB drill with your watch just two days prior.

Jensen: Like I said, MoB is very a serious matter. And Maritime Law requires that crew be regularly drilled in emergency procedures.

Tamoro: One last question, Mr Jensen. Did you like your skipper, Mr Manuel?

Jensen: It doesn't matter if I liked him or not. I had a job to do so I endeavored to do it. It's about the ship, not the people.

Tamoro: But can you answer my question?

Jensen: I just did.

The summary ended with conclusions and recommendations: The missing crew member fell overboard in a period of unsettled weather; the crew member is missing at sea and presumed dead; the crew member was not wearing a pfd or safety line; there were no conclusive findings as to why the crew member was on deck nor how or why he fell overboard; and that the skipper of the vessel was under considerable pressure from the employing company, Pacific Clean-up Solutions (PaCSol) to complete contracted delivery of refuse which may have influenced his decision to sail northwards during storm conditions.

The final recommendation was that the crew of the *Ana Marie* should be detained in their home port until police authorities were completely satisfied that none of the crew played a role in the disappearance and presumed death of their skipper. Only the authorities never got to do that.

Peter shifted in his seat. "There's a lot of ... I mean ... There was a recommendation in the report, after what happened, with the skipper going missing." Peter let the words flow out, worried Jens would stop him. "The *Ana Marie* was on lockdown and the crew were confined to harbor pending a police investigation. And yet you got a job on the *Cirrus* and left the planet."

Peter watched Jens take another sip of his drink, held by the older man's eyes. He sensed a shift in their relationship and knew that his whole plan was balancing on a precipice. He knew that if Dr Lin had known he was going to bring this up, she would not have trusted him to come. She would no doubt learn that he broached the subject with Jens, and he would have to deal with that when it happened.

Peter chose his next words carefully. "You can't do that without help," he said. "And I need that kind of help."

"That was a long time ago," Jens said. Long ago, on a different world, when he was a different man, pushed and goaded beyond his endurance, until he finally snapped, killed a man and threw his body overboard. He lifted his drink to his lips but merely breathed in the scent of rum and mix.

"But he is still on Hokkaido," Peter said. "If it was who I think it was."

"He's retired." Jens said.

"Yes," Peter said. "But he must have influence with the Consortium. I think they'll want this. But first I have to get a meeting. With the *right* people."

Peter tried to appear relaxed, and not at all like he was trying to manipulate his host. In all the interviews Jens ever made, in all the articles or books written about the GLR convoy or the discovery of Pemako, he had never admitted to powerful friends or strings being pulled. Peter nudged his glass. "Can I have one more?" he asked.

"Of course," Jens said, pouring two fingers of rum and an equal amount of mix. He looked across at Peter and shrugged, a gesture that was part of his inner dialogue about the young man talking to him, trying to separate past from present.

"They met when my dad was young, on his OE," Jens said.

"What's an OE?" Peter asked.

"A tradition," Jens answered. "After finishing school, a lot of people spent a year or so traveling around. It's a big thing when you live on an island at the bottom of the planet. 'Overseas Experience'. Go see the world before settling down with a family and a job. Europe, Asia, wherever. In the olden days it was a lot harder to get away. Before my time, and my dad's time. But it's something we do—cultural rite of passage or something. My dad went to Mexico where he met up with a Japanese guy doing the same. They travelled together for a while, and stayed in touch over the years. He came to New Zealand a couple times. The first time was right after I was born. My family were never religious, but he became a sort of godfather to me. That's an even older tradition. Do you know what that is?"

"No."

"Parents used to choose a person or a couple to be there in case anything ever happened to them," Jens explained. "If they died, there would be somebody to look after their child. It was a real honor to be asked to do that. That is what they asked him to do."

"And he worked for the Consortium?" Peter asked.

"Not when he and my dad met. That's the career he went into after," Jens said. "Maybe his OE was a last burst of freedom before he started. When he got back to Japan, he started work, climbed the ladder, and became quite an important player."

"And that's who you called?" Peter asked.

Jen stared at Peter. "Patricia thinks this should happen," he said. "I didn't always like her. When I first met her, I thought she was insufferable. I couldn't stand being around her, but I had to, because I was in charge, and I was responsible for her. Not that she cared about that. I thought she was arrogant, and selfish, and patronizing. But I grew to respect her, and to like her, even love her, like a sister. She is somebody I admire greatly. And she obviously trusts you, which is the only reason

I am telling you any of this. I expect that trust not to be broken."

Peter found himself swallowing again. "Do you think he could get me a meeting?" he asked.

"I don't know," Jens admitted. "But I'll write a letter, one that you can hand to him, and one that only he ever reads. You are to make no copies, and mention it to nobody. Only he can decide what he will do."

"Thank you," Peter said.

7

"You don't look nervous," Michael said.

"I'm not," Peter answered.

"I'm practically having an anxiety attack."

"Just breathe," Peter said. "Deeply, through your nose. Exhale slowly through your mouth. You have nothing to worry about."

"Nothing?" Michael said. "We have *everything* to worry about! If this works, then we'll have funding for over five years."

"More," Peter said. "Now relax," he added softly. "And be quiet. I need to prepare."

"What do you mean, prepare?" Michael asked. "We rehearsed all night!"

"Michael," Peter said. "Relax."

Peter gazed across the waiting room. Wide entrance doors opened into the reception, a perfectly designed purgatory where every soul was made to wait, given time to sit and watch worries and fears surface. A glass wall stood behind them, offering a view of the Sapporo business district. Beyond the busy city center, the green surrounding Hokkaido University offered a welcome contrast. In the center of the room an indifferent receptionist sat behind an imposing desk. She was able to survey every corner of the room, but never looked up. At the far wall were two more doors. Entrance to the inner sanctum.

Before Stepping back to Earth, Peter withdrew the envelope Jens gave him from his satchel and looked at the seal. He peeled back a corner of the lip, stopping when it began to tear. He held the envelope side on, examining the fold. Taking the envelope to the small refreshment machine in his cabin, he dialed in hot water. As soon as the water filled the waiting cup, he held the back of the envelope over the steam. It was an old-fashioned trick, but it might work. Envelopes were extremely old fashioned.

Peter turned the envelope over and picked at the fold, loosening the edges. Emptying the cooling cup, he dialed another hot water. The machine hissed as the contents filled the cup. Peter held the envelope closely over it. Turning it over, he pried at the seal some more. After several more attempts the envelope was open and he withdrew the letter. A small note bearing his name fell out with it. He opened it.

Do not worry about your introduction. Just prepare for your meeting. You'll need a translator if you insist on being nosy, and put this letter back undamaged. You shouldn't read letters intended for another person. Jens.

Chastised, Peter unfolded the letter and looked at the hiragana symbols that made up the most common Japanese alphabet. He passed a scanner bar over the page.

Dear Honorary Father, it began. The translator seemed to struggle with the term, *gifu-ue*.

You will have by now received the family's transmissions sent with the last convoy returning to Earth. My grandchild has grown even more since. Jiao is very clever, nearly as tall as the kitchen table. Being a grandfather is just as you said it would be: an absolute joy.

This note is a form of introduction. The young man standing before you, Dr Peter Taylor, has an important request. Many lives may be at stake. If what Peter believes is true, this may be an opportunity to save those thought long lost, and may also be of benefit to the Consortium. I believe that if he were able to meet with the right executives, they would agree to help him.

I have asked you for help once before, and for that I consider myself honored to be in your debt. But I vowed that I would never again put my own needs before those of our relationship. I find myself breaking that vow. I hope this request is not seen as selfish, although on one level, that is what it is, and that is what I am being. However, I wish you to consider this request without thought to any personal reasons I may have.

I wish that you and Aki are in fine health and spirits.
Your son, Andrew

Peter folded the letter and carefully placed it back. Using some glue, he resealed the envelope. It stayed that way until he handed it to Jens' godfather. It was a gamble. Sometimes it's not what you know, but who you know. To get a high-level meeting at a Consortium, Peter needed to know someone. Or, in this case, know the person who did.

Jens' contact lived over one hundred kilometers from

Sapporo, in a luxurious beach house on Uchiura Bay. The taxi drove at least half a kilometer down a private drive before reaching the place. He told the driver to wait and got out. The sound of waves breaking on the shore followed Peter as he walked to the front door. He knocked and an old man answered.

At a loss for words, Peter handed over the letter. "This is from Andrew Jensen," he managed to say.

The old man didn't invite him in. He opened the envelope in the doorway and read the letter. When he finished, he folded it and put it back.

"Was this your idea, Dr Taylor?" His voice was expressionless.

"Yes," Peter admitted.

"And how will you be reached?"

Peter couldn't read the man's mood. He fumbled for his wallet and withdrew a business card, handing it over.

The man took the card. "Very well," he said without looking at it. "You will be contacted." He closed the door, leaving Peter alone on the front steps.

Two days later he received a call, probably from the receptionist sitting in the center of the room, giving him a time for a meeting. Those two days of waiting, between his brief visit to Uchiura Bay and the phone call, were full of anxiety. Peter didn't like uncertainty, but it seemed to follow him around as a constant teacher. *Nothing is certain*, he would remind himself. *Life is not certain. Worrying won't change or hasten the outcome*. But he was nervous. He let himself hope, and in doing so became vulnerable to disappointment and failure.

But two days later the phone rang offering a time to meet, and all uncertainty evaporated. He couldn't explain it, or share it with Michael, but he felt confident.

He settled into breathing, just like he advised his friend, and stared at the doors on the opposite side of the room, losing track of time.

"Dr Taylor! Dr Hollis!" the receptionist called, snapping Peter out of his meditation. She was standing in front of the double doors, now opened.

"Come on," Michael whispered. He stood over Peter and offered a hand.

Peter grabbed it and was lifted to his feet. He clapped Michael on the back. "Time to go to work," he said, walking forward. He smiled as he passed the receptionist, who stared back expressionless.

Four men sat at one end of a large table made from a single slab of wood. They did not get up or smile. Instead, they stared at the newcomers with the same lack of emotion as the receptionist. Peter and Michael knew who they were. Once the invite was in their hands, they learned what they could of the executives they would have to impress.

At the far end of the table sat Susumo Motoyo, the CEO of HakKor Consortium, the most powerful man in northeast Asia and the Siberian far east. Motoyo was where the road ended—or began, if he saw merit in their proposal. On his right sat Masaru Yamaguchi, known as The Elder. He had a long history with HakKor, rising to prominence in the absorption of the resource rich Amur Basin. There were a lot of theories about how he had wrested *that* from the Russians. To Peter that wasn't important. What was important was the fact that The Elder was someone they absolutely had to win over. Yuji Mikitani sat next to Yamaguchi. The youngest at the table, power hungry and opportunistic, looking for his Basin to absorb and cement his position. On Motoyo's left sat his son-in-law and heir apparent, Guichi Soichiro. An accountant by training, he had an eye for detail.

Peter smiled at the papers each had in front of them—the proposal he had sent as soon as he had accepted their appointment. When Michael realized what they were he glanced at Peter, but quickly recovered. The plan was to sell them the story, offer their proposal through a very well-prepared presentation (which Michael spent hours creating) and only then following up with the numbers. Peter had evidently decided to change the play.

Both men bowed to the executives.

"Gentlemen," Motoyo said. "Please, be seated."

Two empty chairs waited at the other end of the table. Peter and Michael straightened from their bows and sat.

After what he gauged was a suitable pause, Peter spoke. "Thank you for seeing us," he said.

"I was advised by an old friend that it may be of benefit to the Consortium," Motoyo said. "That I hear what you have to say."

"Once again, *arigato*," Peter said. "Thank you."

"Your proposal promises much," Mikitani said, fingering the sheaf of papers in front of him. "But it offers no guarantees. It asks us to take all the risk, whereas you risk nothing."

Peter could feel Michael's eyes on him. Peter looked at Mikitani and smiled softly. "I forwarded our proposal," he said, for the men across the table, as well his partner sitting beside him, "so you would know, from the beginning, what we are willing to offer in exchange for your support." He turned and faced the executives at the far end of the long table that stretched away, making the men seem as out of reach as the dream they came to sell.

"But you are mistaken to assume that we take no risk," Peter said. "Our risk may even be greater. We don't want this project misused, so we choose to trust you. It's because we believe you are trustworthy that we come to you. We bring information that will not only transform your consortium into the most powerful on this planet, it will transform the planet. We could have tried to sell this with a dog and pony show, a flash presentation, but instead we offer the numbers."

"There are many numbers missing," Soichiro said. "Such as the location of this phantom ship."

"The numbers are not missing," Peter said. "They simply are not in the proposal. We will provide the course trajectory of the Seed ship, as well as its estimated location. The math is infallible."

"As you say," Soichiro said. "But unfortunately, that is not all that is missing. There is no inventory of the technology you promise."

"That's because we don't know what technology there is," Peter admitted. He could feel Michael trying not glare at him again. The plan had been to avoid admitting that. At least until they were ready to hand their proposal to the executives, *after* Michael's presentation prepared them for it. "But there most certainly will be technology. The Artifact that Ambassador Jensen and Dr Ling brought back revolutionized space travel. Cryo-technology, weaponry, airlocks, speed, radiation shielding—those are just a few examples. The point is that the Artifact was a mere scout ship, on a seek and acquire mission. As you can see in our proposal, the purpose of the Seed ship was not to scout, but to settle. That ship will have everything the Ruan would require to create another home. It will contain every piece of state-of-the-art technology from their home world."

"*Might* contain," Yamaguchi said.

"Might contain," Peter conceded. "With all due respect, Yamaguchi-san, just as our settlement convoys contain what is needed to build a new world, so too will that of the Ruan. And, Soichiro-san, we have no inventory, because we cannot even imagine what that ship will contain. Not knowing that could be seen as a risk."

"Not knowing that *is* a risk, Dr Taylor," Yamaguchi growled.

"Yes, Yamaguchi-san," Peter answered. "It is a risk. That is why we have come to you, and not any other consortium."

"And tell us, aside from your professed trust in us, why have you come to HakKor?" Motoyo asked. "Why not our larger neighbors? Or have you already? I am sure Beijing would be most interested."

"No, Motoyo-san," Peter said. "We have not approached another Consortium. It is HakKor we wish align with."

"And why is that, Dr Taylor?"

"Because you are hungry, Motoyo-san. HakKor is not the largest or most powerful Consortium, but it wants to be. And because it wants to be, it will take risks. *You* will take risks." Peter scanned the faces across the table, trying to decipher their moods. But his specialty was words, not faces. "If you will permit me?" he asked, indicating his briefcase.

He took their silence as permission, opened the case and took out a data card. "This contains a message that we would like to share with you. I have studied under Dr Lin for the last five years. Dr Hollis joined us to help confirm our findings and offer his expertise. Dr Lin is currently on Pemako, continuing her research. She was unable to leave her work and travel with us. But she recorded this for you. If I may?" Peter asked.

Motoyo gestured with an open hand.

Peter unfolded the card until it was the size of his opened hand, pointed it towards a wall, touched the message icon and sat back. A blue light projected onto the opposing wall and an image of Dr Lin appeared. Peter rested his hands on the arm of his chair, trying not to grip the arm rest. Michael was doing the same. They were used to Dr Lin's way of communicating. They watched the message several times and argued about bringing it, but realized they had no choice. Two young strangers with tales and numbers would never sway a Consortium. If anybody could it was the world-renowned expert on the alien race.

"Gentlemen," the projected image of Dr Lin said. She was wearing her trademark coveralls. She leaned against a wall built by the Originals. The setting wasn't staged, it was where she happened to be working when Peter finally caught up with her with the tablet. However, as backdrops, it was very appropriate.

"I must assume that my colleagues, Drs Taylor and Hollis, have told you what we want and why. I also trust that you are in no doubt as to what you will gain. We have no interest in the technology this ship will be carrying. We give you all rights to copy whatever the ship carries, including the technology represented by the ship itself. We cannot give you the artifacts on board, nor can we give you the ship. They are not ours to give. They belong to the Ruan. This is all in the proposal the doctors present to you. All that we want is to reach the Ruan, to make contact with this species, and to escort them back to Pemako.

"I would not stake my reputation, as I am now doing," she continued, "on a hunch, or a guess. We are scientists, not gamblers. Dr Taylor has found the evidence you need, and Dr Hollis has computed the course of the Seed ship. I stand by my colleagues, as I do this venture. You would do well to do the same." The image of Dr Lin started to walk off the screen but stopped. She came back and brought her face closer to the screen.

"Thank you," she said firmly, and the recording finished.

Motoyo leaned back in his chair, grinning. Peter tried to read the faces across the table again. There was a change.

"Mikitani?" Motoyo asked.

"How big is this *Seed* ship?" Mikitani asked.

"We don't know," Peter answered.

"How many Ruan are supposed to be on it?" Mikitani tried.

"We don't know," Michael said. "What is clear in all the data we have come across is the number two. This could mean two hundred, or two thousand, or twenty thousand. But they are there. Their intention was to find a habitable planet and settle it."

"Soichiro?" Motoyo asked.

"What they propose would be a significant re-direction of Consortium funds," he answered. "They will require a new type of ship to catch and stop the Ruan. The ship specifications alone—"

"Are small compared to potential return," Mikitani interrupted. It was Peter's turn to sit back. He wanted to grin, but didn't want to be obvious. The smallest fish was hooked.

"Let Guichi finish," Motoyo said.

"The ship's specifications call for state of the art technology, some of which only exists in theory. It will take years to complete," Guichi Soichiro said. "And the Donut they will need is not one that we currently possess. That will require acquisition and upgrade. Or a new build, again taking years of effort and resources. You are certainly asking for a lot." The last comment was directed at the other end of the table.

"As you can see, as I hope you can see," Peter said, "it will be worth it."

"A significant re-direction of funds," Motoyo repeated. "But?"

"But not of such a size as to place our current position in jeopardy," Soichiro said. "I have had my department analyze potential negative scenarios. We could survive failure, make the most of what is learned in building and equipping the mission."

"And positive scenarios?" Motoyo asked.

"As is implied in Drs Taylor and Hollis' proposal," Soichiro said. "Unlimited potential applications of the alien technology, all controlled by HakKor."

Motoyo indicated to Mikitani. The younger man opened his mouth to speak, but closed it. He sat up straight and tried again. "Sir. It is my belief that the Consortium should accept this proposal. I would very much like to lead this project."

"Of course, it is. And of course, you would," Yamaguchi said, his voice like a rasp against wood. "And we all agree to acceptance. Dr Taylor, Dr Hollis, thank you for your time, and for this opportunity. We have studied your proposal and would like to begin contract negotiations."

Peter looked at Michael. This time he let himself smile. Beyond that, he was unsure of what he was supposed to do.

"If tomorrow morning is suitable, you can meet our legal department to begin discussing the niceties. It seems that you now work for the HakKor Consortium," Motoyo said.

The four men pushed back their chairs and stood. Peter and Michael did likewise. As Motoyo began to bend at the waist, they bowed deeply, ensuring their backs were straight and their heads lower than the CEO's. They straightened and saw the four men smiling, walking towards them. Motoyo was first to reach out and shake their hands.

"Welcome," he said. "You will be assigned personal assistants, whose first job will be to find you more suitable accommodation than your current hotel."

Tending

8

Peter paused in the doorway to touch the carved lintel before entering the temple. It had become a personal ritual. Leave the street, climb the stone steps, pause at the door. He admired the detail. His fingers traced the scales on the backs of serpents as they wound around the frame. Every carved scale and claw and eye were unique, worried over. The door slid effortlessly when he pushed it. Even that was exquisitely crafted, one panel moving into another, catching it and sliding it open as it moved.

Peter hoped that type of care was also being shown above, as Mikitani kept assuring. Or reassuring. He had to take him at his word, at least until today when he wouldn't have to anymore. Three years into the project and he would finally see the build first hand, and finally leave the cold island that was home to the consortium.

Peter slid the door closed, leaving the hum of the electric cars and hover pods of the city behind. He slowly untied his shoes and took them off. He emptied his pockets and placed the contents in a shoe, then slid the shoes into a cubby. He entered the moya, the center of the temple, and selected a cushion. He sat and tried to put aside the dozens of details that filled his day, primarily around the translation device, HakKor's first potentially marketable product to emerge from their partnership. He fought the feeling that it was his, because it was based on his work and his idea. But as their contract specified that all technology related to the project was the property of HakKor Consortium, he had to let it go.

As it was just past sunrise, he found it easier to achieve some semblance of calm. Typically, he would arrive at lunch and spend the first twenty minutes of his sit trying not to try to let go of his thoughts. This morning felt easier, definitely lighter. There was nothing that more worry would help.

Michael was waiting on the stone steps outside. He preferred the many Living Rooms dotted about the city to sitting on the floor and watching himself breathe. How close to 'God' he wanted to get depended less on the type of day he had, and more on those he spent it with. There was the full-blown mind dissolve. He could handle that once in a while, but when your entire universe dissipates into nothingness along with any sense of self, it takes a while to process on return to 'reality'. Time to process what was still meant by any notion of what reality was. No, Michael preferred to limit the dose as well as the experience, peer at the abyss from a comfortable and comforting distance. By himself.

He enjoyed being a team of one, alone with his formulae. It was familiar. Predictable. Unchallenging and devoid of social traps. But solitude was impossible as the lead of project astrogation. And leading was nigh impossible working with an astrogator whose experience was far more practical than his. Anna Giolino had Stepped before, and not like Michael, asleep in a cryo-pod until it was all over. She was in a Donut Hole with convoy astrogators and manipulating the AI to fold time and space, recently joining the team from a convoy to mining colonies. She was tall, athletic, beautiful. Months in a ship didn't dim the glow of her skin, or her deep brown eyes, or her wavy auburn hair.

Michael tried to deny, to himself, that he found her intimidating. Every woman intimidated Michael. He wondered why it was worse with Anna, or at least he pretended not to know.

Peter was different, at ease with whomever he spoke, regardless of beauty. He and Anna often engaged in conversations a monolingual bystander could only half follow, each wearing the translation receiver pinned to their shirt or jacket, ear bud discreetly whispering the other's words in their own language.

"Seriously, I didn't think he had it so bad." Peter, understandably in English.

"*Lo fece, arrossato e agitato.*" Anna in Italian, looking at Michael and laughing with Peter.

"*Ma è carino,*" she added, smiling and looking down.

Michael was none the wiser without the device, his red and flustered face being described by his colleague whenever conversation strayed into personal territory. And he was unaware that he was called cute. The translator was still prototype, and Michael had yet to try it. In fact, this was the first time he personally saw it in action. In developing a way to talk with aliens, they had stumbled on a device to help their own species communicate better. If it worked as well it seemed to, it was going to make HakKor a fortune.

The rest of the team were fine—hard working and really bright mathematicians. Michael admitted to himself, and privately to Peter, that he just didn't like being a boss or manager or whatever he was supposed to be. It was much more fun in a team of three like they were on Pemako—Peter buried in his recordings, Dr Lin in her findings, he in his numbers, and a warm ocean to swim in whenever he wanted. But then again, beautiful astrogators were not very common at archeological sites on that planet.

Michael pushed these thoughts from his mind and waited. Peter soon came out of the center, smiling peacefully, and patted Michael's shoulder as he walked down the stairs to the waiting company hover pod. Life at HakKor—neither of them had driven nor cleaned up after themselves since Motoyo shook their hands. But now the pampered city life was over.

"Let's go to the upstairs office," Peter said with a grin. "Chitose Space Port," he told the hover pod once he and Michael were strapped in. It lifted gently from the street, banked and flew west over the city, until the urban sprawl was replaced by the green of Shikotsu-Toya National Park. They both watched the landscape pass beneath, leaning into the large window to glimpse Mount Eniwa and the emerald Lake Shikotsu. Then forests gave way to farm fields, that turned into an industrial zone, and the hover pod descended to the space port.

Landing next to a HakKor flier, the door of the pod lifted. Peter and Michael stepped out, grabbed their bags and were greeted by a flight attendant who led them towards the small ship that would take them into orbit. The flier was suspended between the wings of the *Haha Tori,* or Motherbird. They climbed the detachable stairs to the *Chīsai Tori,* or Little Bird, that nestled securely underneath. Three team members were already strapped into their seats. Michael nodded to the technicians he recognized from the lab. Tatsuo Okada and Akira Yasuda were experts in Ruan technology. Their job would be to catalogue any and all equipment on the Seed ship, including the ship itself. Seated behind them was Shinto Doi, the nuclear physicist who had designed the reactor they were using. Anna was either already in orbit, or soon would be. The entire crew had been summoned for a team meeting. That meant the captain was finally on board.

Once they were strapped into their seats, the attendant informed the pilot.

"*Chīsai Tori* ready for flight," the pilot reported to the waiting, larger craft.

"Acknowledged, *Chīsai Tori. Haha Tori* ready for flight," the primary pilot said.

Peter and Michael looked around the flier. With only eight seats, and three of those empty, the small space felt larger than it was. Neither had ever flown in a private orbital flier, only the large commercial variety where space was for seats and seats had to be filled. Tight and cramped. The clink of glass near the cockpit signaled that in-flight refreshments might be quite different as well. They felt small but safe nested under the larger craft, a little bird held in the wings of its protective parent. The huge wing stretched away outside their window, half a football field in length. *Haha Tori* was basically nothing but this massive wing, interrupted by two strong engines and cockpits. Its sole purpose was to take the smaller craft to such an altitude that reaching orbit was a mere rocket thrust away.

The engines of *Motherbird* increased in volume and the mechanical family lurched towards the runway. The flier vibrated but the noise cancelling insulation reduced the roar outside to a murmur. Turning onto the long straight stretch of concrete, the noise and speed increased until the runway became a blur. The green hills in the distance grew closer and the force of takeoff pushed them into their seats, until the hills disappeared underneath. *Motherbird* continued to accelerate as she banked in her climb, an upward spiral taking them to the plane's service ceiling of eighty thousand feet.

As they settled into their ascent the attendant returned and took drink orders. A whisky on the rocks, in a designer glass. Red wine in a small decanter with a goblet. The mathematicians were brought their martinis complete with green olive. Peter sipped his wine as they climbed towards the thermosphere.

Finally, they reached their launch altitude and sat back as instructed. This part wasn't new. A lurch and a fall followed by a kick in the back. They listened to the communication between pilots.

"*Shiawasena hikō, Chīsai Hiyoko,*" they heard.

"He said, 'Happy flying'," Peter said. Michael looked over and saw the translator pinned to Peter's jacket.

"What are you doing with that?" Michael asked. "Those are top secret, aren't they?"

"They're *top useful*," Peter said, "and it won't be missed. I grabbed a few before we left. Got one for you too." Peter handed Michael an ear bud and the small translator. "I mean, what are they going to do, chase after us to get them back? Besides, there's going to be dozens on the ship."

"*Soshite, ichi-ni-san, Kaihō suru! Kaihō suru! Kaihō suru!*" *Motherbird*'s pilot said before Michael could turn the device on.

But Michael didn't need a translation. He understood release. He felt himself float upwards, held in place by the safety straps, as *Little Bird* detached and fell away from the larger ship. *Motherbird* turned sharply for her long descent back to the space port and away from her chick. Michael slammed back into the chair as the small flier's rocket ignited. The craft rattled and shuddered. His vision blurred as the force of acceleration squeezed the air out of his lungs.

And almost as soon as it started, it stopped. The sound. The pressure. The vibrations. The sky darkened until it became black, pierced by countless points of light. They were in space, staring at the vast expanse, mouths open and minds dazed. Peter felt himself rise in his straps as they left the Earth's gravity. His drink similarly rose, threatening to leave his body, but as the ship's thrusters kicked in, he felt both himself and the contents of his stomach settle back into the chair. When the desired acceleration was reached, the thrusters grew silent and he lifted once more. Peter tightened the straps so he didn't feel like he was floating.

The ship adjusted course and they saw their destination, at least the first of the day. Despite the distance, it still looked massive. Michael recognized the shape as a huge asterisk. At the end of each arm was a cuboid docking bay. Their flier adjusted course once more and angled towards one of the cuboids, still hours away. The attendant floated down the aisle and served meals—solids attached to the tray, softer foods and drinks in tubes. Michael sucked absentmindedly on a tube tasting of something Italian, the hub slowly growing larger outside his window. Returning to Earth from Pemako, they had flown cargo class, transiting to a flier with the other passenger, having no time to appreciate the design. Woken from cryo-sleep, herded through immigration checks, strapped into the surface bound craft. Michael smiled as he got to appreciate his surroundings, and sipped a tube of wine.

Midway to the hub the flier slowly flipped and faced its stern towards their target. The thrusters kicked and they were pressed into their seats once more as the craft decelerated. Finally, it rotated until its bow faced the docking bay. A green light filled the view screen, all that separated the vacuum of space from the air in the structure. Michael glanced at Okada and Yasuda. They didn't bother looking up, both engrossed in a book or magazine. Michael shook his head and stared. It was the first time he had seen the alien technology adapted for use. Both the technicians had been involved in creating the airlocks, now standard equipment in hubs and ships, the death of space kept at bay through a curtain of energy.

The flier crossed through the field and into the docking bay; the only indication of passing was a green curtain flickering over the view screen. The craft drifted to a platform, nestled against it and deployed clamps to make the connection solid. As the doors began to dial open, Michael grabbed the arm rests, expecting the air inside to blow out. Instead, the door simply lifted open and he breathed normally.

The attendant reminded them to activate their grav-shoes once outside the flier. Michael bent down and turned them on. He grabbed his bag and stepped out onto the platform. He reached out and grasped the nearest handrail, entering the cavernous space of the docking bay. Hundreds of meters across an entire wall the name HakKor was emblazoned in red paint. Looking down the same distance he could see the floor. Or the ceiling. The only thing giving meaning to up or down was his boots sticking to the decking.

"Sirs, if I could take your bags please," he heard. A young man in HakKor coveralls placed their baggage on a small platform and fastened them down. *"If you'll follow me, I'll show you to your transport."*

"Can't even tell what language he's speaking, can you?" Peter asked.

"No," Michael admitted. "Just the small delay. I think it was a delay."

"That's your brain trying to keep up," Peter said. "There's no delay with my translator. It works as fast as you can hear. You get used it."

They followed their guide to a rounded and polished larger craft. If it ever confronted air it would slip between the molecules. Only it would never fly in air. Shape didn't matter in space, but somebody at HakKor cared a great deal about appearance. Thick oval windows revealed class inside as well as out. Wide faux leather chairs could turn towards the window or the small tables. Not just appearance—comfort as well. It didn't take long to get used to Consortia Class.

Michael and Peter stepped through the hatch and into the plush compartment. Half the seats were already occupied. They found two that were together, sat down and swiveled to face the others.

"You must be doctors Taylor and Hollis," a uniformed man said, before either could say anything. "Welcome. I am Anders Middleton, First Mate of the *Kestrel*."

"Pleased to meet you," Peter said as Michael smiled and nodded in the man's direction. "I'm Taylor, he's Hollis."

"And Dr Doi, it is once again a pleasure. I trust you'll find the reactors ready to go."

"*Arigato*, First Mate Middleton." Doi moved his head, more a nod than a bow.

"As for you," he gestured to the others, "I'm afraid I only know you as names on the manifest."

"I'm Donna Wright," a blond Anglo woman said. Peter turned off his translator in order hear an accent. "Ship's medical specialist. And xeno-biologist."

"Dr Wright," the First Mate said. "A pleasure." He was definitely Norwegian. She … Canadian? A soft North American accent, western, likely somewhere in the plains like Alberta or Saskatchewan.

"Tatsuo Okada, Technical Expert," the first technician said.

"Akiro Yasuda, also Technical Expert," the other added.

"Excellent," Anders said. "It may be a while before you get

your hands on any Ruan hardware, but there will be plenty on board *Chōgenbō* to keep you busy. We've adapted several features from the Artifact, as you know."

Both men nodded their heads as Doi had done.

Michael heard the name *Kestrel* through his translation bud. He liked the name. The kestrel hunts by gaining altitude and hovering as it scans, before swooping down and grabbing its prey. It was a bird that hunted alone, and they would be very alone in their hunt.

"I am Kumiko Mori," a slight Japanese woman said.

"Communications and sensors," Anders said. "Welcome. I'm sure you'll be impressed with our equipment."

"*Arigato,*" she answered.

"The others are already on *Chōgenbō,*" Middleton said, "and as soon we join them, we can have our first full crew meeting. She's about four hours out, so you'll have time to talk, rest, eat, whatever you prefer. But we should be making waves, as the saying goes. Captain," he said towards the bow, "we're ready to depart."

"Copy that," the pilot answered. "Transport leaving now."

They felt the craft gently disengage from the walkway and the thrusters push them towards the curtain separating inside from out. The transport left the light of the docking bay, eased through the green energy field and floated away from the space hub.

"Might be a bit of kick soon," the First Mate warned.

They all settled back into their chairs as the transport's reactor propelled the ship towards its destination.

9

Chōgenbō, the *Kestrel*, was stationed within its construction frame. Everybody in the transport gazed out at its sleek lines. Lights positioned around the frame reflected off the smooth silver surface. Its bow narrowed to a sharp point, sensitive antennae protruding outward. As the curve of the hull widened, strengthened radiation-shielding metal was replaced by the glass view port of the bridge.

The transport pilot slowed the craft as it passed over their new home. Three large view ports formed a line down the side, towards a fin that contained positional thrusters. A green energy field extended from the docking frame to the top of the ship. Technicians could be seen inside, working on the surface of the hull with helmets off and hands uncovered. They moved about a tube the length of a man that protruded from a dome attached to the deck. The electronic shield, creating a heated air pocket around them, allowed them to use their bare hands and work with finer tools than the gloves on the bulkier atmospheric suits.

"Is that a gun?" Peter asked.

"State of the art," Anders said. "Adapted from the Artifact. With some improvements."

"The *Kestrel* is armed?" Peter protested.

"I assumed you were briefed on all aspects of the design of the *Chōgenbō*," Anders said.

"Not all aspects, evidently," Peter said.

"Every ship is armed these days," Anders said. "Seekers lurking in the dark corners of space," he added sarcastically. "It's an unfortunate feature of travel. But it makes sense that if others are armed, we should also be armed, especially on a ship as valuable as the *Chōgenbō*. And we know nothing of the Ruan, or what we'll find when we reach them. It's a wise precaution, don't you think?"

Peter could only nod, unable to argue with the logic. He looked closer at the hull and noticed another protrusion behind the fin. There was, no doubt, a matching copy on the other side. He wondered what other features were built into the *Chōgenbō* that he did not know about.

The transport continued its flight by the ship. At the stern, all pretense of aerodynamics ceased. The body of the ship widened until it formed a large box-like shape containing the reactors that would make it the fastest ship yet constructed. Inside sat three reactors, each a fusion of human and Ruan technology, that could accelerate to achieve speeds that were previously mere design aspirations. The same thrust could decelerate just as quickly as it reached full velocity. It was pure power. Peter looked over at Shintaro Doi as they passed the reactors. They were Doi's babies, and he looked the proud father.

The transport drew close to the port side of the *Chōgenbō*, nestling beside a green glow in the ship's hull. A walkway with a metal frame extended and connected the two craft. There was a flicker of light and a green transparent curtain formed a green-tinted tunnel.

"Docking complete," the pilot announced.

"Welcome to the *Chōgenbō*," Anders said to the party on board. "Grab whatever you brought on board. I'm afraid there'll be no porters from now on. You should find all the belongings that were sent earlier in your quarters." He stooped and picked up his own bag. "But first, the captain would like to meet you. Please follow me."

Anders dialed open the door leading into the walkway. He crossed over the short bridge and walked through the green curtain at the end, disappearing inside the *Chōgenbō*. Doi followed. The others held back.

"*Daijōbudesu,*" Okada said. "*Osoreru koto wanai.*" He laughed.

Michael started to turn his translator back on, but realized that the technician didn't have one. If he could understand Michael's English, then he could also speak it.

"Excuse me?" Michael asked.

"Nothing to worry about," Okada said. "It's okay. Look."

Okada picked up his bag, went over to the walkway and put his hand against the wall of the force field. It vibrated against his palm, but kept it inside the tunnel.

"Space on the outside, air on the inside," he said, walking into the *Chōgenbō* without looking back. "Just stay inside with the air," he added over his shoulder.

All the others followed, one at a time, until the transport

was empty. Each hesitated before walking through the airlock, but passed through.

"This way to the mess," Anders said. "You'll soon learn your way around."

Anders led the party to what seemed like the middle of the ship, where he turned right and walked towards the front. Before reaching the bridge, he stopped at a doorway marked, "Messroom". He motioned towards the room.

"After you," he said.

They filed in. The remainder of the team was already sitting around a large central table. Michael's eyes ran over his crewmates. He stopped and smiled at Anna. She returned the smile before turning her face towards Peter and smiling to him. Peter set his bag down and walked to the empty seat next to her. Michael took one further down the table, next to Komiko, the communications specialist.

A man stood after they all entered. His balding head, and the color of his hair gave his age as late fifties or early sixties. He was neither tall nor short, but still he didn't convey merely average. His energy filled the room. They all knew who he was. Captain Solvieg Olsen had spent a lifetime on HakKor freighters and exploratory vessels. He was Motoyo's personal pick, and there were no objections—not because Motoyo was the CEO of the Consortia, but because Olsen was the best choice.

"Welcome to the *Chōgenbō*," he said. "It's nice to see all the chairs around this table finally occupied." He looked at the one empty seat. "Except for Dr Lin, who will be joining when we reach Pemako. I am the captain of the ship, Solvieg Olsen."

Olsen sat down to murmured greetings and nods. He wasn't one for speeches—he didn't enjoy listening to them, and he didn't enjoy giving them. But he recognized that on some occasions they couldn't be avoided.

"We'll be living together for quite some time," he said. "Which will give you all plenty of time to get to know each other better. *Chōgenbō* is a beautiful ship, built for purpose. That purpose is to track down an alien ship, and bring it back to where it started. There are a lot of unknowns involved with the venture. Personally, I don't like unknowns. But we have no choice. For me, as captain, to be confident of the ship and its crew, is knowing that we are prepared for any eventuality. That will mean a great deal of work. Before we join the Donut, before we Step anywhere, I will need to be absolutely certain that not only the *Chōgenbō* is up to task, but that every one of you are as well."

He let his gaze travel the length of the table. "Everybody will become familiar with every job on the ship. During the next months as you master your own station, you will show and teach each other. You will also second key positions. Communication, piloting, engineering and medical. There is no such thing as too much redundancy."

Olsen closed his eyes, drawing up a name from memory. "Dr Donna Wright," he said, "our medical specialist."

"Right here, Captain," she said.

"We're going to be around each far too much for titles,"

Olsen said, opening his eyes. "Anders, what am I called on board?" he asked.

"Behind your back, or to your face?" Anders answered.

"Better keep it to my face."

"Skip. Cap. Chief. Olsen."

"Olsen'll do," he said. "Dr Wright—"

"Donna."

"Donna," Olsen started again. "After you thoroughly familiarize yourself with sick bay and all the supplies on board, I'd like you to ensure every crew member has the essential skills to keep each other alive. You can draw up your own program of training."

"Yes, sir," she answered.

"Dr Lin will be joining us when we reach Pemako, and we will be fortunate to have two doctors on board. But please give the crew the necessary know-how needed to keep each other alive during an emergency. Always plan as if you aren't going to make it, but you want everybody else to."

"Yes, sir," she said.

"And the same from each of you," Olsen added. "Hiroto and his team will ensure you will all be able to defend yourselves and the ship. Everything in the arsenal, from the cannon outside to what you have in the locker."

"We have guns *in* the ship?" Peter asked.

"We most certainly do, kept secure." Olsen's eyes shifted left as he visualized the manifest. "Taylor?" he asked.

"Yeah," he answered. "Peter Taylor. Peter."

"Peter. Our xeno-linguist," Olsen said. "Welcome aboard.

And yes, we most certainly have guns. As I said, there are many unknowns in what we are doing. We will be prepared."

Peter opened his mouth to speak but couldn't think of anything of value to say. He didn't like guns, didn't think guns should be on or in a ship. Definitely did not want guns involved with contacting those on the Seed ship. But it wasn't up to him. He closed his mouth and nodded to the captain.

"There is one exception to our training regime, of course." He indicated to Anna. "How much our astrogator participates in your departments will entirely be up to her." He turned in her direction. "I will trust your judgement as to how much time you wish to spend learning from the others, and how much you can give to them. You'll be working with a special type of Donut."

"Thank you, sir, I appreciate that," Anna said. "But if you've seen the specs, I just might want a break now and again."

"I have seen them," Olsen said. "Which is why I'm leaving it to you."

"I would like to ask," Anna said, "if I may take more of our mathematician's time than the others. I will need another who can make sense of the numbers."

"Certainly," Olsen said, looking over at Michael, who sat helpless as his face flushed red. Olsen's smile returned.

"I think that's enough talking from me," he said. "You may have noticed we don't have a designated galley slave, so we will all be doing the cooking. Anders will draw up a roster for managing shared meals. We'll come together once a fortnight as a whole company. But you'll be fending for yourselves most of the time. If you haven't spaced much before you will soon learn that when sharing a galley, your crew mates are happier when it is left clean. So, see that it is. But enough for now." Olsen rose from his seat. "Let's get some food and drinks on the table and get to know each other better."

10

Michael set his bag down and examined his quarters. They were comfortable, but nowhere near as comfortable as his apartment in Sapporo. Two rooms and an ensuite washing facility. Water closet, the English had once called them. It was certainly small enough to be considered a closet. Queen sized bed, which was lot better than a single. Refreshment corner with water tap. Desk and study area. Everything was fixed to the deck, except for the state-of-the-art computer system that was built into the wall. It even had a lounge area, with a small coffee table and two comfortable looking chairs. Michael sank into one and decided it wasn't just looks. He smiled as he saw the bookshelves, more than sufficient space to hold the physical books he had brought. It was a nice touch. They looked as if they were made from real wood. The cases containing his belongings, everything he had packed for the duration, were stacked tidily by the entrance, freighted to the *Chōgenbō* before he had even arrived.

He heard a soft knock on his door.

"Yes?" he asked. "I mean, open!"

The door slid into the wall to reveal Anna standing in the doorway. She glanced around.

"Nice!" she said. "I like the color. What is it?"

"I'd need a color chart to answer that," Michael said. "Lavender? And some sort of off-white. Very relaxing. Would you like to come in?"

"No," Anna said. "Maybe another time. Why don't you come out? I want to show you where we'll be working."

"Okay," he said, jumping out of the chair a little too eagerly.

Anna smiled at him and he fell into stride beside her as she walked down the corridor.

"I hope you don't mind me taking you for my own," she said as they walked.

"No, not at all," Michael said.

"Good." She made no further conversation until they reached the research room. Waving a hand over a sensor, she opened the door. Michael followed her inside. A quantum computer occupied the center of the room, with four chairs placed around it. The monitor was mounted in the table top—*was* the table top. It resembled an AI found in a Donut Hole, only much smaller. Counters lined the walls, containing an assortment of equipment. Michael recognized most of it through his work in the HakKor lab planet-side.

Michael stopped gazing around the room and noticed Anna staring at him. He felt his face redden. She smiled gently.

"Listen," she said. "We need to talk." She gestured to one of the seats near the AI. Michael sat, and she took the seat nearest him.

"I want to be sure it's okay, what I did, having you assigned to work with me," she said.

"Yes, of course it is," Michael said.

"That's not quite what I meant." Anna looked down at her lap. "You are so shy," she said without looking up. When she did, she met Michael's eyes.

"I'm going try to make this easy for both of us," she said. "I can see I'm going to have to be a little forward. Michael, I like you. And I'd like to get to know you better. Not as colleagues or friends, but more. I've tried to show you that several times, but you're not very good at reading that kind of thing, are you?"

"No," Michael agreed.

"I think you're a really nice guy, a genuinely good man, which is pretty hard to find, I can tell you. I'm being direct now because, well, working together with any awkwardness or tension would be really difficult for me. And I think if I waited for you to make the first move, we'd be quite a few light years from here. So, I'm trying to be upfront and honest."

She smiled at him. "I've embarrassed you," she said. "Your face is *so* red. I'm sorry."

"No," Michael managed to stammer. "It's okay."

"If you're uncomfortable, if I'm out of order, we can forget it all and just be workmates," she said.

Michael felt his face flush. He looked at his hands, suddenly awkward appendages. He remembered the brush against his arm as they passed the corridor on the way to the mess hall, the slight touch on his hand as she got his attention at the table, asking if he could pass her a drink. His face felt warmer still.

"I would like that," he said, staring at his hands.

"To be workmates?" she asked. The tone of her voice, her disappointment, pierced his heart.

"No!" he said quickly. He forced his head to lift and willed his eyes to meet hers. When they did, he felt a weight lift, and a calmness bathe him. "I mean, I would like to know you better."

Anna's smile grew larger, and to Michael's amazement, his feeling of calm grew even stronger. She reached over and took his hand, squeezing it gently and holding it for several moments. Then she let go.

"Let me show you a few things here," she said, "and then maybe we can make some dinner in that shiny new galley."

"Sure," Michael said through his smile. "Sounds good."

"Look at this," she said.

Anna winked at the table top and a screen materialized in front of her. She showed Michael her hands and then placed them under her bottom. She turned her face to the screen and it began to scroll through a page of data. It stopped on an equation and zoomed in. A section became highlighted, then deleted. Another page opened on the screen, making the display split-screen. Anna's personal account opened. Then two bars appeared in the middle of the screen, pausing the program.

She turned to Michael. "Pretty neat, huh?"

"What did I just see?"

"No hands!" she said. She removed one of her hands from under her bottom and ran her fingers through her hair, brushing it back.

"It's all controlled by facial muscles," she said. "A wink, a twitch of the cheek, making an expression. Computations at the flick of an eyebrow!"

"Cool," Michael said.

"Cool? Is that all you can say?" Anna laughed. "The first thing you need to do is train it for your face, then you'll say more than 'cool'." She could see he still wasn't impressed. "Every second counts when Stepping. And as the backup astrogator, you're going to need some serious upskilling."

Michael nodded, the smile still on his face.

"*Il mio cucciolo*!" she said. "I'm obviously not going to get any work out of you now. Let's go for a walk."

The both stood and made their way out of the door. Once they were in the corridor Michael's hand gently brushed Anna's and he held it in his.

"Now you're getting it," she said.

Peter admired the bridge. Located near the nose of the ship, its bulkheads narrowed towards thick windows that gave a magnificent view out to the stars beyond the ship. Or it would as soon as the *Chōgenbō* left its docking frame. At the moment metal girders framed the vista outside the ship. He had read in the ship's specs that the shielding replaced the lead lining that characterized older ships. Made of the same material as the hull of the Ruan aretfact, it sealed the entire ship, protecting those inside from solar radiation.

In the center of the room sat the captain's chair. Next to it the First Mate's, or Officer of the Watch. They were identical in all aspects except for the aura around Olsen's. Forbidden territory. Peter's grandfather had a chair like that. Whenever he was alone in the room and certain the old man was no-where near, he would sit in that chair. Young Peter would shift his bottom and wriggle his back into the padding, an act of secret rebellion. Older Peter tentatively put his hand on the back of the captain's chair, then removed it.

Along one wall was a seat for the communications officer. In front of her chair were an array of instruments, mounted into the bulkhead as well as on the desk protruding from the wall. A similar station was located on the opposite side of the bridge, where the astrogator, Anna, would work when more traditional navigation was required.

"Come, sit," the pilot told him.

Peter stepped to the front of the bridge where two chairs sat in front of a long console. He looked at the monitor in front of the pilot, a holographic projection of the controls that operate the ship. "Facial control!" he shouted. "No way!"

"Yes, way," the pilot told him. "Sit."

From their interaction in the 'get to know you' session after the captain's speech Peter got the impression that Ar-man Kobarev was a man who suffered no fools. He sat down in the chair next to the pilot's, wearing a serious air. The seat back angled slightly forward, making it impossible to slouch, or relax.

"Until you have aliens to speak with, you will learn how to pilot," Kobarev said. Peter wanted to protest that he had a lot of work left fine-tuning the translation device, but his common sense prevailed.

"Yes," he answered.

"Flying with hands is slow," the pilot said. "Old fashion

has no place on *Chōgenbō*. Once you are trained, every maneuver is executed precisely and quickly. When you are ready, all you will use are your eye muscles."

"Okay," Peter said.

"I have installed program on computer in your quarters," Kobarev said, "You will practice. It is simulator."

"Perfect," Peter said. It seemed agreeing with the pilot was the correct way to respond. "But I'm thinking," Peter tried. "That if we both used the translator, I could keep working out its kinks, and you could speak ... Evenk?"

"Evenki," Kobarev said. "How you know this language?"

"It's what I do." Peter had an exceptional ear for accents and obscure tongues. And, he believed a little research about who you will be working with usually helps to 'prepare for the unknowns', as Olsen would say. Kobarev's service record wasn't classified.

Arman Kobarev, aged forty-two, was born in eastern Siberia and was selected as a HakKor fleet cadet at the age of twelve. The last thirty years of his life had been spent training for the *Chōgenbō*, although that wasn't known at the time. He apprenticed on fliers and shuttles, flew transports, worked his way up to the bridge of a freighter. Growing restless behind those controls, he worked mining moon fragments around Eridani-C. Those pilots required the most skill, and they had the highest mortality rate. It was precise work, running down a hunk of rock, attaching to the fragment, slowing and redirecting it where you wanted it to go, all the while dodging other pieces of the broken satellite. Kobarev never got a scratch.

"Besides," Peter added. "If you speak your mother tongue, you can teach me better."

Kobarev nodded. "Very well," he said. "You give me tomorrow. Tonight, you look at thrusters. Start with baby walks."

"Baby steps," Peter said.

Kumiko Mori changed into her uniform as soon as she reached her quarters. Captain Olsen had told them that he expected the crew, starting tomorrow, to wear them when on the ship, which meant that they would be the only clothes they would be wearing for the foreseeable future. The linguist had stifled a groan, but too late for those around him not to notice—including the captain, who chose to ignore it. While Olsen's orders were cloaked as requests, it was a thin disguise.

Kumiko didn't mind uniforms. They served a purpose. They promoted an atmosphere of cohesion and encouraged discipline and self-care. This was going to be a long assignment, and they would need both. Besides, she liked this uniform. The HakKor designers made something to match the ship—simple elegance; fit for purpose, yet well thought out. Black pants with pockets at the hips and thigh gave them the utility of work, but the cut let them double as full dress. The grey shirt molded to the body and would make, Kumiko thought, anybody look good anywhere. The green collarless jacket was pure class. Pockets on the outside could fit small items, and the pocket on the inside was large enough for a data pad. The fabric looked like natural fiber, but stretch and strength implied a durable synthetic. These clothes would last for a very long time, and need little cleaning. She ran her finger over the insignia embroidered on the left shoulder, a hovering kestrel, seeking its prey.

The lack of any insignia of rank was encouraging. She had served on ships where the captain made a very big deal about station. Olsen had a reputation for being a leader who valued ability more than status, competence over title. What he said in the messroom about formalities was just for the 'doctors' on board—Taylor, Hollis, and Giolino. It was good none of them had introduced themselves with that honorific. They would find out that nobody cared what was in front of their names, just what they did and how well it was done. When and if Olsen used a title in front of their names, they would hopefully know it was a serious matter. The medical officer was a different story. If she were called 'Doc' by Olsen, it would mean he was happy with her work.

She smiled as she dressed, already feeling a part of this new crew, even if she had only met them all a short time before. Kumiko preferred uniforms. They were all she really knew. When she was out of uniform, on extended leave or between ships, she felt uncomfortable, not only with the loose-fitting clothes civilians typically wore, but with having to choose every morning which ones to put on. She had been wearing uniforms since she was a young girl; at school, as a cadet, then as an officer.

She reported to the armory, pleased to see the security chief, who was also wearing his uniform.

"*Tsuji kachou*," she said, bowing. "Kumiko Mori, reporting."

"Welcome, Kumiko," he said. "And you heard the captain. You may address me as Hiroto."

"Yes, Hiroto," she said. She looked from the security chief to the two security crew standing near him. They were Dutch, if she remembered correctly, but couldn't recall their names from the introductions in the messroom. She hadn't gotten to exchange many words at all with them, and tried to remember if she had seen them speaking with any other crew.

She faced them and waited. They stared at her.

Hiroto interrupted the silence. "My security team."

"Koos Rupert," one said.

"Jan de Werk," the other added.

They were also in the uniform issued, but didn't have their jackets. They had added to what they did wear—a sheath for a knife strapped to the thigh, and what looked like a holster attached to each of their belts. Similarities ceased with what they wore. Koos Rupert appeared short next to his crew mate, but was close to six feet. Kumiko had to tilt her head to meet his gaze. His grey shirt hid nothing of his defined muscles; she was not used to seeing men so large on a ship. Time in space tended to make one lose weight, including muscle mass. Jan de Werk stood a head taller than Rupert, his wavy blond hair and blue eyes a stark contrast to Rupert's closely shaved black hair and dark eyes.

Kumiko bowed slightly. "*Konnichiwa*," she said.

"They will be teaching hand to hand combat skills, as well as small arms," Hiroto said. "At the moment I will simply be familiarizing you with the defensive capabilities of the vessel. Gentlemen," he said to the Dutchmen, "you may go now."

They left the room with a word, Rupert leading the way.

"*Amari oshaberide wa arimasen,*" Hiroto said. They are not very talkative. "*They were a gift from the consortium,*" he continued.

"*That is not typical,*" Kumiko said.

"*No, it isn't,*" Hiroto admitted. "*Not every thing about this mission is typical, but it is what is. It is not a typical mission. Come, let me show you the arms locker.*" He led her to a door recessed into the bulkhead, opened it and stepped into a space just big enough for the two of them. Racks built into the wall held an array of weapons, each secure in its own slot.

"*I am sure you're familiar with most of these, which is why I wanted you to act as my second,*" he said.

"*But you have your security team,*" Kumiko said. "*Why do you need a second?*"

"*Because you are from Hokkaido Prefecture, as am I,*" Hiroto replied. "*And you are a career officer whom I believe I can trust.*"

"*Yes, Tsuji kachou,*" Kumiko said.

"*Please. Enough with the honorifics, at least when we are alone,*" Hiroto said. He took a hand gun from its slot and handed it to her. "*Miroku S-14 sounder. Standard issue. Eight charges. You are proficient in its use?*"

"*Yes, Tsuji kachou—I mean, Hiroto,*" Kumiko said.

"*Of course, you are,*" Hiroto said. "*On this rack are the S-4s.*" He indicated to a collection of four smaller hand guns. "*Have you seen this type?*"

"*Seen, yes, but trained very little.*"

"*That is because they are usually reserved for Officers of* the Watch," Hiroto said. "*They work the same, but with only four rounds. They fit into a pocket discreetly. I'll bet you never noticed your officer had one.*"

"*No.*" Kumiko shook her head.

"*They did,*" he said. "*As my second I'd like you to keep one on you at all times. Discreetly,*" he added. He removed one from the inside pocket of his jacket and handed it to her. She held the black weapon in her hand, checked that it was fully charged and that the safety was on. Opening her jacket, she slid it into a pocket.

Hiroto indicated to another rack of hand guns on the opposite wall. "*Plasma guns,*" he said. "*Very unusual to have on board a ship. One charge can puncture a bulkhead. They copy weapons that were found on the Artifact. Ruan weapons. Part of preparing for 'unknowns', as the captain said. If they have this type of weapon, then we will have it too. Active clips are stored in that lockbox, there.*" He pointed to a metal box fixed to the deck plating, with a key pad on it.

"*They are highly illegal,*" he said. "*Like the cannon outside.*"

"*Those aren't projectile?*" she asked.

"*Only in appearance,*" he said. "*And now you, along with myself, Olsen and First Mate Middleton, are the only ones on board who know that.*"

Kumiko nodded. "*What about these?*" she asked, pointing at a rack of clips directly below the handguns.

"*Those are dummy clips,*" he said. "*Used for training. They won't make holes in the ship, but they will knock you off your feet, and hurt quite a bit. Loading and recoil are just what you will experience when charged.*"

"*Come,*" he added. "*Let's get out of this closet. I'll give you the code to the lockbox as soon as you know how to use plasma. Right now, let's have some tea. You were just home, tell me about the season.*"

11

The *Chōgenbō* launched with little fanfare on board. A transport filmed the affair for news feeds. Small tenders stood by to slowly maneuver the empty frame away from the craft and back to the HakKor hangar at the space hub. Inside the new ship, the crew sat around the large table in the messroom. A holo screen illuminated the center of the table.

Michael sat next to Anna, their legs touching under the table. They made no secret of their relationship. The First Mate had been the first to pass them in the corridor as they walked together after leaving the research lab. Michael's first tentative show of affection became public, as he was too absorbed in the feel of her palm against his to let go quickly enough for Anders not to see. Olsen hadn't said anything about crew-based romances, and he didn't have time to before one started on his ship. But he never called either of them to his quarters to talk about boundaries or regulations. Peter smiled at his friend—a little jealous at how things turned out with Anna, but happy for Michael.

The First Mate sat next to the medical officer, and though not touching her under the table, he had tentatively flirted during the hours they spent together in sickbay. Wright had asked Olsen for the use of his officer as a backup medic. With his maritime medical training he was the ideal choice. She had considered and rejected other options, deferring to the captain's recommendation as she knew she would. The security team appeared much too tightly knit to separate, and she doubted whether the two Dutchmen would work with her, or anybody, if asked. The technicians, similarly, seemed too preoccupied with machinery of the mechanical sort, and too inexperienced to focus on the biological. They were better suited to work with Doi in engineering, with whom they sat on the other side of the messroom table. Studying medical procedures for the myriad of things that could go wrong in space would keep the First Mate busy during their time together, and give her time to fend off any advances and assess his motives.

The screen illuminated and the image of Susumo Motoyo filled the space. He held a glass, which he tapped with a spoon. Those around him quieted and he faced the camera. They were having a party below, Consortium big wigs clapping each other on the back. Many of those around the table weren't impressed by the display. All of them were tired from the weeks spent preparing for the official 'launch', and had an indication of how hard Olsen would work them before any Step was taken.

Several of the crew activated the translators Peter had trained them to use. He had found dozens stowed in his lab, and traded in the ones he smuggled up for the newer models on board.

"I want to congratulate all of those involved in getting

the *Chōgenbō* to this momentous moment," Mototyo said. "The designers, the engineers, the builders, and the crew, now watching these proceedings from inside this wonderful ship."

The image of Motoyo was replaced by an image of the *Chōgenbō* from outside. Anders looked at Olsen, who only shrugged. If HakKor decided to transmit a feed to a larger audience, that was none of his concern. The consortium was in full show-off mode, and it was their ship. Olsen took a drink from his coffee cup.

"The *Chōgenbō* is the newest, the fastest, the most advanced, ship in the HakKor fleet," Motoyo said. "Ship building has always been an evolution, and it always will be. This beautiful creation we see on the screen right now represents the pinnacle of ship evolution. She is at the summit of human and Ruan technology, she—"

"Mute," Olsen said. Motoyo's mouth continued to move, but there was no sound. "Let him get this part over with, there's no need for us to suffer."

A laugh at the end of the table made them all look that way. It was the first humor they had seen from any of the Dutch security officers. Koos Rupert looked at the others and shrugged.

"You can watch it all on your private feed later if you want," Olsen said.

"Quite alright, Captain," Rupert said.

"I'm sure he'll be done in a moment," Olsen said. "Yes, here we are. Sound," he said to the screen.

" ... in sea going days it was a tradition to smash a bottle of champagne against the hull of the vessel. Or sake. Earlier still, wine was offered, which replaced the original custom of spilling blood—"

"My mistake," Olsen said. "I *thought* he was there."

"—the purpose of which was to ensure the gods protected the ship, and to guarantee its good fortune and safety." Motoyo raised his glass. "Traditions change, but maintain their threads to the past. Rather than spill our wine, we will raise our glasses and toast the *Chōgenbō*." He paused as those at the party raised theirs. Olsen lifted his mug, and those at the table with a cup or mug raised theirs.

"*Chōgenbō*!" the crew heard the party-goers declare.

"To the *Chōgenbō*," Olsen said. Those around the table murmured agreement.

A young man in an expensive suit approached Motoyo and handed him a silver axe, which the CEO held up for all to see. He showed them the left side of the shiny blade, etched with three grooves, and the right etched with four.

"The three grooves represent God," Doi explained to the table. "The four on the other side represent the four heavenly kings, asking the protection of God."

"This axe is a symbol," Motoyo continued. "It will sever the cord that releases *Chōgenbō* and launches her in her life among the stars. This axe was gifted by those at Handa Shipbuilding, a subsidiary of HakKor Consortium, and once again demonstrating their superior skill at producing the finest ships on Earth and off. It is a gift to our consortium, to bring protection and luck to *Chōgenbō*."

On cue, the young man brought out a piece of wood. At each end stood a dowel of wood carved like a bollard found on a sea-based quayside. A length of cord ran between the bollards. The wood was placed on the table beside Motoyo. He turned to the wooden block and with a smooth downward stroke split the cord in two.

The image on the screen changed to the view of the ship. The tenders attached to the docking frame fired their thrusters and the structure moved forward, giving the impression of the vessel reversing away. Those on board the *Chōgenbō* felt no movement. They watched until the ship was alone, floating in a sea of black with a background of stars.

"Screen off," Olsen said, and the holo screen flickered out.

"Thank you for your time," he said to the crew. "There is some chilled champagne and warm sake, courtesy of Motoyo-san and the HakKor consortium. I'll send your messages of gratitude to head office. Enjoy yourselves, but in moderation. Sea trials start tomorrow."

12

"Peter! *Chīsai Tori* means little bird, treat it like one!" Kobarev growled. "A little bird! Be gentle."

Peter raised his eyebrows, eased off the thruster of the tender and drew level with the *Chōgenbō*. He looked over at Kobarev in *Chīsai Tori ichi*, Little Bird number one, and gave a thumbs up.

"Do not wave at me," Kobarev growled again. "Pay attention and follow."

Kobarev shot past Peter and dropped below the starboard cannon. The small vessel started to leave his view screen but he deployed his own thrusters and followed, matching the experienced pilot's speed. Kobarev maneuvered towards the robotic arms folded under the ship. Three lengths of strengthened alloy, called unbreakable by the engineers, pointed forward, nestled into the underbelly of the ship. A fourth arm stretched towards the stern. When deployed they would lower and splay outward, resembling the talons of a bird of prey. Hovering above its target, the talons would descend and grab it.

"You will learn how to use this soon," Kobarev said. "I want you to see it, remember where it is and what it looks like. Very important."

Kobarev spun his tender in a one hundred and eighty degree arc, until the nose of his craft faced Peter's.

"Do you understand?" Kobarev asked.

Peter wished he could turn off the mic in his helmet. "Yes," he responded.

"Good. Now repeat exercise," Kobarev ordered.

In response, Peter spun his craft to the left until it faced where he had come, hit the port thrusters and spun back, past Kobarev until facing the original direction. He descended one hundred meters, stopped, repeated his turns, and returned level with his instructor. Without waiting for Kobarev to ask, Peter tilted the nose of his craft up until he was perpendicular to the pilot. He kept going and turned a full circle, watching the ship be replaced by open space, then reappear. He levelled out, spun on his axis to starboard, levelled out again and did the same to port. Peter liked flying the tenders more than he anticipated. He took to them naturally and looked forward to trainings.

"Enough with your ballerina bullshit!" Kobarev barked. "These are not play things, they are emergency equipment."

"Yes, pilot," Peter said.

"And don't give me smart ass," Kobarev said. "Emergency requires accuracy and skill. Scenario," the pilot said. Peter stared at his controls, his face a placid mask. Scenario was a favorite word of the Siberian. He had turned off his translator during a training drill on the bridge days earlier and listened to the word as Kobarev spoke it in his native language. It had a melodic ring. But it was forewarning of serious action, and worse ear-bashing if not taken as seriously as the pilot demanded.

"Crew member injured at beacon location," Kobarev's monotone instructions began. "Suit compromised, bleeding oxygen. Locate crew member, deploy airfield, return with crew member to docking bay. Beacon initiated now."

A light began flashing on Peter's console. Peter moved his cheek and *Chīsai Tori ni*, Little Bird Two, shot past Kobarev and smoothly flipped over. Peter scanned the hull of the *Chōgenbō* with his eyes, flying upside down towards the beacon located near the bow of the larger vessel. The silver plating of the hull passed beneath him. He manipulated a facial muscle and the tender swerved around the port cannon, then back to its original course. He clenched his jaw and drew back his lips, and fired his own bow thrusters, slowing and turning the tender over. He visualized the invisible strings connecting his face to the console, bringing himself closer to his target. He came in fast—Kobarev would say too fast, and rebuke him once inside, but Peter moved his right ocular muscles and fired his hull thrusters. *Chīsai Tori ni* froze a meter from the surface of the *Chōgenbō*.

As he came to halt, three magnetic couplings shot out and attached themselves to the hull plating. As soon as they affixed, he activated the barrier and created an atmosphere. Unbuckling from his seat, he floated to the tender's airlock, propelled by a light kick on the arm rest. Checking the atmosphere was stable, he opened the hatch, activated the gravlock on his boots and stepped onto the hull. After five steps he retrieved the beacon and returned to his ship. Face before the console, he retracted the couplings, banked up and over the larger ship and approached the green light of the docking bay. Kobarev fell in behind and parked *Chīsai Tori ichi* beside its sister craft. Peter stepped out *of Chīsai Tori ni*, beacon in hand, smiling at Kobarev.

"So," the pilot said. "You have saved injured crew mate."

Peter held up the beacon.

"But wipe smile from your face," Kobarev said. "You come in fast, you become a danger. What happens if hull thrusters fail? Answer me that Dr Smart Ass! I tell you what happens, you die, crew mate dies, we all die as you plow into the ship like a missile."

Peter stopped smiling as Kobarev stepped over and took the beacon from him. He tried not to flinch as the pilot reached one of his thick hands out and placed it on his shoulder. "You are learning fast," Kobarev said, the growl gone from his voice. "You will make good pilot. But remember this—it is easier to slow down if you are going slow. I have watched comrades die doing what you did, coming in fast and full of confidence. Everything we do must be done safely. It is how you will live to be old like me."

Kobarev squeezed Peter's shoulder. "Come, time to rest."

Olsen leaned forward in his chair, put his elbow on his knee and cupped his chin in his hand. He gazed out of the view screen. It was a gesture crew on the bridge recognized as the moment before an order was issued.

"Arman, are you satisfied with ship's thrusters?" he asked.

"Yes, Captain." Kobarev couldn't shake the habit of calling

Olsen what he was rather than by name. It was how he addressed the ranking officer on any ship he worked. Other crew had followed suit and it became the name used by most on board. His stated preference about titles and names seemed to dissipate like oxygen out of a small hull breach.

"Good," Olsen said. "And you're happy with your second? That he can control the ship with precision?"

"Yes, Captain."

"You hesitated," Olsen said. "What is it?"

"He is too confident," Kobarev replied. "He needs more humility when it comes to his abilities."

"He's young," Olsen said. "That will come. Is he following on his own screen? I want him up here once we're confident with the reactors."

"He is."

Olsen got up from his chair and stood behind the pilot.

"Nothing left for it then," he said. "Let's fire her up." Olsen couldn't see the smile spread across Kobarev's face.

"Aye, Captain," he said.

"A good opportunity to test out those sensors under motion," Olsen said to Kumiko Mori, sitting at her monitors.

"Yes, Captain," she answered without turning.

"Get those Dutchmen online," he told her. "Let them practice with whatever's out there."

"Doing that now, Captain," Mori said, having trained the security men to work the sensitive sensors.

"Chief engineer Doi," Olsen said over ship coms. "Are you prepped for Acceleration?"

"Yes, Captain," Doi reported. "Reactors are standing by."

"Excellent," Olsen said. "Attention crew. We will be initiating Acceleration in A minus ten minutes. Ensure you are secured. Acceleration will continue for a period of two hours at two point two Gs. During that time stay at your assigned stations as you have been instructed. At the end of Acceleration, we will flip, assess performance, and then initiate Decel. Countdown is on monitor. Time to put those coffee cups away."

Those in the messroom listened to the message. Michael shifted in his seat and tried to hide his excitement. Rupert and de Werk made no effort to disguise their boredom. The shorter of the two refused to look at the holo screen and its reducing numbers. He continued to drink his coffee. After another minute elapsed de Werk stood, took his colleague's cup and secured it, and his own, in the galley. Anna and Donna finished their conversation and checked the straps securing them to their chairs.

Doi studied the console measuring reactor output. The Ruan had leap-frogged fission power and made human understanding of fusion juvenile. From power generation to fuel injection, the technology brought back with the Artifact radically advanced the field. Ships already held the power of the sun in their drives. Now they held even more. Doi likened the difference to that between a G class star like Earth's sun and that of an O, or, as he explained to everybody except the technicians Okada and Yasuda, Earth's yellow sun and a very hot and extremely luminous blue giant. Where a G class star had an effective temperature of up to six thousand kelvins, an O class star was more than thirty thousand.

Whereas the basic design of the old Spherical Tokamak reactors was essentially the same, their inner core contained a strengthened magnetic field and extended tubing to contain the plasma heated to temperatures of almost one hundred million degrees Celsius. The Ruan had cracked the problem of confining fuel at very low pressure but at extremely high temperatures. All Doi needed to do at this point in his explanation was start to discuss magnetic field ration and beta numbers and eyes would glaze over.

What it all translated to was that just one of *Chōgenbō's* reactors was more powerful than the eight used together on a space freighter convoy a mere two decades earlier, and the need for tons of fuel to keep them running was reduced to kilos, which could be continually recycled with minimal loss. A ship like *Chōgenbō* could theoretically maintain acceleration for centuries before the reactors cooled and power output ceased. Three engines, used alternately, would make that time even longer, but Stepping meant that they would never have to do that. Doi remembered the first time he figured out where the name Donut had come from. Sitting in class as a young student, he stopped the lecture for a moment when he burst out laughing. The reactor of the Ein-Ros (as it was originally called), stationed near a star, captured the immense power of photons being emitted which was funneled into the toroidal confinement area that resembled a donut. The new technology, applied to Donuts, meant they could harness more power, travel farther, and even store enough energy to carry out multiple Steps after one recharge period.

One Ruan scout ship had advanced human technology by

generations. If they managed to capture a ship the size that the researchers claimed … Doi tried not to think too much about the possibilities. *Toranu anaguma no kawa zan'you.* Don't count the skins of badgers which haven't been caught. He understood the passion driving Tatsuo and Yasuda. Their selection for this mission would make their careers. If they caught the *anaguma.*

Each of the technicians monitored the reactors. Doi passed his eye over their chairs to see they were secured, and buckled his own. He watched the countdown reduce. He sat back as it hit zero.

The ship vibrated and a hum filled the engine control room. All three studied their monitors, projected in front of them. Doi flicked an eyebrow and another schematic filled his screen. He sank into the chair as acceleration increased.

"Reactors at desired output," he reported to Olsen.

"Happy with their performance?" Olsen asked.

"Very pleased, sir," Doi said. The reactors were almost at idle compared to their full potential. Of course, if they were at full power, they would create a force strong enough to burst the crew's internal organs under the increased gravity. That's where the cryo-pods would be needed, and why any Ruan they might find would be sound asleep.

"Very good," Olsen said. "Flip programmed for two hours. Take care moving about," he said to the rest of the crew. "You weigh twice as much you used to."

For Kumiko Mori, Flip didn't come soon enough. She struggled to stay focused on the scanners as well as the two security men acting as her back-up. They were good at spotting objects—de Werk was first to note a convoy returning from its Donut—but they both needed more practice in interpreting size. Kumiko would program more simulation drills. She squeezed her eyes shut and opened them, but the pain between her temples remained. Maybe the Doctor would have something for her to use during future exercises. She had come to expect the pain in her head like some expect seasickness on the ocean. It didn't stop her from hoping it wouldn't come.

As the *Chōgenbō* reached the end of its acceleration period the thrust that sank her into her seat ceased. The weight bearing down on her head was lifted. Her body began to float, but was restrained by her safety straps. She rested, knowing the time would be brief.

"Mister Doi," Olsen said.

"Reactors performing wonderfully," Doi reported. "Standing by for Decel at bridge discretion."

"Doctor Wright." Olsen asked. "Any concerns to report."

"None, Captain," she replied.

"Well, Arman," Olsen said to the pilot. "Flip and Decel."

"My pleasure, Captain," the pilot said. "Watch and learn, young man," he said to Peter.

Peter heard the man in his ear and watched his screen. He couldn't see Kobarev moving his face, but he saw bow thrusters activated, watched the ship begin to rotate as the bow rose up until the vessel travelled through space as if standing on its engines. The motion continued until the *Chōgenbō* lay flat, belly up, as Kobarev described the maneuver. But Peter knew the pilot was a perfectionist, or at least demanded a tidy performance. Port thrusters fired and the ship rotated on its side and 'righted' itself. Peter looked at Michael and Anna and smiled. With the lack of gravity, they were unaware of the maneuver. And in space, upside down or right side up carried little meaning.

"Very nice, Mr Kobarev," he said on his private line to the pilot.

"Next time it will be you, so I hope you paid attention."

"On my mark, Arman," Olsen interrupted. "And, mark!"

The reactors flared and the crew once again felt weight return, pressing down until they sank deep into their chairs. The pain returned to Kumiko's head, but she ignored it. She reduced power even more to the scanners and waited for Rupert and de Werk to report their findings. At full power they would register every ship and satellite within five astronomical units, an area equal to that between Jupiter and the sun. The monitor would be a static cloud of objects, useless in the inner solar system. She adjusted settings, until only inert metallic objects would register, at a distance of thirty-five million kilometers, one quarter of an AU, give or take a few klicks. She waited. Finally, de Werk reported in with two objects. She narrowed the search area and he located the third, a derelict satellite that had fallen out of its orbit. Kumiko reassessed the usefulness of the sensors. They would revolutionize salvage work.

"Pinpoint each object and create profile," she said over her line to the two security men. "Rupert, increase search field until you find your own three. Show me when we're finished."

Kumiko closed both her eyes for a moment, savoring the darkness, but opened them and kept them on the monitor until Decel was complete. When they approached the Ruan ship, she would need to be clear minded and focused, whether under acceleration or freefall.

Finally, the two hours ended. The reactors were powered down and the *Chōgenbō* floated motionless. Olsen congratulated the crew on the first of many drills to come. Two hours became three, and then four, as the captain and the engineer explored the reactors' capability. There were six quiet days as the cryo-pods were tested. Half the crew put the other half to sleep, monitored their readings, and after three days changed places. Each exercise brought them closer to the Donut and their first Step. Olsen tried to act dissatisfied with his crew's, or the ship's, ability, but gave up any pretense and grinned openly.

The last test was out of his control and he placed his trust completely in the ship's systems. Each retired to their cryo-pods, and placed the injector below the bottom rib. They felt a slight pinch as a thin tube pierced their skin and located their livers, injecting the chemical that would protect their bodies at low temperature. The pods sealed them in, soft foam enveloping their bodies as they drifted into a frozen slumber while the reactors fired at sufficient force to increase the gravity in the ship to twelve. At five g's blood stays at the feet and the average human will pass out. With a suit designed to force blood out of the lower extremities, and with specialist training in breathing and tension techniques, they might stay conscious up to a force of nine gravities. But not for long. Gray-out occurs, a graying of vision because of reduced blood flow to the eyes. Blackout, when vision is totally lost. Loss of consciousness, with blood flow to the brain reduced. Then death.

Humans didn't need to pursue cryogenic technology with any real seriousness. Worm hole breakthroughs made that unnecessary. To travel to the nearest stars, they harnessed the power of a star and folded space, creating a gravity well large enough to bend time and space—an Einstein-Rosen bridge from one point in the galaxy to another. To get from here to there, put them both in the same place and step across. The Ruan had only one way to reach a distant star, a journey that would take decades, if not centuries. So, they figured out how to travel vast distances at high velocity and live to see the end of the road. They slept, nestled in shock resistant pods, their bodies cooled until their molecules ceased moving.

Before entering her cryo-pod, Donna Wright stopped at each crew member, checked their vitals, ensured their body fluids were readjusting so that their cells would maintain stasis and not burst. Satisfied, she entered her own pod. Acceleration, flip and Decel were programmed; there was nothing to do but sleep.

Exactly as programmed, the ship accelerated, and continued to accelerate at immense speed. At a set time the reactors went silent. Thrusters rotated the ship until the stern faced in the direction of travel. And just as programmed, the reactors fired once again, reducing their speed incrementally until the vessel stopped, many, many kilometers from where it started.

Olsen woke at the same time as the ship's medical officer. His pod opened; he removed the tubes that kept him alive, walked among his sleeping crew. He stretched his back, opened and closed his hands. He pulled up a monitor and checked the data. He was pleased. Hull integrity was unchanged. The ship's sleek lines weren't created just for show, but to handle the immense pressure of multiple g's. All internal systems were running at optimal. No evidence of damage anywhere. The AI that held their lives in its processors reported all well. Tracking down and capturing the Ruan ship was going to mean a great deal of reliance on the ship's computer.

Olsen went to his quarters to change. By the time he had washed and dressed, Wright was welcoming the others as they slowly emerged from their slumber.

Most people held that you didn't dream when in cryo-sleep. This was not Michael's experience. He tried to speak with others about his 'dreams', but never felt heard. So, he stopped talking about what he experienced—not images, not stories from his subconscious, nothing physical or auditory. But ... something beyond the senses. Something that asked him to let go of any preconceived manner of understanding, like when he took a stronger dose of GLR, which he preferred not to do. Because of that something. He wondered if it was similar to death. Or if it was death, lurking in the cold.

Michael sat on the edge of his pod, rubbing the spot just under his bottom rib. He looked at Anna and returned her smile. He never liked cryo-sleep. But now he had no choice.

Olsen wanted several more trials before Step, and finding the Ruan meant Michael would revisit that dark place many more times.

13

Olsen summoned the crew to the mess hall and let them view the Donut through the holo screen. It wasn't hard to miss. At twenty-five kilometers across, it was one of the largest Donuts ever constructed, and designed for one run. Pemako. Its size and improved technology meant that it could cover the ten thousand light years in a single step. Having someplace worth going had encouraged a great deal of research and development. The product of all that effort lay in front of them. The view screen filtered out the corona of the sun behind the giant disc, which was almost five hundred square kilometers of surface area absorbing the sun's photons and converting them into the power needed.

Olsen kept his speech brief. "Well done," he said to assembled crew. "Thank you for all your effort. I am very pleased with you, and the ship. I've notified HakKor we're ready to Step and they have given clearance. Get some rest."

The *Chōgenbō* approached with the dozens of other ships bound for the distant planet. Most were transports, filled with thousands of colonists asleep in their cryo-pods. Kobarev had piloted one; lonely work, with only the bare minimum of crew. A job was a job, but he found it easy work, which meant it was boring. For the colonists, the trip lasted a week, maybe two. Leave Earth on a flier, process through to the docking bay warehousing the cryo-pods, enter and sleep, then wake up with a water filled new world in the view port. For the pilot, it was a three-month trip to the Donut, followed by another three months to their destination. And the same back. One run, one year. The trip used to take at least three Steps, with stops to recharge the Donut's power cells, making the round trip close to a decade to complete. For Kobarev, one year was enough, and at the end of his first run he applied for a transfer and was posted to the *Chōgenbō*.

Most of the ships approaching the Donut neared their apportioned docking bays at the outer rim. Many more were already secured. Five times larger than the older generation of Donuts, there was room along the eighty-kilometer circumference for a lot more freighters. Anna squeezed Michael's hand and pointed to one of four circular areas in the surface of the large disc.

"That's ours," she said.

He peered closely at the smaller disc. He saw the docking bay built for the *Chōgenbō*, the only ship to travel on it. The giant Donut made it appear small, but he knew it wasn't. Under its surface area of over three square kilometers ran hundreds of kilometers of containment tubes filled with high temperature plasma made stable through a powerful magnetic field. Once charged, it had the capacity to Step multiple times, if the distance of the Step were not too great.

Kobarev disengaged from his monitor and turned his face to Peter. "You can park," he said. "Do not damage ship."

Peter smiled and locked his eyes onto his screen. He checked momentum, adjusted angles with thrusters. He brought up another screen, programmed his intended actions, let the AI add minor corrections. When first practicing on his simulator he took such corrections as failure. Now he appreciated the fine tuning provided by the quantum computer. There is always human error, he came to admit. That kind of computing was not a threat, but a tool. He glanced at the bottom corner to see that override was engaged. Kobarev trusted him to take her in, but not blindly. If he strayed too far off course, the computer would automatically bring them back, and Kobarev could take over. Neither would allow any damage, not even a scratch.

Slowing the *Chōgenbō*, he guided the ship closer to its docking bay on the smaller Donut. The surface was rippled with retracted arms like the talons beneath them. To move the Seed ship through space, they needed to affix it to the Donut. Not knowing the size or shape of that vessel meant this one was equipped with a variety of tools. Peter looked forward to unfolding them, exploring the Swiss army knife contraptions engineered into the disc.

Kobarev had taught him how to catch prey with the *Kestrel's* talons. Accelerate, flip, decelerate towards target, approach with claws extended, stop at the exact moment of contact, and grip the prize. Its application, if misused, was worrying. It made an excellent tool for capturing and boarding another ship. One practice target, a HakKor freighter, was surprisingly easy to catch. Once secured they were invited on board by the crew for a needed distraction.

"You think you are first to think of that?" Kobarev asked, laughing. "Work in the Belt, or around Eradani—very good pirate training. But you want to be a pirate! Find and board an alien ship! All you need is an eye patch."

Peter guided the *Chōgenbō* over the surface of the Donut, until the bay lay directly beneath. He lowered the vessel, and as it reached the bottom, activated the couplings that secured it. Kobarev nodded and Peter disengaged his eyes from the monitor.

"Well done," Olsen said from his chair behind him.

"Two days until Step," the captain said over ship comms. "Tidy and secure all stations, and then relax. You've earned it."

"This might be your last chance to Step sleeping," Anna said. "You'll be with me in the Hole from now on."

"I have thought about that," Michael said.

"Have you ever experienced a Step?" she asked. "I mean, conscious through the whole thing?"

Michael shook his head. He put his hand into his pocket and fingered the vial at the bottom. He knew he would have to experience Step after they reached Pemako, but he wanted to delay that as long as possible. Anna had described it in enough detail to put him off the idea.

"Have you ever slept through a Step?" he asked.

She pursed her lips and furrowed her brow. "I really don't think so," she finally said. "My first Step was as a cadet. Besides, I hate cryo-sleep."

"I know what you mean," he agreed.

He closed his hand around the vial and took it out of his

pocket. "We don't have to sleep, though, and as this might be our last opportunity ..."

"Yes?" Anna looked at Michael sideways, a smile beginning to form.

"I mean, seeing that you're not involved in this Step, not even on call ..."

She hit his arm. "Just say it!"

Michael opened his hand and let her see the vial. "I was thinking we could do it the old-fashioned way."

"You've got to be kidding," she said.

"You're not on duty."

"True," she said. "But what if something happens?"

"Out of your control," Michael said. "There's a whole team in that gargantuan Donut managing the Step, and you weren't invited. Take advantage of it."

"Well ..." she said.

Michael could see she was wavering and gently pushed her over the edge of decision. "It'll be special. Just the two of us, sitting on the rim of the universe." He had spoken to her a little about the café scene at Sapporo, the Twin Cities in Minnesota where he studied, even on Pemako. But he saw she had little experience besides early experimentation, before she trained as an astrogator. Astrogators tended to be very focused individuals with little time or inclination to sit on the edges of the universe.

"There are different doses," he said. "This is a really good level to just let yourself dissolve and realize what you're a part of. I'd really like to do that with you."

He met her eyes and took her hand with his free one. "I'll

be right there with you," he said. "We can cuddle up in bed, take a dose and Step, all cozy in God's Living Room."

She was nervous, he could see that. He squeezed her hand gently and smiled. "Okay?" he asked.

She gave a faint smile. "Okay," she agreed.

With an hour to go before Step, Michael made Anna stop tidying her quarters and sit beside him. The pillows were pushed against the bulkhead at the top of the bed so they could lean back, slightly upright. When she was reclining beside him, they spent some minutes talking softly. Michael described the waters of Pemako, their calm warmth, the gentle lapping that could be heard at night. He told her about the winds, constant in their direction, depending on season. He asked her to close her eyes and image feeling the warmth of the sun against her face. As the final hour turned into minutes, he asked her to let go of thought, and sit in the quiet. Then with five minutes before Step, he put a pill in her hand. She held it in her opened palm beside his. He smiled at her, leaned over and kissed her cheek, and then raised his palm to his mouth. She copied the motion, and when he put the pill in his mouth and swallowed, she did the same. She leaned back against the pillows and closed her eyes.

The hit was almost instantaneous. Anna's world went black. She fell into the darkness. Michael told her not to carry expectations, to let go of what she thought, or what she thought would happen.

"When we dream, we expect images," he had told her earlier. "Maybe that's why it's hard to remember dreams.

What if the dream wasn't an image, but a sound, or a feeling? A sensory experience, outside of images or concepts? You have to totally empty yourself of expectations of what you might experience, so that you can actually experience."

If she could have thought in the moment after she took the pill, she might have held a mantra or a reminder. *Expect nothing,* it would say. But any intention was whisked away by the power submersing her, like a dead leaf torn from the branch of a tree in a winter gale. She lost sensation of arms, legs, torso, as she tumbled in this wind. She felt her body tingle, as if it were made entirely of electricity. Every cell vibrated, every atom moved, until she lost track of what was inside or outside her body. Until she lost track of that elusive container holding a sense of identity, that frail concept known as *Anna.*

Colors began to form in the void. Green, yellow, blue, red. They began to coalesce, to take shape, until they formed patterns, geometric structures that slowly grew edges that fit with other colored shapes. She, whatever that was in this place, was a detached observer, mesmerized by the fractals, shapes that gave way to shapes that gave way to shapes within themselves. There was no sense of scale as she fell deeper and deeper. But beyond the shapes, beyond the patterns, patterns and shapes she knew were the building blocks of the known universe, there was something more.

The observer formerly known as Anna looked, and saw crystalline lights bordering the geometric play. Each light, each of the many thousands spiraling out and around and within, contained a spark, like a red gem that shone within the brightness, with a brightness of its own. She tried to bring herself closer to the lights, and heard them sing. She felt joy as she listened. It was a song that filled her, that touched her physically, until she became the song. She came close to a thought, a brief awareness. *They* are singing. And she knew she wasn't alone, that she was surrounded and held in this pulsing nest of movement and sound and love.

She began to fall into a crystal. She became blinded in the white glare of its aura, until she reached the red core. And she fell further, into the glow. Within the red she saw deeper shades, deeper colors, and fell towards them, knowing there was no end, only invitation.

14

"We've been summoned," Anna heard beside her. "Crew meeting."

She slowly surfaced, feeling her consciousness return to her body. She wiggled a toe. Moved a finger. A smile spread across her face.

"Welcome back," Michael said.

Anna remained lying, propped against the pillow. She could feel Michael beside her. She kept her eyes closed.

"I don't want to come back," she said.

Anna couldn't see him, but she knew he was smiling. "We never really leave," he said.

He gently stroked her hair. Physical touch was important in grounding. He had brought a strong dose. He moved his hand to hers and pressed down, letting her feel the weight.

"We have time for a hot drink," he said. "But Olsen wants us on the bridge within the hour."

"Reality sucks," she sighed. Anna opened her eyes and saw Michael's smile. *He had such a gentle smile*, she thought. *Such a gentle man*. She looked at him, still seeing shadows of white crystal lights with red gems buried deep within.

"Take me back there sometime," she said.

"Definitely," he said.

Michael sat up on the bed, resting his forearms on his knees. He opened his hands and closed them into fists, squeezing hard. Then he opened them again, as wide he could, feeling the fingers stretch as they spread outward. His grounding. Standing, he let the soles of his feet feel the deck beneath them—his toes, the balls of his feet, the heels. He stepped over to Anna's refreshment cupboard, removed two mugs and filled them with hot water. He looked at her on the bed, slowly stretching and returning to the here and now. He chose black tea, put a bag in the water, added a touch of milk as she had taught him, and brought it over to her.

"I don't remember that as being so intense," she said, taking the mug.

"Maybe that means you were more open to it this time," he said. "Or that it was good stuff."

"Maybe both," she said thoughtfully, sipping her tea.

"But we're here now, ten thousand light years from home," he said. "Not a bad way to Step, huh?"

"Not a bad way to Step," Anna repeated.

"But we have another one soon," he said. "And you're driving."

"I know," she said. "But they can wait for once."

Michael watched Anna sip more of her tea, her eyes meeting his over the rim of her mug. He felt the calm he had just left in his own trip to the Living Room fill him, and realized it was the same feeling he had whenever he was near her, or, more and more, whenever he was thinking about her.

Michael followed behind Anna and Kobarev, the pilot shuttling them to the Donut Hole. They left the bridge and headed directly to the airlock. Peter was disappointed about staying behind.

"Both pilots do not leave ship," Kobarev told him. "So, you stay and man the helm."

"But we're not going anywhere!" Peter protested. "I need to learn how to drive a Donut—"

"You do not drive a Donut," Kobarev said. "Pilots do not drive."

"Okay, but—"

"No buts."

Kobarev spoke in that tone Peter had grown very familiar with. Discussion was at an end. Anymore attempts and familiar names would come out. *Baby. Whiner. Spoilt child*. Peter did his best to avoid those. He answered as the pilot trained him to do so in such situations. He shut up and nodded. But Kobarev wasn't finished with him.

"Let us say couplings break and *Chōgenbō* is set adrift, who will steer her to safety if you are going for ride?"

"Yes, true," Peter agreed, nodding.

"If there is disaster in Donut and I am killed, who will then pilot?"

"Yes—"

"You are back up pilot, that is your job."

"I know—"

"Take care of *Chōgenbō*."

"Yes, Pilot Kobarev."

Peter watched their backs as they exited the bridge. Michael didn't pay attention to the entirety of the interaction. Part of Michael wanted to exchange places with Peter. Get to stay on board the *Chōgenbō*, rather than descend into the heart of the Donut. He knew it was a rare privilege, that he was stumbling into the domain of a very select few who sat in the middle of the great device that folded space and time how and when they wanted. The sunward facing side of the disc harvested the immense stores of power needed for Step. The Hole, located at the center of the disc, was where all that power was manipulated.

Anna tried to make him feel at ease, but gave up. She remembered her first Step in a Hole. She was nervous. It was normal. And Michael had been running the numbers through countless simulations. Once the computations start, she knew he wouldn't have time to worry. Let him 'enjoy' it now. As they entered the airlock connecting the *Chōgenbō* with the elevator taking them to the Hole, Kobarev took the lead.

The elevator doors closed and Anna took a seat while the men stood for the journey. The Donut was small only in comparison to the one it rode on, but it was still a journey of over a kilometer. Twenty minutes later it stopped and the doors opened. Anna placed a hand on Michael's arm.

"Let me show you around the office," she said.

Michael had imagined the center of the Donut to be clinical in appearance—stainless steel work surfaces, rigid chairs, high-tech sensors beeping or flashing, white walls. Something like a sick bay, but without the warmth. Cold. Clinical. Mathematical. What greeted him was a warm room, with sofa-like benches around walls painted in an apricot hue. They seemed to mimic the glow at sunrise or sunset. The lighting was neither too bright, nor too dim. Comfortable. The computer console, the brain of the Donut, took up the center of the room. He knew it wasn't the actual computer, whose internal organs occupied much more of the structure. The table, with the screens built into it, had two large and accommodating chairs around it. The astrogators, sitting at the console, would peer into the complex workings, follow the computations, and sometimes make small adjustments.

Anna handed Michael her small bag and pointed to a door.

"We'll be staying in there," she said. "Drop this in there and have a look."

She turned away from him and sat in one of the chairs near the console. She tilted the monitor in front of the chair until its screen was level with her face. Her hands began to tap on a keypad built into the table. Michael went through the door she had indicated, into a large apartment, complete with living room, kitchen, bedroom and adjoining recreation room. It made his quarters on the *Chōgenbō* resemble a walk-in closet, and he wouldn't be surprised to find one or two of those, just as big, somewhere in the apartment.

When he returned to the central control room, Kobarev sat in a chair similar to Anna's, but away from the table. He had activated a split view screen, showing four views. One was filled with stars, the other three were black. Michael stood beside him and pointed at the dark screens.

"What do those show?" he asked.

"Nothing yet," Kobarev answered. Michael waited for more, but the pilot offered nothing.

"Twenty minutes to release, Ma'am," Kobarev said.

"Thank you, Pilot Kobarev," Anna replied.

Michael took a seat near Anna, tilted a monitor, and ran his hand over the surface of the table searching for the key pad.

"Just touch here to activate," Anna pointed. "Then it will look just like when we practiced."

He touched and the key pad illuminated under his fingers. He looked at the monitor, displaying what was shown on Anna's. Lines of numbers moved across the screen. He gazed at the display until he began to see the three-dimensional nature of the equations speeding by.

"Find the vectors representing our position and their alignment with destination. You'll see lots of change as soon as Kobarev moves us away from Mother. That can't be helped. It'll be good practice. Once we're stationary at Step point, we'll be able to admire the math."

Astrogation was largely admiration, Anna once admitted. The human mind couldn't keep up with the AI. It could only keep an eye on it. And, properly trained, act as an emergency backup.

"Tell me when you see destination vectors," she said.

"Right there," Michael said, letting his finger follow the numbers as they moved across the screen. "It's wavering. Why is it wavering?" he asked.

"Because it anticipates change," she said.

Michael looked over at the back of Kobarev's head. The pilot sat still, except for the movement of his eyes.

"Release in two minutes, ma'am," he said without turning.

"Thank you, Pilot Kobarev," Anna answered as before.

"Initiate countdown at twenty seconds," she said. "I want to see how you handle this." The last sentence was said under her breath, to the monitor.

"Yes, Ma'am," Kobarev said.

Michael watched the two, fully engaged in their work, extremely professional in their task. He had seen Anna's serious side. This was another level.

"Twenty seconds, Ma'am," Kobarev said. "And nineteen, eighteen, seventeen."

Michael swiveled his chair until it faced Kobarev and the screen in front of him. The pilot continued the count, until he stopped at three.

"Initiating release," he announced. Michael turned to see Anna, peering at her monitor. Michael grabbed the arm rests of his chair when Kobarev spoke again.

"And we are released," he said calmly. "Initiating lift."

Anna didn't answer, but continued to stare at her screen. Michael could see the corner of her mouth lift in a faint smile. He turned again towards Kobarev's view screen. Two of the dark screens started to show a crack of light that continued to grow.

"Permission to come closer?" Michael asked.

"Of course," Kobarev said. "Just do not touch. Anything."

Michael got up and walked closer, until he could look directly over the pilot's shoulder.

"I didn't feel anything," he said.

"And you will not." He could see that Kobarev was smiling. "This is not a flier."

"That it isn't," Michael agreed. "Those," he said, pointing

to the two illuminated screens. "The sides of the docking bay?"

"That is correct," Kobarev said. "And as more light filters down, you will see the bottom."

"Wow."

"Yes, wow is correct," Kobarev said. "I am flying a Donut."

"Have you done this before?"

Kobarev laughed. "Nobody has done this before!" he said. "I, Arman Kobarev, am the first. It is why your friend Doctor Pilot Peter Taylor is whining like little boy. He is missing this. There!" he said, blinking. He lifted his palms and rubbed his eyes.

"Ascension in progress," he said, turning to Anna.

"Thank you, Arman," she said. "Congratulations. How long until Decel and positioning?"

"Decel in eight hours, positioning in another eight, Ma'am," he said.

"Call me Anna," she said.

"No, Ma'am," Kobarev answered. "The astrogator is always 'Ma'am'."

"Even if the astrogator is a man?" Anna asked.

"I have never Stepped with a *male* astrogator," Kobarev said. "I would prefer to walk, if that were the case."

"Lucky for you, then," Anna said. "Why don't you take some rest?"

"Thank you, Ma'am," Kobarev answered. "I will do that."

The screen displayed the countdown, red numbers growing increasingly smaller. The Hole took on an even deeper silence. Kobarev sat in his chair facing his split view screen. He was now superfluous, staying in the Hole as a redundancy. A safety backup. The thrusters built into the Donut allowed him to maneuver it away from the larger disc, to a distance where their Step would cause no disturbance in the surrounding space. They also allowed for emergency maneuvers once Step was complete.

Michael watched the seconds march down to that moment. His expression was apprehension mixed with anticipation, and the definite desire to be somewhere else. Michael breathed deeply, and exhaled slowly, trying unsuccessfully to do so without shaking.

"Try to relax," Anna said. "Watch the monitor. Focus on the coordinates."

Michael did so, watching the equations. He noticed a slight variation, let it pass, continued to stare at the numbers until he thought he began to see a location in the code, an actual physical place.

"Why did you ignore that," Anna asked.

"What?"

"You know what, I hope," she said.

"A small difference between numbers?" he admitted. It came out as a question.

"I told you before to ignore nothing. Everything has significance," she said. "There are always slight disturbances in the continuum. The AI corrects for them, but that isn't what we always want." She continued to stare at her screen. "Don't nod, I can't see your head move."

"Okay." This was a new tone for her. Coldly efficient and professional.

"There it is again," she said. "I am making correction."

Michael saw the number, twelve decimal places beyond zero, change back to its original.

"You say, 'concur', if you agree with the correction," she said. "If you don't agree, say 'object'. That doesn't happen very often. But what you don't do is just sit there silently."

"Okay," Michael said. "I concur."

"Just 'concur.' Keep it brief. Keep your attention fixed."

When the countdown reached sixty seconds Anna leaned back in her chair and squeezed her eyes tight. She opened them, blinking rapidly. She rubbed her neck. "There's nothing more we can do," she said. She turned her face to Michael and smiled. "Sorry about the snap," she said. "Each correction might be mere meters, but they can add up. We're Stepping near a planet. Too close to its gravitational field and we may not be able to recover."

Michael started to glance at his screen, at the ever-reducing red numbers, but Anna stopped him.

"Never mind those numbers," she said. "It's better to just let it happen."

Michael started to respond, to open his mouth. He felt it opening. And then he felt it keep opening, as if his lower jaw stretched wider and wider as the top of his head elongated towards the roof. He heard the sound that came out of his mouth, a sound that continued as seconds seemed to merge into years, a vowel transcending reality. His ears vibrated with the "oh" that escaped. His eyes widened as he saw the sound, a vibration pattern dancing away from him, bouncing off the opposing wall, ricocheting onto another. His eyes continued to widen until his vision blurred, and he was left with physical sensation, his body being dissolved molecule by molecule, reassembled and repositioned, stretched and bent, folded and … He forced his eyes to close, but even the darkness behind his lids seemed warped.

The sensation of hands returned, and Michael used them to hold on to whatever was near, grasping the armrests of his chair. It was a tenuous link, but he seized it. Sound entered his consciousness, vibrations taking form. He listened.

"Michael, open your eyes," the vibrations told him. "We're here."

He kept his eyes shut. "I don't like this," he said. "I don't like this." He felt more vibrations, coming from within himself, that he somehow knew was a sob. He felt touch, a hand on his shoulder, another on his chest. A presence above him.

"Open your eyes," he heard. "It helps."

"It does," another voice said. Kobarev. "Do as she says."

Michael gripped the armrests tighter and forced his eyes open. Light flooded in. He felt his back pressing against the seat, his legs bent at the knee, his feet on the deck. His eyes began to focus. The shape in front of him took solid form. Anna's hands were still on him, pressing him back.

"I don't like his," he said again.

"Nobody likes it," Anna said. "But it's over now." She moved a hand, rubbing his upper chest. "All together now?" she asked. "Ready to admire the view?"

"She is beautiful!" Kobarev called loudly.

Michael took in his surroundings. Kobarev stood in front of his view screen, hands on hips. Anna grabbed Michael's arm and helped him stand. They looked where Kobarev was gazing. The screen was no longer split, but displaying one view, which took up the entire panel. Floating in a sea of black was a beautiful blue orb, littered with the greens of its many archipelagos. Small poles of white decorated the top and bottom. The white clouds swirled around the northern hemisphere. A storm approached a group of large islands. Michael leaned forward, trying to recognize them. The storm would pass to the south, as they tended to do, working their way around the globe until playing out among a southern archipelago.

His hand searched for Anna's, found it and held it gently. The damp warmth of her palm grounded him, bringing him fully to this place.

"Welcome to Pemako," she said.

15

Jens furled the head sail, set the helm to auto and climbed on to the deck. Loosening the halyard, he lowered the main sail, letting it drop in neat folds within the lazy jack, a simple arrangement of lines ensuring that the sail lay directly on top of the boom. He tied it down and covered it. Moving forward he picked up a coil of line, tossed it towards the stern, and re-coiled it, each oval a perfect copy of the one preceding it.

He checked the anchor mounting and the pins that held it in place. Opening the bow hatch, he poked his head below and eyed the sail bags. They were stacked neatly in their proper place. He was tempted to drop down and restack them, but forced himself to close and secure the hatch. He returned to the main mast and re-coiled the halyard, hanging it back on its cleat. He readied the mooring line on the port side.

Jens breathed out slowly, pretending it wasn't a sigh. Returning to the cockpit he rested his hand on the tiller and put the helm back on manual. He knew a visitor was waiting on shore. The flier was easy to spot in the clear blue sky. He had watched it come over the horizon directly off the star-board bow, hovering over the property before descending and disappearing from view. He was at least an hour out, so the guest had time to have a cup a tea and catch up with his wife.

Jens suspected they had already had a chance to catch up, that they had spoken several times before. Fran threatened she would call, and she never made idle threats. Although, he wondered who actually called first. Regardless, the ambassador's sails were growing increasingly longer in duration. A night up the coast had turned into a week or two circumnavigating the island or visiting those nearby, where he would anchor for a night or two before sailing back home. Hikes behind the homestead turned into ridge walks lasting days.

At home, he smiled lovingly at his wife, and she gave him the space he seemed to need. She knew him better than to try to coax out the reasons behind his restlessness. She seemed to already intuit reasons he couldn't quite articulate. She knew that he would process them at his own speed. But if it became too intolerable, she would put her foot down. She was a woman of immense patience, within limits.

"If you want to go, just call her," Fran said, taking a direct route she knew wouldn't work. She had watched her husband wander into the woods only to emerge a day or two later. Or sail off on his boat. She originally hoped the look on his face might change after these breaks, but when he walked up the path, she couldn't fail to see the furrows on his forehead as deep, if not deeper, than before.

"You know you want to," she added. "Just do it."

"What about the cooperatives?"

"What about them? You set them up and let the partners

run them," she said. "That's why you have too much free time."

"I'd be gone too long."

"We'll manage," she countered.

"And what about Jiao? She wouldn't recognize me when I got back," Jens said.

"Of course she will," Fran said. "And you'll have new stories to tell her. She's growing tired of the same old tales."

"Is that why she rolls her eyes?"

"Yes," she answered. "I didn't think you noticed."

"I'll miss you," Jens said.

"No, you won't," Fran said. She softened her tone. "You'll focus on what you need to do and won't waste thoughts on things you can't change."

"I won't even have a role," he protested.

"That's nonsense, and you know it."

"And if something happens? If I don't come back?"

"You always come back, even when you don't want to."

"I'm serious," Jens said.

The discussion had lapped itself. Another full circle. Fran took a deep breath, exhaling slowly. "So am I," she said. "You need this. It's okay. We'll be okay."

Jens nodded, but didn't argue. He could take her words out on the water and try to reconcile them with how he felt.

Jens slowed the yacht as it approached the jetty. He cut the engine as it neared, and climbed out of the cockpit. From the deck of the ship he stepped over to its mooring. A practiced maneuver, muscle memory, the whole thing done without thinking. He took the line he had prepared on deck and looped it around a docking cleat, steadied the vessel with his free hand and brought the stern in close. Using the line waiting on the jetty, he secured the yacht. He grabbed his bag, powered down the reactor and locked up. He walked towards the house, past the unattended HakKor flier tied to the jetty. *Executive* class—she was certainly traveling in style.

Jens smiled as he walked up the path, feeling lighter than he had in a very long time. Decisions tended to do that. He put his bag down on the front deck and opened the door. The two women were sitting on stools at the kitchen counter.

"Patricia," he said. "It's so nice to see you!"

She stood up and faced him. "You almost sound like you mean it. We heard you practicing that line as you sailed in."

"Yeah, well, it's true," he said, as he put his arms around her and held her tight. "It's been too long."

She stepped back and studied him. "My god, you've aged," she said.

"Sorry I'm late, hun." he said to Fran. He stepped over and took her in her arms. She resisted the display in front of their guest, but he didn't give her an out. When he released her, she smiled and shook her head.

"You've been spending too much time on your own," she said.

"No argument there," he said. "But what can I say, I like the company." He went to the sink and washed his hands, drying them on a tea towel.

"And just what are you ladies scheming about?" he asked.

"You," Patricia said.

Jens grabbed an apple from a bowl on the counter and took a bite. He stared at Patricia as he chewed. "Nice flier," he said, still chewing.

"They're sparing no expense," she said, "so I'm spending it."

Jens swallowed. He looked at his wife. An unspoken discussion took place in the few moments that passed silently between them. Finally, she nodded.

"When are they arriving?" Jens asked.

"In about a week," Patricia said.

"That's not long," Jens responded.

"What, do you want to do more sailing?" Patricia said.

"No," Jens said. "She's all battened down." He took another bite of his apple, chewing slowly.

"Andrew's been following their progress," Fran said.

"Of course he has," Patricia said, staring at him. "And from what Fran tells me, he has been acting increasingly restless the closer they get."

"HakKor doesn't give much away," he said. "I doubt many buy the 'exploratory mission' story," he said.

News from Earth travelled at the speed of Donuts, and broadcasts were transmitted after each Step. He had watched the feeds describing the build of the new, state of the art 'science vessel'. She was touted as the fastest ship yet developed, with her own multi-Step Donut. He read about her successful trials and her imminent departure for Pemako. HakKor were vague about mission objectives, so there was a selection of theories. Some closer than others.

"As soon as word gets out that you're on board, other Consortia will put the pieces together," Jens said.

"Insignificant," Patricia answered.

"Patricia says you don't have to be in orbit until the end of the week," Fran said.

Jens smiled at his wife, telling her that he loved her, that he would miss her, and that he thanked her, in the silent language passing between them. He would tell her the same when they were alone together, using his voice.

"That's good," he said. "Time for a catch up with old friends, eh?"

The tender fired its forward thrusters to slow its progress as the *Chōgenbō* filled the view screen. Jens looked over the shoulder of the pilot, admiring the lines of the ship. The streamlined nose and silver plating gave it a sleek and aerodynamic look. He grinned, remembering the lead-lined rectangular boxes he first sailed in. Ruan technology recovered from the Artifact had changed how all ships were built, but this ship was built to impress. Just who it wanted to impress was a matter of conjecture. Sail trials had been covered by all feeds and followed by millions. HakKor was showing off.

But for the purpose of first contact, if that ever happened, it would also do. Jens' eye travelled down the hull, past the cannon, and to the tail of the ship.

"She's got a fat ass," he said.

"Nothing but power back there," Kobarev said. "Power you have never seen or felt before." He turned and looked at

Jens. "She can push up to fourteen g, more! And Decel faster. That is beautiful fat ass!"

"It sure is," Jens said.

Kobarev turned back to the illuminated screen in front of him, made facial gestures those behind couldn't see and slowed the transport even more. The pilot took the tender underneath the *Chōgenbō*, and pointed it at a haze of green light. He angled the nose of the shuttle up and for the briefest moment green filled the view screen. It was soon replaced by the docking bay of the larger craft.

"Welcome home, *Chīsai Tori ichi*," they heard over the comms. "Airlock sealing behind you."

"Many thank you," Kobarev said. He raised an eye at the screen in front of him and the door of the shuttle began to open. Jens and Patricia stood and grabbed their bags.

"Leave those," Kobarev said. "I will take."

"*Spasibo*," Jens said.

"A good try," Kobarev said. "Welcome to the *Kestrel*."

Olsen stood waiting as Patricia stepped out of the shuttle. Behind him Peter and Michael stood with their arms at their sides. Their green jackets and black pants were identical to the captain's. *Playing sailors now?* she thought. Fine. Captains seemed to love their uniforms. Jens asked her to don one on the *General Xing* on their long return to Earth, all those decades ago. She laughed at him then. She hoped she wouldn't have to laugh at this captain.

"Dr Lin, welcome to the *Chōgenbō*," Olsen said. He made a fist with his right hand and held it in the palm of his left, bowed deeply from the waist, and held it for a long moment.

"It is a pleasure, and an honor, to finally have you join us," he added after straightening. "I am Captain Solvieg Olsen."

"Thank you, Captain Olsen, but there's no need for that kind of behavior," Patricia said.

"As you wish," he said. "Your colleagues have been eager to see you, so I will leave it to them to show you to your quarters."

"Once again, thank you," she said.

"We can meet once you have settled in." Olsen stepped aside and let Patricia join Peter and Michael. He turned towards Jens.

"Ambassador Jensen," he said. "I am honored to have you aboard." He reached out a hand.

Jens grabbed his hand and shook it.

"I certainly hope that's true, Captain," Jens said.

"It is," Olsen said. "Your skill and experience are—"

"Enough of that," Jens interrupted. "I know how I would feel if somebody like me invited himself on my ship."

Olsen laughed. "You didn't invite yourself, you were recruited," he said. "Dr Lin wanted you, and that's why you're here. I'm told she usually gets what she wants. In fact, I *was* told that, by Motoyo himself. But I think I can see it for myself."

Kobarev passed them carrying four bags, two in each arm. Jens stopped him, opened one of the bags and pulled out a bottle.

"Twelve-year-old whiskey," he said to Olsen. "Oldest on Pemako. Shall we have a sip and talk about what my role will actually involve?"

Olsen took the bottle and examined the label. "Just a sip," he said. "We're prepping to join our Donut."

He led Jens to his quarters, which were slightly larger than those of his crew. He motioned to a chair and Jens sat. Olsen brought over two glasses, one with a small amount of whisky, the other twice as much, which he handed over. He touched his glass to Jens', took a sip, and sat opposite.

"Not bad," Olsen said.

"There's no need to lie," Jens said. "Give them points for trying, anyway."

Olsen took another sip, winced, and set the glass on the table. "Seriously, it's passable. Probably better with a mixer."

"Well, it's an offering of sorts," Jens said. "An apology for the imposition."

"I've already told you, there's no need for an apology," Olsen said. "I'm glad you're here. Really."

Jens picked up his glass, closed his eyes and breathed in the drink. He took a sip. Opening his eyes, he looked at Olsen. "Any particular reason for that?"

Olsen shifted in his seat. "Experience is always welcome on a mission like this," he said.

"I don't think there has ever been a mission like this," Jens said.

"Exactly," Olsen admitted. "Which is why I could use more experience, especially of the type you have. I've made it policy that every section head has a second. A back up. You can never have too many redundancies going into an unknown."

"Agreed."

"I want you to be my back-up," Olsen said.

"Don't you have a First Mate?" Jens asked.

"Yes, of course," Olsen said. "Anders is very competent. But there are quite a lot of other duties that go along with that responsibility. Call it a second First Mate, if that makes any sense."

"I don't think he would like me stepping in his way," Jens said.

"He is aware, and happy with the arrangement. Leading with the great Ambassador Jensen! He has a sealed envelope containing orders in case I become … incapacitated. For whatever reason. He'll assume command, as is proper, but he'll have you for help." Olsen picked up his glass, drained it and swallowed.

"A sealed envelope?" Jens asked. "Sounds a bit old fashioned."

"Call it dramatic effect," Olsen said. "At the insistence of HakKor, orders and instructions for our return, whatever the outcome might be. Just get to know as much about the ship, and the crew, as you can before we start this hunt. I've given you access to all data, including that marked 'Captain's Eyes Only,' or any communications from HakKor. You can log on to the ship's computer from your cabin, just like me. And that includes security feeds."

"Okay," Jens agreed.

"Just introduce yourself as a xeno-something. No, wait. A *Mission Specialist*. That should satisfy the crew," Olsen said. "Though they'll all know who you are. Hopefully no one will ask for an autograph. Now let's go to the bridge. Kobarev will be parking the ship in the Donut. He's a very good pilot."

Harvesting

16

Michael went over the numbers again. The Seed ship was a generation ship, of sorts. Its passengers wouldn't be handing over the helm to their children and grandchildren because they were all frozen in cryo-sleep. The only generations passing were those on Earth, for not long after the Seed ship left Pemako, or *Ruanae*, as the Originals called it, the last of their species died. There were no more generations to pass there. When they left, the Roman Empire had just reached its zenith on Earth. Their technology had allowed them to conquer all the lands around the Mediterranean Sea. They built roads, aqueducts, sanitation systems for entire cities.

To the Ruan, the Romans would have appeared to be stone age ignoramuses playing around a small pond. But it was all timing. By the time Rome's descendants, like Anna Giolino, were capable of plotting a course to Ruanae, all they would find were ruins similar to those left by the Romans. Humanity had managed to scatter itself across star systems to ensure the survival of the species. It had survived past pandemics, before it had the ability to seed other planets. That, Michael reflected, was a bit of pure luck. Now there were colonies on dozens of planets.

Rome was brought to its knees by a pandemic, and the ancient world probably never really recovered from it. Dr Lin compiled a list of epidemics and plagues, which she made Peter and he study. "Just for perspective," she had said. The Antonine Plague was brought back to Rome by soldiers returning from conquests in Asia. It was named after the emperor of the time, Marcus Aurelius Antoninus. It killed up to five million people, twenty five percent of those it infected. It may have even had as high as a thirty five percent mortality rate. Marcus Aurelius himself would be a victim. Her list got depressingly repetitive. Plagues and flus killing millions.

"But that's the worst of it," Dr Lin concluded. "Sure, pandemics were bad, but death rates have always gone down. We're a lucky species."

Michael knew her better than to think her callous. He saw how upset she got at new sites. She didn't dwell on whatever thoughts caused that deep sadness to cross her face, and she pushed it someplace deeper before resuming her work. It was, after all, entirely about perspective. During their pandemic, the Ruan had faced a one hundred percent mortality rate. Michael couldn't imagine what that could be like. He knew that indigenous peoples on old Earth knew. Europeans brought a host of diseases to North America, which decimated up to eighty percent of the population. In some Pacific islands, like Tahiti, it may have been as high as ninety-five percent. A lucky species.

Sometime in their past, in a desperate act to preserve their species, the Ruan sent some away from their diseased kin. Michael had bragged about the math, even calling it easy.

Now the weight of the equations immobilized him. An entire expedition, possibly an entire species, hung on him getting it right. Michael started to examine those numbers again.

"Going over them again won't change anything, son." Olsen stood in the doorway of the lab. "You are needed in the Hole, and I am needed on the bridge."

"I'm sure I can fine tune," Michael said without looking up. "The variables are—"

Michael didn't hear Olsen step across the room. The captain's hand on his shoulder caused him to start.

"You've done all you can do," Olsen said. "It's time."

"Time," Michael repeated. He put both hands on his desk and looked up at Olsen. The captain tried to smile reassuringly, but didn't quite pull it off.

"Come on, son," he said. "I'll walk you to the airlock."

Michael sent the coordinates to Anna as she waited in the Hole. As soon as Michael stood, Olsen gripped the young man's elbow. They left the lab and walked side by side down the corridor. As they passed the mess hall, all those within stopped talking and watched silently. Closer to the airlock they passed the engineer, Hiroto Doi, and technician Tatsua Okada. Both men stood still against the bulkhead and let them pass. Michael tried to make eye contact with them, but their gaze didn't rise above chest height. At the airlock, Olsen released Michael's arm and patted him on the back.

"We're all counting on you," he said. "Let the hunt begin."

"Thank you, sir," Michael said.

Olsen heard the doubt in Michael's voice. "You've worked very hard," he said. "Time to put it all to the test."

Another pat on the back forced Michael to take a step forward, into the airlock. He didn't turn until he was in the elevator. When he pressed the control to the Hole, he saw Olsen, still standing where he left him. Olsen gave a nod; the elevator doors closed and the small room began its trip to the center of the Donut.

"No pressure," he said to the empty room. "We're *counting* on you. Arrgh!" He sat down, rested his hands on his knees, fidgeted with his fingers, clapped his hands, stood again. Just when he thought the journey would never end, the elevator stopped and the doors opened. Anna was bent over her console. Michael took the chair next to Anna. She looked up as he did, her eyes meeting his and almost stilling the turmoil he felt.

"Nice numbers," she said. She smiled gently. "You've done well."

Even though he wanted to, they didn't need to say more. She had listened to his fears and doubts for nights, gave up trying to reassure, and even sent him to sleep in his own quarters under the pretext of needing her rest in preparation to Step. He liked to quietly do his computations, ignored by all those around. He wasn't used to being the center of attention. Anna had watched him squirm under the pressure of eyes and expectations.

Now they peered at their screens. *She is right,* Michael thought. The numbers were nice. He stared at the red numbers in the corner, counting down to Step.

"Around the first star, after over one hundred years—"

"One hundred and twenty-three years, four months and sixteen days," Michael said.

"Sleeping the whole time," Anna continued. "Imagine what they missed."

"A lot of darkness, a star getting brighter, then a lot more darkness," he said.

"Oh. Come on," she added. "That system must have—"

"You don't have to do this," Michael said.

"Do what?"

"Distract me from that." Michael didn't take his eyes off his screen. He lifted a hand and pointed to the diminishing red numbers. "I want to be ready this time."

"There is no getting ready," she said. "How can you get ready to be pulled across lightyears?"

"I really don't like this part," Michael said, closing his eyes.

"Don't be a little girl, though that might be an insult to little girls," Anna said. Only her words were lost as the Donut initiated Step.

Michael turned to see Anna studying her monitor. He breathed in deeply and slowly, trying to stop his body from shaking. He flexed his hands, made them into fists, opened them and stretched his fingers.

"We're here," she said, keeping her eyes on her screen. "And we're due on the bridge." She folded her monitor down. "Are you staying or coming?" she asked across the table.

"With you," he said.

"*Una piccola ragazza*," she said. "You're a little girl. Now get out of my Donut."

Standing, she placed a hand on Michael's shoulder, let it slip down to his wrist, then took his hand in hers. Gently pulled, he rose and they walked to the elevator. Anna sat smiling as they made their way back to the ship. She started to speak, looked at Michael's face, and stopped. She was told Stepping was like sea sickness for some. The first time on a boat, a person can't really know if they'll feel sick or not. Sometimes people adjust, get used to it, stop feeling queasy. She never minded Stepping. Part of her actually enjoyed the sensation. She didn't think Michael would ever really enjoy it, but she hoped he'd get used to it. They might be doing quite a few more Steps.

They felt the ship disengage from the Donut a few moments after they notified Olsen they were aboard. Anna guided Michael directly to the bridge. Half the crew were present, clustered around Kumiko's monitor. Dr Lin stood over her left shoulder, Olsen over her right. Ambassador Jensen peered over Dr Lin's head. Peter gave Michael an excited look when they entered, made a fist and shook it as if they had won a game.

"Sensors are now on!" Peter said.

"Anything?" Michael asked.

"No, not at all, it's way too early for that," he said.

"Enough," Olsen and Dr Lin said at the same time.

Olsen turned to greet Anna. "Thank you, Astrogator Giolino," he said. "Donut status?"

"All systems fine," Anna reported. "Accurate Step. Charge at seventy-two percent."

"Good," Olsen said. He turned away from the screen

and shook Anna's hand. "Well done." He smiled at Michael. "Now to see how good your math is," he said.

"Please," Kumiko said. It wasn't a request, but a rebuke.

Olsen nodded to Anna and Michael and resumed his place, staring over the communication officer's shoulder. Michael stood next to Jens and saw the monitor between his and Dr Lin's heads. Kumiko stared intently at a round black screen, with green waves pulsing from the center. She placed a hand over the headphone covering her right ear. The others watched her hand expectantly. The scene was frozen as a minute passed. Finally, she took her headphones off and set them on her console.

"Anything?" Peter asked.

Kumiko laughed. "Nothing. Nothing metallic, anyway, and nothing travelling at high speed. This might take a while," she said.

"It is like needle in haystack," Kobarev said. He did not join the others clustered around the communications station.

"Indeed!" Kumiko agreed. "But more like a needle moving very quickly through a lot of space." She raised her hand and waved the others away. "Now we wait and listen. This is all speed of light. Very slow. Our sensors have travelled ... maybe five AU. About the distance from Jupiter to the sun. In about seven hours, they would have travelled fifty. Seventy hours, you get it."

"But you can see what was there. The light," Jens said.

"Yes, we can see light that was there," Kumiko said. "But we're not looking for light. We're trying to detect technology."

"Three days," Michael said. "Five hundred AU in three

days. Sixty-nine hours. Five thousand AU in six hundred and ninety hours. Twenty-nine days."

"You're the mathematician," Kumiko said.

"Five thousand AU is tiny space," Kobarev said. "Less than a light year."

"Zero point eight of a light year," Michael said.

"Which is why your math has to be accurate," Olsen cut in. "I suggest we let our astrogator and mathematician rest. Crunch your numbers while we search, and prep for a possible second Step. Hopefully that won't be necessary, but I want to see your data. The rest of you," he said, "let Kumiko work. Three days. If nothing is found, we'll discuss it then."

Anna took Michael's hand and led him out of the bridge. He started to smile as they neared her quarters, but his mouth began to curve downward as they walked past her door. It was a straight line when she stopped in front of sickbay. She tilted her head and glanced at him from the corner of her eye, then touched the door. It slid open. Anna gripped Michael's hand tighter and pulled him into the room.

"I have a patient for you," she announced.

"It's about time." The ship's doctor set down the screen she was reading and smiled at Michael.

"What's this all about?" he asked.

"Stop it," Anna said. "You know why you're here."

"No, I don't," he protested.

"It's okay, Michael," Donna said. "You've been self-medicating, which is a good start. But I can tell from the dark rings under eyes that it isn't working very well."

Michael bit his lip and looked from the doctor to Anna.

"It's true," Anna said to him. "I need your mind sharp right now. You're not sleeping, and you're twitching under the pressure."

"Come, sit down, Michael," Donna said, patting a sick-bay examination couch. "Thanks, Anna. I'll send him home when we're done."

Anna nodded. She pointed a finger at Michael. "Do what she says." She leaned over and kissed his forehead before leaving. The door slid shut behind her.

"You're using GLR to try to relax," Donna said. "That's not what it's for, and you know that."

"It does the trick," Michael said.

"No, it doesn't," she said. "Lack of sleep and anxiety. It's not helping, at least not how you're taking it. Look at your leg twitching away. You're needed right now. You can't just keep trying to manage by yourself, or what you fear will actually happen."

Michael put his hand on his knee and tried to sit still.

"If you want to just relax at night, I'll give you some CBD with a nice level of THC—"

"A joint?" Michael asked.

"If that's all you want," Donna said. "But that's not what you need."

"And what do I need?" Michael asked.

"Perspective," Donna answered. "You think this is all on you, everybody waiting for you to find the Ruan in the middle of this nothingness." She spread her arms wide, palms out. "The odds of them being out here are slim, and you know it."

"Not so slim," Michael said. "Their course is predictable—"

"Listen to you," Donna said. "You still think this is going to work." She sat down on the table next to Michael. "And it might. It just might. But the sooner you give up trying to be the hero, the better you'll feel."

"I'm not trying to be a hero," Michael said.

"Yeah, right." She hopped off the table and walked over to a work bench. Opening a cupboard mounted to the bulkhead, she moved bottles aside, taking several out until choosing one. Holding it up, she showed Michael.

"This ought to help, if you let it," she said.

"What is it?"

"Perspective," she said. "Two drops under your tongue, three times a day."

"Perspective?"

"Exactly. Combine it with some exercise, even a distraction or two, and you'll start to feel better." She handed the bottle to Michael. He unscrewed the cap, withdrew the dropper and looked at the liquid inside.

"Go on," she said.

"What is it?"

"I told you."

"No, really."

"It's GLR," she said. "A nice percentage, the level you need, not what you've been taking. I want you to micro dose. You should start to feel a little better after a sleep or two, but it will be subtle. You'll have to look for it. Examine your mind. That will help. Go on. Two drops."

Michael put the dropper in his mouth and squeezed two drops under his tongue.

"Good," Donna said. "Just remember, aside from your friend Peter, I don't think anybody on board really believes we're going to find that ship. And I gave Peter the same medicine and advice I'm giving you. Give up, and relax. You'll be able to focus more on your work. You can see more when your mind isn't clouded with emotion, which includes hope."

Michael sat holding the bottle in his hand. "Okay," he said.

"Just try," Donna said. "Now get out of here. Get something to eat, take some rest, and then check your numbers or whatever it is you do."

Jens walked into the galley looking for a quiet place to eat. He was out of practice being around others, or even being inside. Solitude was a precious commodity on a small ship. He noticed the Dutch security man too late to back out of the room without causing offense. Tall, blond, well built, he was a walking Nordic stereotype. Even his name. *Something* de Werk. Jan, that was it. Jens nodded in greeting.

De Werk watched Jens walk into the galley, fill a mug with coffee and return to the table area. He indicated the chair opposite. "Ambassador Jensen," the man said. "Are you enjoying the ride?"

"Please, 'Jens' will do," he answered, trying to decide if the Dutchman was being polite, or an asshole.

"Jens," de Werk repeated. "Nice ship, eh?"

"Yes, it is," Jens answered.

"I bet a lot more comfortable than what you sailed in the day," de Werk said.

"No, not really," Jens said. "Just a bit shinier."

De Werk laughed. Jens felt himself warming to the man. He looked as hard and welcoming as an iron bulk head—until he smiled. His otherwise stony face lit up with humor, even warmth. Jens knew it would better to be somebody the big man smiled at than scowled at.

"Our freighters were beat up and boxy, but they were spacious," Jens said. "I can't walk down the corridor in this boat without bumping into somebody."

"I think they went for looks more than access," de Werk agreed. He looked down at his hands, then up at Jens. "Hard to defend."

"I've noticed that," Jens agreed. "It could use another bulkhead or two between the airlock and the bridge. But at least the bridge has doors."

"And the reactor room," de Werk added. "The doorway to the control room is much too wide. Once that is breached, there is nowhere to hide. One stun grenade and the room is taken."

"There's plenty of cargo boxes that could be stacked around the room," Jens said. "To about chest height. Lashed to the deck."

"Oh," de Werk laughed. "Doi would love that, cluttering up his room."

"Yeah, but who cares?" Jens asked. "Security first."

"I like your attitude," de Werk said.

"It's kept me alive," Jens said. "The armory is impressive. I was surprised to see plasma."

"Standard issue. Had a play with the cannon yet?"

"Just a little," Jens said. "Nothing live though. I'd like a bit more."

"We'll make that happen. Sounds like we have a couple of days. Tsuji and Mori were reluctant at first, but they finally gave us access."

"They didn't give you access? Neither you nor Rupert?" Jens said. "That sounds odd."

"This whole set up is odd," de Werk said. "Maybe Tsuji had a grudge, having a team imposed on him. Whatever. All I know is that orders came and we followed them. Report to Sapporo for transportation topside, ship duty. The big boss interfering for some reason. But I'm not here to ask questions, just to do my job. Tsuji takes his serious, which is good. Mori as well. Career are that way."

De Werk pushed his chair back and stood. "Do you want some food? I am getting some."

"Sure, thanks," Jens said.

De Werk went into the galley, and returned a few minutes later with two bowls of stew. He set them both down with spoons. He breathed in appreciatively. The two men ate in silence. De Werk waited until Jens pushed his bowl away from him before speaking.

"You have seen them," he said.

Jens let a moment pass before he responded. He knew who de Werk meant. He had been waiting for this conversation, but was undecided about having it. "Not really."

"You know what I mean."

"I know what you mean," Jens said.

"If you don't want to tell me, you don't have to," de Werk said. "But I am security, so I should know as much as I can about what I might have to fight. You can only learn so much from data feeds or seminars."

"Do you really think we're going to find anything out here?"

"Doesn't matter what I think," de Werk said. "I need to be ready. It's my job."

Jens stared at the man across the table. He had commanded professional security in the past. They were a nightmare on leave, and thankfully they were usually somebody else's nightmare, but they were very focused on the job. Jen decided to talk.

"I'll tell you what I know," he said. "But it isn't much."

"It's still more than anybody else," de Werk said.

"I sprayed with the room with rounds from my sounder," Jens started. "Three, maybe four, hit their target. But I couldn't see anything."

"We have glasses now, infrared," de Werk said.

"Yeah, and certain doses of GLR, I know," Jens said. "Might be wise to start taking that."

"I am," de Werk said. "You?"

"No," Jens said. "Not yet. When you spend a good deal of time on Pemako you start to adjust to the pheromones that made them invisible, or translucent. But I'll take the doses just in case." Jens got up and walked into the galley, returning with two mugs of coffee. De Werk smiled when a mug was set in front of him.

"Three rounds," Jens said. "And it didn't kill it. I saw movement on the deck—only because it had fallen in the blood of the astrogators it had just slaughtered. Three rounds, at least, and still moving. That's strength."

"Fucking tough," de Werk agreed. "But a knife finished it. That one?" de Werk pointed under the table at Jens' leg.

Jens moved a hand to his leg and removed a knife from the sheath strapped to his thigh. He took it by the blade and passed it across to the security man. De Werk took it reverently, his examination of the steel an act of worship.

"Beautiful," was all he said.

"Japanese steel. Priceless," Jens said. "In more ways than money. It was a gift from a dear friend. Friends. It saved my life, and probably a lot of others."

"Is it true? Where it was made?"

"Yeah," Jens said. "Every knife bears the trace of its maker; in the way the steel is folded. This one was made by a winner of the Masamune Prize. It should be in a museum."

De Werk turned the knife over and examined it closely, then gave the blade back. Jens returned it to its sheath.

"But I wouldn't advise getting that close. If you even could. They're bigger, faster and stronger than us. In an even fight, it wouldn't be very even. I know who I would bet on. All I had was surprise, and a gun. Theirs were useless; thank god for that. They wouldn't recharge for some reason. Those tech boys could probably tell you why."

Jens took another drink of coffee. "This coffee isn't strong enough. Needs a shot of something."

"I'm on duty," de Werk said.

"Yeah. I guess we all are now," Jens agreed.

"I know they're taller and stronger and faster," de Werk said. "Those corpses you brought back certainly were. But … I'm just asking. How would you handle them now?"

"I don't know what to tell you," Jens said. "If they outmatch us in a fair fight, then we don't fight fair. Go in with everything. Fast. And if that isn't possible, go in smart."

"Smart."

"You know what I mean. If you can't win toe to toe, then don't fight that way. Don't even fight, if at all possible."

De Werk pursed his lips.

"Just words, I know," Jens said. "We have no idea how many are out there, no idea of their defenses, or their offences. They might all be dead, or it might be like poking an ant hill."

"A lot of unknowns, as Olsen says."

"So, prepare for as many situations as possible," Jens said. "Starting with that reactor room. Nah, on second thought, let's start with something fun. Why don't you show me those cannons?"

17

After three days, Michael and Anna returned to the Donut Hole. Michael watched the numbers count down. Anna reviewed the coordinates, before finally sitting back and handing it all over to the AI. Until now, she had always Stepped towards a target where accuracy was essential. A star. A planet. Donuts could disappear due to small errors. Donuts had disappeared, as well as all the ships and personnel travelling on them. Anna never wanted to be *that* astrogator, or even be a part of *that* team.

She smiled at Michael, embellished with a wink. She could tell him that it would be over soon enough, that it was only temporary, but knew it wouldn't do any good. He would probably take it as teasing—which it would be, to a degree. He smiled back weakly. She could see the trepidation in his eyes, but also the resignation, which was good. *I'll have to thank the doctor*, she thought.

After Step, Anna checked the numbers and, satisfied, reported to the bridge. Donut on location, power at sixty-one percent. She and Michael left the Hole and made their way back to the ship. Olsen, Dr Lin, Jensen, Taylor, Middleton, de Werk, even the technicians, Okada and Yasuda, were gathered around Mori and the scanner. They waited in the doorway as minutes went by, noticed only by Kobarev who nodded a hello before turning back to his monitor. The group behind Mori slowly started to dissipate. Okada and Yasuda passed Michael without looking up. Jens patted him on the shoulder and thanked Anna.

When Olsen noticed them, he nodded. "Three days, folks," he said to those left on the bridge. "Let's see what we can find while some more numbers are being crunched. Once again, thanks to our astrogator for a successful Step."

After the third Step the crowd behind Mori was smaller. Dr Lin was at her place, looking over the communication officer's shoulder. Olsen was seated, watching from his captain's chair.

"Donut status?" he asked without turning.

"Step accurate. Power at forty-nine percent," Anna replied.

"How many Steps until recharge?"

"Two. I wouldn't advise more than that," she said.

Olsen swivelled in his chair to face them. "Thank you, Astrogator Giolino," he said. "Calculate two Steps, then to the nearest star to recharge."

"Yes, sir," Anna replied.

"Three days to crunch numbers," he said to Michael.

The fourth Step was almost routine. At fifth Step, only Dr Lin stood behind Mori looking at the scanner. When Michael entered, she walked over and placed her hand on his arm.

"You're doing great," she said. "These things take time."

"I don't understand why it's not here," he said. "Maybe it doesn't exist."

"You know that's not true, there's just more variables to consider," she said. "And make sure you work more with Mori," she added before leaving the bridge. "She knows a great deal about searching."

Michael turned and followed her before he could hear Olsen tell whoever was near that they had three days.

Step to a star, and three months in close orbit to recharge. Middleton assigned a training regime to keep boredom at bay. All crew drilled under Tsuji and Mori with sounders, plasma and cannon. Jens acted as instructor in safety drills. He seemed to take pleasure in the mock disasters and attacks, cutting gravity without warning and turning it back on when it was least expected—at least until several sprains made the ship's doctor put a stop to it. Peter wondered how the boarding of another ship was considered a safety drill. De Werk and Rupert especially enjoyed those drills, wearing atmosphere suits as well as energy fields, walking the outer deck, weapons in hand. Okada and Yasuda kept up with the Dutch security men, both agile and quick learners. Kobarev used the time to refine using the claw, with Peter in a tender as practice on the dark side of the Donut. Peter watched Okada and Yasuda walk beneath the tender, their bodies cloaked in the green hue of the energy field as they probed for unguarded hatches, and snuck into the ship for another boarding drill. Then the large claws from the raptor closed over Peter, blocking his view.

Kumiko Mori joined Michael and Anna in the lab, retracing their Steps, and exploring possible courses the Seed ship could have taken. The math, Michael admitted, was anything but easy. They studied the systems the ship should have passed, the slingshots that would have affected its velocity, but it was impossible to account for what they couldn't know. Accidents happen. Systems fail. False readings of life or atmosphere that might cause the ship to stop. Anything. The only way to account for any of those variables was to assume they didn't happen. He retraced his original computations, checked his numbers and plotted the exact Steps they had just taken.

"You are cast netting," Kumiko said. "That's what it looks like."

"What is cast netting?" Anna asked.

"It is fishing with a net, one that you throw out into the water," she answered. "My father used to fish this way. The net is circular, just like our scans. You throw out the net, and it covers a wide area of water. What is in that area can be caught. Our sensors throw out a pulse, like a net, radiating outward."

"And?"

"Your Steps are sequential," she said.

"I don't understand," Michael said.

"We're throwing a big net, following the projected course. But we're leaving out more than we're covering."

When Michael and Anna didn't respond, she got up, grabbed three cups from the cupboard and returned to the work bench. She placed the cups in a straight line. Going back to the cupboard she grabbed three more and made the line of cups longer.

"These should really be balls or something spherical because that's how we see," she said. "Look—Step, Step, Step,

Step, Step, Step." She pointed to the areas beside the cups, then drew a tangent from each one at right angles until a grid started to appear. She put her finger on a space in the grid.

"Step here next," she said. She moved her finger to another grid. "Then Step here." She moved her finger, pointing to other grids. "Then here, and then here, and then here."

"That's a lot of Steps," Michael said.

"What's the rush?" Kumiko asked. "You said if there is a ship, it would be in this area. Let's explore the area better. It's why the *Chōgenbō* was built. Quit thinking of this as a quick trip. Nobody else is."

At the end of three months, they Stepped again. Three days passed, and they Stepped yet again. At the end of another three days, another Step. And another, before returning to the star to recharge and train. After each Step Kumiko studied the scanner, its silence reporting failure. When she was off watch, de Werk or Rupert took her place, waiting.

After the seventeenth Step, the scanner spoke. Rupert sat at the station, at first wondering what he touched or pressed to start the alarm, but leaned into the screen as Middleton joined him. They both saw it—a quick motion near the bottom of the monitor, a smear of green light, now gone. Rupert switched off the alarm, and they continued to stare at the empty screen.

"Should I wake her?" Rupert asked.

"It's the most excitement we've had in months," Middleton said. "Yes, I think you should wake her." He returned to his chair and woke Olsen.

Rupert stood as Kumiko entered, happy to vacate the seat and hand over responsibility. The communication officer's hair was mussed and she rubbed her tired eyes. She played back the data that Rupert saw. A green smear of light, hundreds of AU distant, on the screen for mere seconds. She reviewed the information offered by the sensors, staring silently at what they showed.

"Well?" Olsen asked.

"Definitely moving fast," she answered. "And definitely metallic."

"Iron could mean an asteroid," Middleton said. "A rogue S-type. Or M-type."

"Possible," Kumiko said. "They are very metallic. But ..." She returned to the screen, replaying the few moments the smear was shown.

"But what?" Middleton asked.

"It is moving very fast," Kumiko said.

"How fast?" he asked.

"Very," she answered.

"We don't have to speculate," Olsen said. Nobody had noticed the captain enter the bridge. "We know it's there. Let's go see it."

Kumiko smiled. "I will wake Dr Lin," she said. "She will be most excited."

"And our mathematician," Olsen suggested. "He and our Astrogator will need to get to work. Can you work out where we need to be to get the readings you need?"

"I can't," she said. "But they can."

"Good," Olsen said. "Let's put on some coffee and get started."

Michael hugged Anna when they saw the blip. It was on the screen for all of three seconds. He tried to hold back his emotion but started to cry into Anna's shoulder. Then he cried and laughed at the same time.

"What does it mean, then?" Dr Lin asked.

"It ..." Michael started but couldn't form any more words.

"It means it's the ship," Anna said. "It has to be." She squeezed Michael in her arms, then tried to push him away, but his arms were locked firmly.

"Nothing else can travel that fast," Michael finally managed to say. He stepped back from Anna and looked at the screen. "Play it again," he told Kumiko. She did.

"See?" he asked.

"It's fast," she said.

"Yeah," Michael replied. "Have you computed its trajectory?" he asked Kumiko.

"No," she said. "That's why you're here."

"Right," he said. "I'll get on it. We can Step closer."

Michael and Anna rushed to the bridge as soon as the Donut emerged from Step. One small Step to get closer, to observe, to measure. They watched the light make its way across the screen. Kumiko widened the range of the scan and it appeared to move slower, but only due to the vast distance covered in the sweep.

"That's fast," Michael said. The bridge was crowded, all

those present hanging on his words, weeks of doubt forgotten.

"Just a Step away," Peter said.

"Yeah," Michael agreed. "We can Step right to them, but all we'd see was a blur as they passed by."

"Any idea how fast?" Olsen said behind him.

Michael didn't turn. "No, but I will as soon as we get more data."

"Very good," Olsen said. Michael felt a hand on his shoulder. "Well done. *Very* well done. As soon as you're ready, let me know," Olsen added.

Michael and Anna returned to the lab. After four hours she left and went to her quarters. After a few hours sleep she returned to find Michael still at work. His original monitor had reproduced, and he now worked on four simultaneously. She made hot tea and brought over. He took the mug without taking his eyes off the screens, took a sip and set it back down.

"Thanks," he said.

She waited for more, but he seemed to forget she was even there. She left and made her way to the mess room. It looked like a communal meal. Everyone not on watch was sitting around the table, waiting. Anna went into the galley and started to make a meal, looked at those around the table and added ingredients. Donna came in and started to help. No words were exchanged as they worked together. When the meal was ready, they brought it out. Shintaro Doi smiled at them, jumped up and brought over plates and utensils. Middleton left the room, returning minutes later with bottles of wine. He smiled as he opened the first. Folding a napkin over his forearm he walked around the table and filled glasses. When that bottle was empty, he opened another and continued his round. He was opening the third bottle when Michael came in, sat next to Anna and scooped some lasagna onto a plate.

He took a bite, closed his eyes, and let out a sigh. "That is so good," he said. He opened his eyes and grinned at the all the faces pointed at him.

"Well?" Middleton asked.

"I just gave Olsen all the data," Michael said. "He'll be here soon to tell you the game plan." He pointed at the bottle. "Can I get some of that?"

18

Peter waited until the others left. Dr Lin said her words of advice, which could be counted on the fingers of one hand. De Werk walked around the Hole, and its living quarters, as the others talked, checking the weapons locker with Michael before he also left. There was an air of impatience that made the farewell seem less sincere than it actually was. They were leaving two friends alone in the depths of space for what would be months, possibly more. And they were leaving them on the donut, the only way to get home. But they were all eager to go.

Peter didn't have anything special to say to his friend. When he got his chance, he hugged both Michael and Anna.

"You're going to be alright?" he asked. "You don't need anything else?"

"We're well stocked," Michael answered.

"Not really what I meant, but okay," Peter said. "It's going to be a long time."

"Like a vacation," Michael said. "Peace and quiet."

"I bet," Peter said. "No pressure."

"No computations, no Steps," Michael said.

"He needs this break," Anna said. "I need a break. But we'll be following you as soon as we get your signal."

Peter stood back and nodded. Michael had a look in his eyes that was almost peaceful. That was probably thanks to the doctor. But he was tired, which made him look haggard, older. Exactly how Peter felt himself. They were all tired, and they would all get to sleep for a very long time, very soon. When they woke, they would send coordinates back to the pair in the Donut, and messages that would take longer and longer to reach them. Peter put a hand on Michael's shoulders and smiled weakly before turning away.

The others waited in the elevator. As soon as Peter joined them, the door closed and it made its way back to the ship. They didn't speak. There was nothing to say. The course was set and the decisions made. Fears were best left unspoken. All systems would be in the hands of the ship's AI. It would hold all their lives in its quantum circuits. While they slept in their cryo-pods, it would accelerate to such a force that any living thing on deck would be crushed under its own weight. It meant surrendering all control. Peter realized that most of his crewmates, including himself, were control freaks.

They left the Donut, Doi collapsing the airlock behind them. Once on board the ship, Kobarev took the vessel away from its docking bay and started accelerating on their new course. Doi checked and rechecked the reactors as more power was applied. They accelerated to one G, matching the artificial gravity they had been living with. Then Kobarev disengaged from his monitor and shut down his station. He stood, looking for a reason to delay his walk to the cryo-chamber. He noticed Middleton doing one more scan of the bridge for forgotten or loose items. A coffee mug that might be pulverized as it slid across a deck or was flung into a bulkhead. Kobarev joined him, but the ship was secured. Everything, from personal gear to galley equipment, was stowed for just this occasion.

Wright was checking and rechecking all the cryo-pods. While the AI held all their lives, she felt like she had a more immediate hold. Any technical fault would kill. She went over each pod until it was occupied. All the Japanese crew were already under. She wondered if it was cultural, the way they dealt with fear, or how they could surrender to fate. They just got on and did what was required. She gave Peter a sedative to help him lie down, inserted the tube that provided the chemicals to ensure vitrification. He was far away by the time she closed and sealed his pod. All it took for Dr Lin, or Patricia, as she preferred the doctor to call her in private, was the offer of the same sedative. Even with her former student asleep she felt the need to prove her toughness. She thanked Donna, lay back and closed her eyes, wincing slightly as the injection was administered.

The ambassador enjoyed the scene, trying to ease the moment with a joke, but Patricia was already sinking into sleep. He wanted to drag this out, be one of the last, but he wasn't the captain. He wasn't even an officer. Donna didn't quite know what he was. But she liked him, so wanted to put him out of his misery.

"Your turn," she said in her best doctor voice—authoritative, knows best, final say.

"I'll just check in with Olsen one more time," he said.

"No," she answered. "Into your pod. I have everything ready."

She guided him to the cylinder and to her surprise didn't have to pull too much. He climbed into the bed and lay back.

"Comfy?" she asked.

"That's not possible in one of these," Jens said.

"Well, you won't be in for very long," Donna said. "Four months, maybe five."

"You really know how to put a guy at ease," Jens said.

"And without even trying," she said. "Little pin prick here," she raised the injector but hesitated. She shook her head, put it her satchel, and pulled out a small white pill. "Unless you would rather …?" she asked.

Jens smiled. He relaxed, closed his eyes and opened his mouth. Donna shrugged, and placed the pill on his tongue. Jens sank deeper into the abyss and was under seconds later. She inserted the tube and adjusted the chemical flow, closed and sealed the lid.

The security team hung as far back as possible, but the doctor tone worked again. She herded the Dutchmen to their pods, sedated them and sealed them in. Kobarev and Middleton followed. Olsen entered his after all the others were asleep.

"Thirty minutes," he reminded her. "That's all you'll have."

"As you've said already," she answered.

"Then acceleration will really kick in. Fast, and hard," he said. "If you're out of your pod you won't be able to get in. You won't be able to move. You'll be—"

"Captain, it's time," she started in the voice she used on the others, but softened her tone. "I'll be right behind you," she said. "And the next thing you'll see is me waking you up."

She didn't give Olsen a chance to reply, injecting the sedative into his arm as she spoke. She prepped him for cryosleep, closed and sealed his pod. She walked around each pod a final time, watching the thick glass view screen slowly frost over, each person already hidden in the foam padding encasing and protecting their frail bodies. She approached her pod and sighed as she stepped into it. Her thoughts raced like she imagined the others did at this point. Entering an unnaturally induced sleep from which she might never wake. Would this be her last conscious sight, thought, sensation? She pushed the idea from her mind and let her eyes wander slowly around the room that held their pods, lingering at each one, trying not to think of them as coffins. She inserted the tube into her abdomen, allowed the chemicals to enter her body, and closed the lid of her pod. That last part she had to do consciously. No comfort from sedation. No way to avoid the feeling of cold invading her body, exploring her skin, her muscle, her organs, from the inside. That was the feeling she really dreaded, the feeling she shielded the others from, or least tried to—freezing from the inside out.

As she sank deeper into sleep, the reactors increased their thrust. The ship flew faster, and then faster, accelerating to match the object detected by the sensors. If it were a race, the *Chōgenbō* was already ahead. Once the course was plotted, it was simple to know where it would be in several months' time. The problem was matching its velocity, and not watching it barrel by on its way between the stars; or miss it and continue on another, endless trajectory. One gravity of acceleration became two, and then three. But the reactors were designed for more, and continued to create the thrust that propelled them forward.

After one week, the ship was accelerating at six gravities. After two weeks it had increased to eight. The mites that had hitched a ride on Kobarev's blanket from home, that had survived the fumigation and quarantine because the pilot did not declare it, lost their grip on the thick fabric. They slipped to the deck below, pinned down by the weight of their exo-skeletons. The eggs laid in the weave of fabric slipped from the fine silk webbing fixing them in place and shot downward, dissolving in a microscopic explosion as they hit the flooring. By that time their parents were a tiny pool of liquid within a shell that finally collapsed in on itself as the force of gravity reached ten, and then eleven, and then twelve.

As the weeks turned to months, the *Chōgenbō* flew faster than any human ship had ever dreamed. If it were leaving Earth, its current speed would still take over fifty years to reach the nearest star, Alpha Centauri. But they didn't want to go to a star.

Donna woke as she always did from cryo-sleep, gasping as if held under water for too long. She glimpsed light through the side of the lid of her pod. It was open several inches, but no more. It should have hinged fully open when the chemical cocktail that caused her body to revive was injected. Instead of the fogged view plate, she should be looking at the ceiling of the cryobay. She lifted her hand, pleased that it wasn't stuck in place by the padding that protected her body. Her last memory before 'sleep' was being smothered in the blue foam as she grew colder and colder in the encroaching darkness.

She pushed up against the lid and it moved. She pushed again, this time with both hands, and it opened fully. She gulped in the air and squinted her eyes. The air was all wrong, discolored. Her mind began to claw its way back to clarity. She realized she wasn't seeing the air, but the light filling it. Red light. Flashing. Red was not good, her groggy mind reasoned. Red, for some reason, was never good. Except in China, where it symbolized good luck. Donna had visited China, to attend a friend's wedding. She lay back again and closed her eyes, picturing the dress she wore, how handsome the groom was —then she snapped her lids open. Using all her strength, she sat up, put a hand on each side of the coffin-like chamber, and heaved herself upward. She pulled herself to the right-hand side, lifted her body out and tumbled onto the decking.

Donna stayed on the floor only long enough to catch her breath. Rising to her elbows, she crawled to the pod and used it to pull herself to a standing position. Scanning the room, she saw all the pods were intact, and the life support monitors showed a steady green light, as they should. Olsen's pod was closed like the others, but the light was flashing. Donna shook her head, took a hand and slapped her own face. Clenching her jaw, she staggered over to the pod on numb feet. Releasing the lid, she lifted. Olsen helped from the inside, pushing upward, and the lid swung fully open. Donna saw he was breathing and pushed off from the pod, moving her heavy legs to the locker containing her medical kit. Opening the door, she grabbed the bag, reached around in it until she found what she wanted. Gripping the device in her fist she punched it against her thigh.

She immediately jolted back, dropping the empty syringe. Awareness surged through her. She grabbed another syringe from the bag and took it to Olsen. He watched through groggy eyes as the doctor raised her fist and slammed it into his leg. His eyes widened and he grabbed her arm.

"Get up!" she yelled.

"What happened?" he asked.

"I don't know, that's your job," she said, turning away towards the nearest pod. By the time she was checking the third, Olsen was up, leaning against a work bench and studying a monitor.

"*Min Gud*!" he said.

"What is it?" Donna demanded.

"Get everyone up, now," Olsen barked. "Kobarev first. Then officers. Send them to the bridge."

"What's happening?" she asked.

"Do it now!" he called as he left the room.

Donna carried her bag to each pod and repeated a procedure that should have not have been needed. Manually activating each pod, she roused the inhabitant, the preprogramed stimulant bringing them to consciousness quickly. As soon as each crew member was awake, they asked the same things; she ignored their questions, checking their vitals instead. When she was satisfied, she let them go to the bridge, or the reactor room, or the armory. Thankfully, Olsen had turned off the flashing lights.

By the time Jens and Patricia reached the bridge, each officer was already at their station. The two stood in the back and tried to deduce what was happening through the actions and orders of the officers. As soon as the view screen was activated, they didn't need any more clues.

A large disc filled their view, running from one edge of the screen to the others, displaying a mere fraction of what was outside. Patricia reached over and took Jens' hand. They watched as cameras mounted on the outside of their ship panned up to reveal more of the disc that dwarfed the *Chō-genbō*. Both wanted to ask questions, but they waited. Olsen was speaking to both Kobarev and Mori, having two different conversations at one time. The pilot didn't turn from his controls, only tilted his head slightly and increased the distance between their ship and the disc.

Mori was similarly focused on her scanners. The back of her head twitched as she examined the data scrolling across the screen at a rapid pace.

"Anything?" Olsen asked.

"No, sir," she answered, though Jens and Patricia didn't know what thing it was she was looking for.

Peter entered and Jens flung out his arm to stop him. "Wait," Jens whispered.

A large grin spread over Peter's face as he realized what he was seeing. He wanted to shout, to wave a fist in the air, to dance. He turned to Jens and Patricia, eyes wide and mouth open. Patricia only nodded. Jens lowered his arm, but patted his palm downward. Slow down. Calm down. Peter took a deep breath. Olsen leaned over Mori. Middleton sat at the security console, his words to Tsuji lost in the short distance to the doorway. Peter pointed at Kobarev and Jens nodded. He sat next to the pilot in a flash, bringing up and engaging with a monitor.

"Nothing?" Olsen asked Mori.

"No, sir," she reported. "Nothing yet."

"Good." Olsen turned and saw Jens and Patricia for the first time. "It turns out you were right, Dr Lin."

She tried to reply, but for perhaps the first time—at least Jens had seen—she was at a loss for words.

"Please," he said. "Join Kumiko. She is looking for any of your Ruan that may be awake. Thankfully, she hasn't detected any yet."

Patricia noticed she was still holding Jens' hand, and let go. She walked slowly towards the communication station, as if in a daze.

Olsen leaned forward and spoke to the pilot. "I want distance," he said.

"You and me both," Kobarev answered.

"Why are we so close?" Jens asked.

"We aren't," Olsen said.

Jens tilted his head, trying to reconcile what Olsen said with what filled the view screen. He stared at the object, seemingly fixed in place, but it slowly grew smaller in the screen, fractionally at first, then noticeably. The curve of the disc became more apparent, until the edge was visible.

"It's massive!" Jens gasped.

"Just wait," Olsen said.

Kobarev increased the distance and more of the disc was revealed. It was hundreds of meters thick, and was many more in diameter. The farther away Kobarev took them, the farther they saw across the disc. Finally, they could see half-way across to where a large cylinder projected out of it. Jens followed the cylinder as the view screen displayed more, until it ended at another disc.

"My god," Jens said.

"My sentiments exactly," Olsen said. "But what you're seeing … well, there's more." The captain sat back in his chair.

"I want you to lend Mr Tsuji a hand," Olsen said. "If you don't mind? I think he'll appreciate your experience."

"Anything," Jens answered.

"I'm not sure we're quite prepared for this," Olsen admitted. "But seeing as we didn't know what to expect anyway …"

Jens started to go, but Olsen placed a hand on his arm. "Wait a moment," he said. "We'll just let him know you're available so he can assess and plan." Olsen leaned into the comms on the arm of chair and told the security chief he had one more on his team.

"Just what is Kumiko looking for?" Jens asked.

"Activity," Olsen said. "Any type. Especially life, but any systems, anything *activating*." He said the last word through clenched teeth. "Our AI woke us when we matched velocity," he said. "They have AI as well, which means they can see us."

"But nothing?"

"Ms Mori?" he asked loudly, tension or stress bringing out a formality he had not previously shown.

The communications officer turned away from her monitor. "No, sir," she said. "Signs of systems. There is power on the ship. But ... nothing. All discs read the same."

"Discs?" Jens asked quietly.

"Discs," Olsen said. "Mr Tsuji will fill you in."

Tsuji handed Jens a sounder as soon as he arrived at the armory. Jens chose a shoulder holster and took three extra clips. He looked at the plasma, and Tsuji took one off the rack. He opened a lock-box on the deck and withdrew a clip. After checking the safety, he took it by the barrel and handed it to Jens. Tsuji glanced at Jens' hip pocket and Jens slipped it in.

"I want you to wear this, too," Tsuji said. He pulled a small pack off the wall. Aside from the strengthened cylinder in the center, it looked like any day pack. Jens put his arms through the straps and Tsuji helped him adjust them. He clicked the sternum strap together and pointed to the disc in the middle.

"Do you remember how to work this?" he asked.

"Hit the button and the emergency field surrounds me," Jens answered.

"Two hours oxygen and power," Tsuji said. "Only for an emergency. And wear the glasses at all times."

Jens took the pair Tsuji offered and put them on. He saw the heat radiating off the security officer's body. Wright had administered the GLR percentage that enhanced his visual acuity, but Tsuji left nothing to chance. Jens appreciated that.

Tsuji walked out of the armory and into the corridor. "Rupert and de Werk are in the port and starboard cannon. I'd like you to take topside, be my eyes up there." He stopped walking and looked Jens in the eye. "I need a steady hand as well. Don't use that cannon unless ... well, as you told de Werk, you have to act first."

"Understood," Jens said.

"Comms will be open," Tsuji continued. "So, communicate. You're the only person that has seen one of these Ruan, at least one that wasn't in a laboratory. I need your assessment. I'll be on standby with Okada and Yasuda, prepping a tori." Tsuji pointed to the hatch leading to the cannon, slapped Jens on the shoulder, before abruptly turning and making his way to the docking bay.

Jens climbed the ladder leading to the hatch, opening it and entering the tube leading to the cannon. He continued to climb until he emerged into the dome housing the weapon. Strapping himself into the seat, he checked the controls, using his eyes to direct the swivel of the barrel; up and down, left and right. *Designed for a pilot*, had been his first impression when de Werk took him through the procedure months earlier. Once satisfied it was operational, he looked up and through the dome.

"My god," he said, for the second time since he was pulled out of cryo-sleep.

Kobarev had increased the distance from the ship, enough for Jens to see the entire disc, as well as the one connected to it. He looked past those and saw another, and another, and still another; five huge disks floated before him, all connected by the central cylinder. At the end of the row of discs was a large rectangular structure he could only assume was the reactor, or reactors, that propelled the ship.

He suddenly remembered why he was at the cannon, and studied the structure carefully. If powerful reactors were housed in there, they were definitely off line now. He scanned the discs and they appeared to be equally quiet. Kobarev was moving the *Chōgenbō* forward with the bow thrusters and the front of the alien ship came into view. A cylinder protruded from the disc, and attached to that was a cone-like append-age, extending for hundreds of meters. Jens studied the cone, looking for light, for movement, anything.

"It looks dead," he said into his comms.

"Or sleeping," Tsuji answered. "Our sensors woke us when we matched velocity. Theirs might if they detect us."

"Theirs should. But it doesn't look like anything's detected us," Jens said.

"That's also what Mori is reading," Tsuji said.

"I take it Olsen is going to land the *Chōgenbō*?" Jens asked.

"On the cone," Tsuji said. "He is assuming that is the bridge."

Jens watched from his perch, entranced as Kobarev began to bring the *Chōgenbō* closer to its target. Under the ship, the large talons were extending. In the wild, a kestrel hovered above its prey, wings extended and talons aiming forward. They hunted by sight, very keen sight, hovering on the wind or a thermal or the power of its own wings, watch-ing. Game typically blends into its environment, colored and camouflaged. A grasshopper on a rock two hundred meters away would actually be invisible to the kestrel. It would blend in, unseen—until it moved. The slightest movement attracted the raptor's eye, letting it hone in on the creature. A slight movement of a wing, and the kestrel swooped and grabbed its meal.

The eyes of the *Chōgenbō*, its scanners based on alien technology, saw for millions of kilometers. Its winds were solar, pushed along by three state of the art fusion reactors. And its swoop took months. Masayoshi Katsuya would have thought it beautiful nonetheless. As a boy, Jens only knew him as Yoshi, an infrequent, but always welcome, visitor to the family home. His godfather loved birds, especially the raptors, graceful killers. We all kill to survive, he told the young Jens, but so rarely is it done with grace. *Grace*—he didn't mean some divine assistance or love, but smoothness and elegance of movement. Yoshi watched the hunt and the kill in business, and all he saw was a crude dance. He was, he could admit privately, a crude, yet efficient, dancer. His superiors took notice of his skill and he rose rapidly in the consortium, above and beyond his peers, until he wielded an enviable amount of influence. He still did, including the naming rights of its latest ship. Leaving the city, raising his glasses, and watching the grace of the chōgenbō in the hills behind his home, was a balm and a sanctuary.

Kobarev increased speed and tilted the nose of the vessel up. Jens thought of his godfather as he lost sight of the cone, when the *Chōgenbō* took a stance directly above it. Stars twirled past his viewing dome as the ship swivelled one hundred and eighty degrees to face the array of discs.

"Jens?" Tsuji called.

Jens blinked back to awareness, scanning the disc in front of him. "Yes, here," he answered.

"Hand over to the AI and join me in the docking bay," Tsuji said. "They're talking about a boarding party. That will be us. Let's be ready before we're asked."

Jens leaned forward and switched the cannon over to auto. AI might be fast, and accurate, but they didn't have a gut, and didn't feel fear. Jens could never bring himself to trust or rely on something lacking either of those. He got out of his seat, patted his shoulder holster and his pocket unconsciously, like someone would check for their wallet and keys, and climbed back down into the ship.

19

Kobarev continued the decent of the *Chōgenbō* as Peter read the numbers. Five hundred meters. Four-fifty. Four hundred meters. It was unnecessary—the pilot saw all the data on screen, as well as the prey below, but it kept the young man occupied, like an expectant father told to go and boil some water. Kobarev operated the descent with his eyes, but took the talons in his hands, each finger linked into the system. Opening his hand, the three talons stretched open, ready to latch on. He blinked and thrusters slowed the decent. The middle finger of his left hand extended the end of the primary talon, revealing the pad that would adhere to the surface of the cone. He did the same with thumb and little finger. Adherence pads extended from the other two talons. To Olsen, it looked as if the pilot was typing an invisible message on an invisible keyboard.

"One hundred meters," Peter said. "Eighty—"

"That's enough," Kobarev said. "Be quiet now. Contact in ten seconds, five—"

The pilot rubbed his hands, raised them to his face and massaged his forehead before burying the heels of his palms in his eyes and moving them left and right.

"Attachment complete," he said, with his hands still on his face.

"Well done, very smooth," Olsen said. "Ms Mori, anything?"

"No, sir," she said. "All systems appear dormant."

"*Appear* dormant," Olsen said. "Let's go see for ourselves."

Olsen led the boarding party off the ship. Jens wore his sidearms on the outside of his atmosphere suit, weapons designed for the thick fingers of gloves. His knife was still strapped to his leg under the suit; inaccessible, but comforting. The two Dutchmen checked each other's suits, plasma rifles slung over their shoulders. Each had a sounder on one hip, as well as a long knife strapped to a leg. Years ago, Jens had seen an over-eager and under-trained crewman slice his own suit and nearly die from asphyxiation as his oxygen escaped, but he knew those two were experienced enough to handle a sharp blade in a vacuum. Tsuji was in conference with Olsen and Mori. The communications specialist had weapons strapped to her waist as well, but was staying on the ship. A moment later Tsuji came over, gave Jens' suit a cursory look over and smiled.

"I am pleased you are with us," he said.

I wish I was as pleased, Jens thought, trying to calm his heart and breathe normally. He couldn't think of a suitable response, so nodded.

"Rupert will walk point, de Werk will follow us," he said. "You will be with me. We'll keep it tight."

Jens nodded again.

"We're heading to a part of the hull that looks like an airlock," Tsuji said. "You have the kit?"

Jens turned sideways to show Tsuji the pack on his back.

"Good," he said, before calling out, "Helmets on!"

Jens sealed his and fell into step several meters behind Rupert. Tsuji walked just to the side and half a meter behind. A thin cable connected them, running through Jens' belt and back to de Werk, where it continued on to the hatch of the *Chōgenbō*. Jens lifted his foot from the deck, stepping forward and onto the alien craft, wondering what it may sound like from the inside of the ship. He lifted the other foot and placed it down, one foot always glued to the hull. Rupert had his rifle unslung, scanning the area before them.

Tsuji pointed to their target, a slightly raised rectangle, barely standing out from the polished cone of the massive ship. They walked around the hull, leaving the *Chōgenbō* behind them. The first disc towered above, rising from the cone like a sheer cliff. Jens tried to estimate the size, using his height as a gauge, but gave up. If it had been a building, he could have counted windows and floors, but there were none. He tried not to dwell on what might be inside. The lights of one of the *Chīsai Tori* swept past them and onto the disc. Taylor, or Kobarev, in the little flier, watching from above.

When they reached their target, Rupert continued to scan the hull while de Werk stood over the security chief as he knelt beside the plating. Jens bent and examined it with him.

"An airlock?" Tsuji asked over comms.

"I don't know," Jens said. "But it has to serve a purpose."

He reached down his gloved hand and felt the rise of the plating, running his fingers along the meter-long ridge. He knelt next to Tsuji and continue to explore, using the other hand to feel along another edge, continuing around until he had examined the entire shape. Jens had boarded ships before. Every ship had a way in. Every ship also had ways to defend itself. He looked up and along the hull, expecting to see tall figures approaching through his thermal lenses, but all he saw was cold metal and colder space. If they knew they had boarders on their hull, they would already be here, he realized. He relaxed and focused on the metal in front of him. Labs on Pemako reproduced what the Ruan had made from their minerals, intensely strong yet light alloys, just like on the Artifact. Jens had experimented with some sheets in his own workroom. Awkwardly shrugging off his pack he clipped it on to their safety cable and opened it. He pulled out a hand-held cutting torch and attached the power cell.

He pointed the torch to a slight protuberance, only noticeable once he felt it. He used his free hand to point at another farther along the shape. Tsuji dipped his helmet and raised it. A nod. Jens turned on the torch and ran it slowly along the ridge, doing the same with the other. The two glowed. Jens shifted back and waited, but nothing happened. He grimaced and he cursed himself silently. If there was pressure behind what he thought was a hatch, it could have blown open, and blown them off the hull.

Jens signaled to Tsuji to step back. He reached into his pack and withdrew a hammer and the closest thing he could find to a chisel. He heard a muffled protest over his comms, a female voice being silenced. As he hit it with the hammer, he imagined Patricia saying, 'is that your best idea?' Jens held the chisel in the cut he'd made and struck it with the hammer.

He hit it again and leveraged the chisel, feeling the gap widen. Repeating the procedure on the other cut, he felt the plating give. A small gap formed between it and the hull. Inserting the chisel, Jens widened it until he could see an inky blackness beneath it. He reached towards the pack but Tsuji had a light sphere ready and handed it over. He took the chisel from Jens and pried the plating back further. Jens squeezed the sphere, activating the light, and dropped it into the space.

"What do you see?" Tsuji asked.

The sphere drifted two meters down and illuminated a crawl space. The bottom had a small window in it. The other side showed nothing but black.

"We're in," was all Jens said, not taking his gaze away from the hatchway. "Almost."

Jens showed Tsuji the cutting torch, gave it a slight push and it floated to the other man. Tsuji ran it against the other side of the hatch and Jens could feel it loosen. De Werk stood over Jens' shoulder, aiming his rifle into the crawl space as they lifted the panel. It came away from the hull where Tsuji cut, and drifted away from the men. De Werk leaned over, barrel first.

"Clear," he said.

Jens placed an energy generator near the opening and activated it. The green field spread over the opening. He adjusted the height and increased the diameter until a small dome encased Tsuji, de Werk and himself. Reaching across the hole, he took the torch back from Tsuji and attached it to his belt. Grabbing the edge of the crawl space, he unclipped from the tether and deactivated his grav-boots. He pushed forward.

His face plate was soon against the window, the light from his helmet showing an empty room on the other side.

He studied the door. The *Cirrus* and the *Sunrise Blossom* had several emergency escapes, some with escape pods, others for crew to reach the hull in key places in order to effect repairs. This door wasn't too different from those. They were designed to be opened from the inside, so that only those who were welcomed could enter. However, they usually had an emergency override, some with code that, as with all code, could be hacked. On his own ships he instructed the technicians to install a booby trap in case the wrong person wanted in. He searched the door until he found a small panel built into the frame.

"We need a tech," he said.

"Send one of the techs," Tsuji repeated to the *Chōgenbō*.

Jens took another look in the dark room, peering at the walls and the decking. He pushed gently against the door, felt his legs being grasped and was soon back on the deck. Tsuji clipped him onto the tether and he activated his boots. One of the technicians stepped through the energy field and stood with the small party. Jens tapped the side of his helmet and his faceplate retracted. The technician did the same and Jens was pleased to see Akiro Yasuda rather than his colleague. He seemed the brighter of the two, or at least the more amiable. Jens knew the young man liked a challenge and he had one for him. He explained the small panel and what he thought it was, as well as what it might be able to do to uninvited guests. Yasuda nodded as Jens spoke, closed his faceplate and descended into the hole.

"Keen," Jens said.

"Close your helmet, Jens," Tsuji said.

Jens tapped his helmet again and his view plate descended. He stepped back with Tsuji so that they weren't over the crawl space, in case Yasuda and anything else blew out. They heard a faint humming over the comms as the technician worked. The tune was almost recognizable. After a moment his feet rose out of the chamber. When his belt cleared the rim, Tsuji grabbed it and pulled the man out.

"Do you want me to open it?" Yasuda asked, upside down.

"Can you?" Tsuji returned.

"I don't think they're trying to keep people out," Yasuda said. "The controls seem to have two choices, open and close."

"I'll do it," de Werk said. He handed Jens his rifle, unholstered his sounder and looked into the crawl space.

"Just press the top one," Yasuda, now upright, said. "It should open inward."

De Werk entered, reached the hatch, and peered through the window. With his free hand he pressed the top switch on the control panel the tech had exposed. The hatch clicked inward several centimeters and stopped. De Werk waited, but nothing more happened. He holstered his sounder, clutched the side of the hatchway and pushed on the door. It gave some more. He placed a foot in the crawl space, leveraged against the wall and used all his strength to push.

The door swung open and he sailed through the gap, turning at the last moment so that his shoulder hit the opposite wall. He bounced off and started to float towards another wall; he activated his grav-boots and came down upright.

Pulling out his sounder he turned a full circle, checking each direction. He took a deep breath, exhaling slowly as he surveyed each wall in turn.

"Clear," he said, pleased nobody had seen his entrance—until remembering that the crew on the ship were watching through his helmet cam. "The room is empty. It is some sort of ante-chamber."

"On our way," Tsuji said.

Yasuda entered through the hatch feet first, activated his boots and stood upright. Tsuji entered the same way, followed by Jens. Rupert came last, pushing de Werk's rifle across the room and unshouldering his own. De Werk grabbed his weapon with one hand and pointed to a doorway with the other. It was a larger hatch, over two meters in height.

"Are you seeing this?" Tsuji asked Olsen viewing from the ship. "Opinion?"

"Seeing very clearly," Olsen answered. "We're just observers, Mr Tsuji. This is your mission."

"Yes, sir," Tsuji answered.

He pointed to Yasuda, and then to the door. Yasuda found the control pad, pried open the cover plate and inserted a power cord. De Werk knelt in front of the door and Rupert stood to the side, weapons raised.

"Okay," Tsuji said.

Yasuda touched the pad and the door slid open. Rupert's helmet light pierced the gloom on the other side. He stepped past de Werk and into the empty space, swept the room with his gun, and took a knee. Rupert followed, stepped past him, and took up a position against a wall.

"Clear," he said.

Tsuji entered with the others. Jens reached into his bag and withdrew another light sphere. He squeezed it in his hand until it began to glow. He pushed it away from himself to light up the room. It was larger than the one they had just left. Tall cabinets lined the walls, each with indentations where a handle could be expected. He walked over to one, his boots clicking with each step. Putting his hand into the indentation, his fingers found a catch and he pulled. The door swung smoothly open and he stood looking up at a Ruan.

Jens tried to jump back but his boots held firmly to the decking. He pulled out his sounder but was shouldered aside by Rupert, who thrust the barrel of his rifle toward the alien. His helmet light scanned from head to foot and he lowered his weapon. Yasuda floated across the room, activated his boots, and opened the door next to it, where another figure hung.

"Suits," he said. He leaned back and tilted his head up to see the helmet attached to the one in front of him. "These guys are huge." Moving closer, he lifted a sleeve, found the control panel he suspected was there, and tapped it. The suit's control pad and the helmet face plate began to illuminate.

"You'll have time to play later," Tsuji said. "Let's not activate anything yet. Shut it down."

"Yes, sir," Yasuda said, tapping the panel and watching the light fade. "Unbelievable! Still operational!"

"Jens, you've seen the Artifact," Tsuji said. "Does the layout look similar at all?"

"Not at all," Jens answered. "That was tiny compared to this."

"We'll split up and search," Tsuji said. "Send the other tech," he said to Olsen. "De Werk, go with Jensen, and Okada when he arrives. Take the doorway forward, we'll take that one. Keep your comms open."

"Yes, sir," de Werk answered.

Yasuda opened the aft doorway and the small party disappeared. Minutes later Okada floated into the room, activated his boots and stood before Jens and de Werk. He seemed to twitch from excitement, a wide grin visible through his faceplate. De Werk pointed to the door with his rifle and took up a firing stance. Okada quickly accessed the control pad, inserted his power cell and the door slid open.

"Not like they're trying to keep folks out," Okada said, but was pushed aside by de Werk, who stepped through the doorway, the barrel of his gun and his light scanning the next room.

"Clear," he said. "Pop a light, Jens."

Jens took a sphere out of his pack, squeezed it and let it drift it into the room. De-activating his boots, he pushed off and glided into the illuminated space. Floating past the glowing sphere, he reached the far door.

"This isn't a room," he said, looking through another view plate into absolute darkness. "It's a corridor."

De Werk walked down the hall as Okada followed Jens, floating. "Why are you guys so jumpy?" Okada asked. "Mori scanned the whole cone. No heat signatures at all. I can see about turning on the lights if you want. It'd be easy."

"It might be easy," de Werk answered. "But I don't want

you turning anything, or anybody, else on yet. You see how big this corridor is? That's because these things are big."

He indicated to the next door and took up position as Okada worked the control panel. As the door slid open Jens popped a light and floated it in, while de Werk stepped forward scanning as before. After two steps he lowered his weapon and waved the others in.

"You'll want to see this," he said. "And pop a couple more lights."

De Werk grabbed for a foot as Okada floated by, but missed. Okada stopped at a large chair mounted in the center of the room. He activated his boots and walked around it, whistling softly. Jens floated another sphere into the shadows and more seats became visible. Each seat was positioned in front of a flat surface. Okada stepped over to one, lightly running his hand over the opaque face. He went to another, whistling again.

"This is it," he said.

"The bridge," Jens confirmed.

"Absolutely amazing." Okada spoke each syllable individually. "We're going to need to turn some of this on," he said more quickly.

"That can wait a while," de Werk said.

"We need the linguist," Okada said.

"He's landing that little ship now," Dr Lin cut in. "And I'm on my way."

"Patricia, it isn't clear yet," Jens said. He clenched his jaw before he spoke again.

De Werk put a hand on Jens' arm.

"Doctor Lin, Ambassador Jensen is correct—"

"The doctor is on her way," Olsen said. "I tried," he added on a personal line to Jens.

"I'll bet," Jen replied.

"Sir, are you getting this?" de Werk asked.

"Very clearly," Olsen answered. He had the view of each of the party's helmet cameras displayed on the bridge view screen. He brought one up larger.

"Still no sign of crew," de Werk reported.

"Tsuji has found them," Olsen replied.

Yasuda opened another door and Rupert entered, light scanning and weapon raised. He took a kneeling position and Tsuji stepped past, sounder in hand. He withdrew a light, squeezed it, and pushed it forward, watching it drift into the space. This room was different, yet very familiar. He holstered his gun and walked towards a rectangular box. Bending down, he examined a control panel built into it. He motioned Yasuda forward.

Yasuda looked at the panel and brought out his power cell. He tried several connections before putting it away.

"Well?" Tsuji asked.

"Nothing," he said. "No response at all."

Tsuji stood, wiping the top of the box with his gloved hand. He peered in, but couldn't see through the glass. He found the door latches and released them. Rupert pointed his rifle at the cryo-pod. Tsuji stood and pulled out his plasma pistol and indicated to Yasuda. The technician approached the lid, placing both hands on it.

"Are you sure about this?" he asked.

"Open the lid, Technician Yasuda," Tsuji said.

The young man lifted and it gave, swinging open. The protective foam was retracted into the walls of the pod, probably decades or centuries ago when the power failed. Rupert moved the barrel of his rifle closer. Tsuji's hand tensed as he leaned forward. The shape of a head emerged, large and angular. Wide shoulders, long torso, legs stretching to the bottom of the pod. Tsuji lowered his gun and peered in.

Its eyes were closed, the lids stretched tight, shrunken and dried to the bone beneath. Its jaw gaped, pulled open by the dried macular muscles in a voiceless scream. Thick bones showed through the thin garment fused to the flesh beneath. Broad chest, long torso with sunken abdomen, thick legs ending in sharp and bony toes. Tsuji turned away.

"Open the others," he said to Yasuda.

Rupert followed the young tech from cryo-pod to cryo-pod, standing above the box, rifle poised, then lowering his weapon as lid retracted and another gaping mouth shouted silently.

"All twelve, sir," Tsuji reported. "All cryo-pods non-functional, and the crew inside long dead."

"Any other cryo-pods? Any evidence of more crew?" Olsen asked.

"No, sir," Tsuji said. "My team have swept the entire cone. Dr Lin's opinion—"

"Yes, she has told me."

"I think she's right," Tsuji said. "The design makes sense. This is the crew quarters of the bridge. Taylor has been using his device. The pods have titles, and what he thinks are names." He walked over to a pod, knelt beside a plate and pointed.

"See this?" Tsuji asked.

"Clearly," Olsen said.

Tsuji brought a finger to the plate, moving it as if writing in the air. "That first part Taylor thinks is a name. His device just produces letters, lots of consonants, nonsense. But this part," he touched the figures on the plate, sweeping lines that flowed back on themselves. "Taylor says this is a title. His device read this one as 'talker.' Maybe communications? One over there," he pointed, "comes up as 'controller'. I'm thinking that means Captain. His device needs some work."

Tsuji stood and walked out of the cryo-bay, down a wide corridor lit by light spheres and finally into the bridge.

20

"I want you to split up and enter the disc," Olsen said over comms. "I'm on my way over. Tsuji, Rupert and Yasuda will go with me into the center. Mori is getting some rather interesting power readings from there. Jens, take the tori with Dr Lin, de Werk, Okada and Taylor, and access the disc from the outer rim. You can make a start now."

The other tori maneuvered towards the top of the disc, as Kobarev set Olsen down beside the airlock into the cone. As soon as he was out of the tori, it lifted and returned to the *Chōgenbō*. Tsuji, Rupert, and Yasuda were waiting beside the entrance to the corridor connecting the cone to the disc. Yasuda had his power pack already connected. Olsen pointed at the door as he approached and the tech opened it. Tsuji entered first, weapon raised, indicated it was clear and the others followed. They walked down the wide corridor until stopped by another door. Yasuda set up his device, waited for Olsen to give the nod, and they proceeded.

After another door, and another segment of corridor, they stood in front of a larger passageway; the entrance to this one made of two large doors meeting in the center. Yasuda whistled.

"These are outer doors," he said. "What are they doing in a corridor?"

"Can you open them?" Olsen asked.

"Oh, yeah," he answered. He started to attach his power cell but stopped. He placed it back in his tool bag.

"What's the problem?"

"Nothing, Captain. Power is on." He studied the key pad, touching the upper left corner.

The doors slowly and smoothly opened, sliding into the hull on either side. They entered, stopping at an inner door. As Yasuda touched the control panel, the doors they had just passed through slid shut. Olsen waited, knowing the doors in front would open as soon as a stable pressure was registered. That was how airlocks worked. He puzzled over the design for a moment, an airlock inside of a ship, then filed it for later as the others walked by him and into the disc.

Olsen walked behind Rupert. The security man still held his sounder, but was beginning to relax. They seemed to finally be starting to believe the flawless sensors that showed no life forms moving about the disc, other than their own. Tsuji opened a door by simply touching the control panel, and he and Olsen strode through. He turned right at a junction, guided by Mori on a private line. Tsuji opened another door, this one built for the interior of a ship. Yasuda heard a whistle over the comms and pushed past Rupert to see. Stopping in the door way, he also whistled.

"That's beautiful," he said.

"Anders," Olsen said over the comms. "I know you're

short-handed over there, but can you spare Doi? He's going to want to see this."

"He'll be over shortly," Middleton answered.

"She's still going," Yasuda said. "After all these years. Amazing."

A reactor nestled in the center of the disc, bathing the boarding party in its blue glow. Yasuda started to walk around it, admiring the sheer size and elegance of the machine. It dwarfed the reactors on the *Chōgenbō*, not only in size, he suspected, but also in sophistication and power. The reactor on its own made the trip worth it, if they could get it home. He tried to trace the fuel source, its drip feed into the fusion reaction chamber. He itched to examine it. He was sure the technology he was looking at would soon be powering their ships, and making them all very rich.

"Leave it, Yasuda," Rupert said. "We're moving on."

Yasuda hesitated before joining the others. The beauty of the reactor was one thing, but the scale of it bothered him. It was obviously well designed, but looked oversized for the power needs of the disc. He'd wait until Doi had a closer look to find out more.

The men followed Olsen. He walked with purpose, as if he had been on the disc before—but it was Mori analyzing the interior from her monitors on the *Chōgenbō*, guiding him. They walked through another doorway, down another corridor, and into a chamber with rounded walls. Rupert floated a light sphere into the room, followed by another. Yasuda walked to the center where a raised dais stood. He recognized similarities with the room in the cone. His hand passed reverently over the panels without touching. Olsen stopped and watched the technician as he left the dais and examined the various stations. Yasuda paused at one, touching the panels. The Captain took a half step forward, instinctively cautious, wanting to stop the tech, then paused, yielding to the young man's apparent confidence. Yasuda pulled out one of Taylor's translating devices and held it over the illuminated surface. He spoke to Olsen on a private line.

"This is the control room, I'm sure of it," he said. "I'd say it was the bridge if we hadn't already seen that on the cone."

"It looks that way," Olsen agreed.

"This is the support systems, sir," he said, pointing to the center in front of him. "Everything's here. Lights, artificial gravity, atmosphere. As far as I can tell, it's all functional, just like the reactor. Just dormant."

"You can activate it?"

"That's what I'm asking your permission for," Yasuda answered.

"And it's not linked to anything else? Like cryo-pods? I'd rather not wake up the locals."

"As far as I can tell," Yasuda said, "it's only support systems."

"Try them, one at time," Olsen said. "Lights first."

Yasuda touched the panel and the light spheres became superfluous as the room was illuminated.

"Gravity?" Olsen asked.

Yasuda touched another panel and waited. He felt weight return to his body, pressing him down. Clicking his heels, he deactivated his grav-boots, and tested with a little hop.

Rather than continue to drift upwards, he came down in the same spot.

"Mr Doi," Olsen asked. "Are you at the reactor yet?"

"Yes, sir," Doi answered. "Just arrived a moment ago. It's increased its power output."

"Stable?"

"Yes, sir. Very. It's a magnificent machine," Doi said.

Yasuda smiled. "Atmosphere?" he asked.

"Do it," Olsen said.

Yasuda worked another panel, and then stepped back and waited. He monitored the readings projected on the inside of his visor, measuring the vacuum around them. Trace elements began to appear, then increase, as the atmosphere in the room began to resemble that on Pemako.

"Mr Doi," Olsen said. "We're turning on some key systems, as you can see. Let me know if that reactor isn't happy with it."

"Yes, sir," Doi answered. "Though I doubt much can upset her. I could use Yasuda when you're finished with him."

Olsen watched Yasuda working over anther panel. "Mr Yasuda?"

"I've located their database," he said. "It might take a while to crack."

"Leave it for now, it can wait," Olsen said. "Go give Doi a hand." He reached up and started to remove his helmet. "And thanks for the air."

De Werk gripped his gloved hands in his lap, resisting the urge to grab the controls of the tori. Taylor sat next to him in the pilot seat, unmoving, except for his eyes. De Werk couldn't see Taylor's eyes. To him the pilot just sat passively while the small craft turned to starboard, levelled out, then began to descend towards the enormous disc below them. The security man shifted in his seat, feeling completely helpless.

With a subtle eye movement, Taylor landed the tori next to what was unmistakably an airlock. The wide door set into the rim of the disc acted as a welcome beacon. Jens, de Werk, Okada and Dr Lin checked each other's helmets before Peter opened the hatch and debarked. Okada headed straight for the lock, his magnetic boots making progress slow. De Werk was pleased with the pace, mentally preparing himself to board the alien ship. The crew of the cone may have been long dead, but this was a new unknown. He took a stance, weapon in hand, in front of the lock as Okada examined the control panel. Jens waited with a light sphere behind the tall Dutchman, with Dr Lin and Taylor further behind.

"It's like the cone—they're not trying to keep anybody out," Okada said. "I can open this when you want. There's power registering."

"Okay," Jens said. "Do it."

Okada pressed the panel and the lock slowly slid open. Jens gently floated the sphere into the opening and it slowly rebounded against the door of the inner lock. They followed de Werk into the chamber and waited as Okada worked the next panel. The door behind them cycled shut, and with a signal from Jens he activated the inner lock. A light sphere floated past Okada and de Werk, lighting the way. Large lockers lined the wall. Jens opened one and saw what he expected

—Ruan atmosphere suits, kept serviceable over the centuries due to the lack of atmosphere and gravity. He grabbed a sleeve and pulled, half suspecting it to dissolve in his hands, but it held firm.

"Next chamber looks like a warehouse," de Werk reported. He peered through a window in the door with his helmet light as Okada worked on the panel.

The area brightened as Dr Lin and Taylor stepped closer, light spheres in hand. Jens gave the nod to the technician and the door slid open. He floated a sphere into the space, slightly faster than de Werk's careful step into the room. De Werk scanned the empty space as the sphere was swallowed by the darkness.

"Float your spheres," Jens said to the two behind him.

The lights drifted past, adding a small amount of illumination.

"This place is empty, at least of life," de Werk said. "Mori doesn't read any heat signatures, and no movement."

"I see that on my feed," Jens said. "Let's take a look for the next door."

As they walked forward shadows began to form on the bulkheads and deck. The darkness beyond their light spheres began to dissipate, and the room grew larger. Within minutes the light spheres were lost, and the lights from their helmets were useless as the ship's lights came on. An immense space opened before them. Jens withdrew a sounder from a hip pocket. After months in the confined space of the *Chōgenbō,* he suddenly felt very exposed, and vulnerable, in the vastness around him. The others crouched beside him, a slight motion that indicated their unease.

"Somebody found the lights," de Werk said.

"Yeah, but who?" Jens said. "Captain, we have lights here. Is that your doing?"

"Roger that," Olsen replied. "Doi is at the reactor, which is still humming, and Yasuda is getting other systems on line."

"Any locals?" Jens asked.

"We have a dozen, all in stasis," Olsen said. "Keep exploring. I'll watch through your cams."

Jens felt weight return and tentatively deactivated his boots. He remained on deck. "We have gravity," he said to the team.

Okada deactivated his boots and walked to a container nearby. He held one of Taylor's translators over a plate mounted on it, walked to another nearby and used the device again. Taylor caught up to him at the third. He could see Okada speaking quickly, but heard nothing over his comms. A private line, probably to the other tech.

"What do you read?" he interrupted.

Okada looked over quickly and stopped talking. He chinned the open line. "Equipment," he said. "Lots and lots of equipment. This container says fliers. Literally, that's what your device is saying. That container there, it reads land vehicles. I can't wait to pop these open."

"It looks like you'll have quite a few to pop," Taylor said.

They both looked across the room at the rows of containers stretching out of sight, lost to view with the curve of the disc. Okada was at another container before Taylor noticed he had moved. The tech was speaking quickly on his private line again.

"Time to move on," Jens said over the line. "We're checking out the level below."

"I'll catch up," Okada said. "I can survey this area more."

"You'll get your ass over here now!" Jens said. "There'll be plenty of time for that later."

Taylor tried to see Okada's expression, but the tech turned and shoved the translator into a pocket before he could. They both walked to the others, who were waiting by a door.

"Take it easy, Jens," Dr Lin said on a private line. "We've got this with you."

Jens bit back the response he wanted to give. He knew his friend meant well, and that he was wound too tight. Instead, he took several slow breaths, turned to her and nodded.

"I'm reading atmosphere," she said as they arrived at the door. "Breathable. Same gases as the atmosphere on Pemako."

Jens checked the readings and touched his face plate, hesitating. After a moment he touched the control with his chin and it retracted into his helmet. He took a tentative breath, then another.

"It's a bit stale, but it's good," he said. "Open them up, but keep your helmets on."

Face plates retracted and they tasted metallic, recycled air.

"Let's see where this leads," Jens said. He turned off the channel to his team now that the sound could carry to them, but kept his private line to Olsen open.

Okada opened the door as de Werk took a stance in front, sounder raised. As the door retracted, he stepped through and scanned an empty ramp. He lowered the weapon and reported, "Clear," but the group was already walking right behind him. The ramp sloped for almost one hundred meters before leveling out and ending at another door. De Werk stood once more with his sounder raised, his left hand holding the right, which held the gun. Okada worked at the controls and in a moment the barrier slid into the wall. De Werk lowered the gun and the others filed past.

No one spoke as they slowly fanned out across the vast room. They stopped at various locations, used a translator to try to make sense of the labels, but on most could only read a jumble of consonants, interrupted by the odd vowel. Or the device simply stated that the word was not in its data. But they didn't need the labels to tell them what they were seeing. They were not too dissimilar to what they had on the *Chōgenbō*. What silenced them was the sheer number. Stretching as far as they could see in either direction, until the curve of the disc interrupted their view, lay row upon row of cryo-pods.

Taylor breathed in, an audible gasp. Dr Lin walked to the nearest row of cryo-pods and examined the panels on each before moving to another row. At the third she stood. "They're all operational," she said. "They're still alive."

She headed to another row before anybody answered. Jens heard her talk animatedly but couldn't catch the words. Conferencing with Wright on a private line, no doubt. He held his sounder at his side, peering across the vast room. De Werk maintained discipline, scanning the area for movement, but there was nothing other than Taylor and Okada moving from row to row—examining labels, control panels, trying to see into the pods. Bending over the nearest pod, Jens could only see the protective foam hiding the Ruan within. He stood on his toes and tried to take a count of the cryo-pods in the chamber before reporting in to Olsen. He got somewhere in the hundreds before they were lost to view.

"We found the Ruan," he finally said. "All in stasis, and alive. At least the ones we've checked. There's a lot. The whole area is nothing but cryo-pods."

"We've found the same on the level above engineering," Olsen replied. "The whole disc is full of them. But we'll take a longer look later. Time to pull back to the *Chōgenbō* and take stock."

"See you there," Jens said. He chinned his team's channel, not feeling like shouting. "We're returning to the ship. Our ship. Right now. There'll be time to explore later."

Jens stared at the technician, making sure he didn't need additional encouragement. Okada followed the others to the ramp leading up.

"It's simple math," Middleton explained. "The momentum and the mass can be handled by our reactor, but it'll take a long time."

"The reactor was never designed for so much mass," Doi said.

"But it's the mass we have," Middleton replied. "Nobody knew what we'd find would be so large. And it was designed for stress. We can slow it down, but—"

"How long?" Olsen interrupted.

"We'll be in cryo-sleep during Decel," Middleton said.

"What I asked was, how long?"

"The figure we received from Anna and Michael, based on the data we sent them, is nearly five years. Four years and eight months, to be more precise," Mori said.

While the others explored the alien vessel, she had communicated with the astrogator and mathematician on the Donut. Their messages travelled at light speed. It took light from the sun a little over eight minutes to reach Earth. Forty-three minutes to reach Jupiter. After three hours it would reach Saturn. The latest response from the Donut took more than four days. And the time lag increased with every day that they remained attached to the Ruan ship.

Rupert whistled softly and shook his head. The others stood staring at the first mate.

"Almost five years, at the twelve g's you are using for your calculations?" Doi's question sounded more like accusation.

"That's right," Middleton said. He turned from Doi, hoping to avoid or put off the inevitable argument about structural integrity, and ended up facing the captain.

"Five years in cryo-sleep?" Olsen asked.

"Four years, seven months, and thirteen days," Middleton answered.

"Some of us have families to get home to," Jens said, trying to keep his voice level. He could hear that he wasn't succeeding.

"That is one option," Olsen interrupted. "And we're here to explore options. Using the *Chōgenbō* we can rendezvous with the Donut in the time our astrogator and mathematician have calculated. We don't need to question their computations. But we need to look at all of our possibilities."

He sat at the mess table. Jens recognized the tactic and sat as well. When the captain sits, the crew do too. The table forced them all to sit in a circle, smoothed the power balance by placing them all at the same level, and helped calm the situation.

"There are other options," Olsen said. "I want to hear them now."

"Anna and Michael sent other numbers," Mori offered.

"Go on," Olsen said.

"The *Chōgenbō* can decelerate for rendezvous in one year and three months. That is at high gee."

"Why the difference in times?" Wright asked.

"Because the only mass in that equation belongs to the *Chōgenbō*," Kobarev said.

"What does that mean?" Peter asked.

"It means leaving the Ruan ship," Dr Lin said. "Absolutely not!"

"We're not making decisions right now," Olsen said. "We're only exploring options."

"Well, surely that can't be one of them!" She slapped a hand on the table. "You seriously can't even be entertaining that. There are thousands of them. Thousands! You'd be condemning them to death!"

"We could take samples of the technology—" Okada suggested, and flinched when Dr Lin shouted again.

"What!?"

Olsen stood slowly, his arms spread and palms facing

down, as if physically trying to contain the energy around the table. He reclaimed his authority as Captain.

"Nothing is being decided right now. As I said before, we are only here to explore possibilities. Leaving the Ruan ship is one, only one, among the several being discussed. Arguing will only waste time. I want to hear potential solutions, and nothing more." He remained standing when he finished, his mouth a straight line across his face. The others were forced to look up at him, reminding them all of the hierarchy on the ship.

"We could use their reactors," Peter said.

"They have very large reactors," Kobarev added. "We had a good look on our approach."

"We flip the ship and initiate a Decel," Peter added. "That would have to cut our time to rendezvous."

"We know nothing about them, and their bridge is dead," Doi said.

"Along with the entire bridge crew," Tsuji added.

"But there are others we can wake who could tell us, who could fly it. There's thousands of them, as we saw!"

"Absolutely not," Jens said.

"I don't mean wake thousands," Peter said, "Just those that can fly the ship. Their cryo-pods have labels."

"That your translator can hardly make sense of," Jens said.

"The symbols are technical, that's the only thing," Peter protested. "I can get to work on it now and refine the translations. We can wake engineers—"

"Nobody is doing anything at the moment," Olsen said.

Peter tried to argue, tried to appeal to Jens, the other

captain at the table, the only one with actual experience of living Ruan, but that was a dead end. Instead, after more arguments that seemed to only circle around themselves, they were all dismissed and sent to their rooms like naughty children.

Reaping

21

Peter left the messroom and walked down the corridor. He clenched his jaw as tight as his fists. He had said his piece in the meeting, what he viewed as an endless pointless meeting, and then bit his tongue. He fumed inside. The old men would prefer to talk than act. Their days of acting were over, that was clear. All those stories of voyages and fights. Peter would have spat if he weren't so self-conscious about cleanliness on the ship. Olsen kept a tidy ship—at least he could do that! What kind of captain had a group meeting about what to do? Peter walked up to his quarters, stopped and looked at the door, and then walked on. Reaching the docking bay, he put on an atmosphere suit.

He ran a hand around his neck. He always worried about the seal, about what would happen if he stepped out into the vacuum of space with his helmet loose. The readout displayed on his face plate did little to reassure him. He would worry, whatever it said. He stepped through the green-lit energy field and down the ramp leading to the deck of the Seeder ship's cone. A tori would save time, but it would also alert those on the *Chōgenbō* bridge that somebody was leaving the ship. He looked up at the towering disc. It was a long way away.

He reached into his hip pocket and withdrew the grappling hook he had taken from stores. Peter switched off the safety and held the implement in his hand. He had never shot one before, but assumed it was the same as a sounder. Point. Press trigger.

Peter crouched, aimed his body, de-magnetized his boots and pushed off. He left the surface of the cone and watched the disc fly by. The fact that he had never used a grappling hook, or flown untethered through space began to hit home, but it was too late to change course or change his mind. As the outer rim of the disc neared he stretched out his arm and gripped the hook with both hands. He pressed the trigger and watched as the grappling hook shot out towards the disc. It soundlessly stuck fast. Peter continued his ascent, flying past the disc and into the nothingness beyond it until the line had played out. The device tried to rip itself from his grip, but he held tight, and his body jerked at the end of the line. He retracted the line and the surface of the disc grew closer.

Bending his body as he neared, he landed feet first, his grav-boots activating on impact. He detached the hook and pocketed the device. He lifted a foot and headed for an air-lock, one of many on the rim of the disc. The boots were easy to use. Just lean back more when walking and make sure one foot was always on the deck. Peter walked forward. Unlike the cone, the discs seemed to invite entrance. He reached the lock and withdrew the power pack 'borrowed' from Yasuda.

Using the device, he opened the airlock. Peter stepped in and closed the lock behind him. He waited as the atmosphere pressurized and the inner lock opened. As he walked into the waiting room, the inner lock door automatically closed behind him. Peter unclasped his helmet and took it off, breathing the recycled air in the disc. He walked past cases of supplies, the type of thing Yasuda and Okada got so excited about. Peter held his translator over the panel on a box. *Moving parts*, it said. He shook his head. The app needed work, that was for sure. *Moving parts for what?* he thought. *Did they move, or were they used for moving?* He would have to lift the lid and look in order to add more precise language to develop the app, but there was no time for that now. He reached a lift tube and stepped into it, floating to the floor below. Cryo-pods filled the vast space that greeted him. He walked past them to the nearest lift tube and stepped again. There were thousands of cryo-pods on this deck, but only one that he wanted to see.

Peter had walked through this floor on their first visit. He had held the translator app over cryo-pods and read nonsense, until he realised the jumble of consonants and vowels might indicate names rather than items or roles. Proper nouns rather than common or concrete. Except many of the pods had their name plates removed, or covered, replaced with other symbols. Peter headed towards one he had scanned earlier, a cryo-pod whose name plate, if that was what they were, was replaced with a series of symbols that registered on his device. A common noun. A title. The type of title they would need if his seed of an idea was to succeed.

He stopped at the pod he was looking for. Passing the translator over the name plate he read, *clinic.* The word on its own made no sense, but looking at the field of cryo-pods, he was certain that there was not a clinic in the pod in front of him. What might be there, though, was a person who worked in a clinic. The tail at the end of the script must be a suffix, like '-ian' at the end of electric, or politic. Clinician, then. Peter scanned the plate again and changed the meaning to *medic*. He stared at the cryo-pod and changed the meaning again, to *doctor*. Hope, more than reason, guided his work.

He had told the others what they needed to do. But all they did was find reasons to do nothing. Return to quarters, rest, meet back in the messroom in four hours. Olsen was a spacer, he must have a good indication of the distance the ships were covering as time ticked past. But instead of listening to him, Peter was accused of impatience.

"You have made it very clear how you feel, Dr Taylor," Olsen said, enunciating each word clearly and slowly. Peter didn't need his device to understand the translation: Shut up.

"At one tenth the speed of light, every minute counts, let alone hours," Peter said. He looked around the room, but all he saw were the tired faces of people who didn't get it. Nobody wanted to sleep for almost five years, they all wanted to get home, but they seemed happy to keep waiting. Five years was a lot of time for things to go wrong—like cryo-pods failing, or Donuts getting lost. The sooner Michael and Anna could meet them, the better!

He caught Jens' eye. "Jens, you know this is the only way, why are you willing to do nothing?" he asked.

"I know it is *a* way. It is not the only way, yet," Jens said. "And we have no way of knowing what might be unleashed."

"Unleashed? What are you talking about?" Peter shot

back, desperation and frustration in every word. "They know how to stop their ship!"

"Maybe," Jens said. "And maybe not. All the crew on the cone are dead. That was the bridge of this ship."

"We know—"

"Enough!" Olsen barked. "We've been around this bush too many times. Now clear the room and clear your heads. Return to your quarters." His measured tone was gone. "We'll reconvene in four hours. Until then this matter is closed." He stared hard at Peter as the others began filing out.

Peter withered under the older man's glare, turned and followed them out, jaw clenched as tight as his fists tucked into his pockets. Olsen needed to lead and he was holding a town meeting. Why was he waiting? The solution was simple. And Jens, probably still scared of monsters long gone, long dead, was now afraid of what was sleeping. Peter saw how carefully the man walked around the cryo-pods, a hand always near that knife that belonged in a museum, but was instead strapped to his thigh, or the sounder in his pocket. They would all rather keep talking, which they would no doubt do once more when they came back to the messroom.

Kneeling before the pod, he gazed at the control panel. A faint flow of light indicated its systems were functional. The cryo-pods were similar to those used on the *Chōgenbō*, or any freighter. The controls were based on the Ruan technology found on the Artifact. But Peter had only lain down inside cryo-pods and waited for sleep, letting trained technicians manage it. He had never paid attention to the how's or why's of its workings. He passed the translator over the panel, reading each button. They were translatable. His finger hovered over the pad labelled *re-animate*. If what was inside was a doctor, and actually revived, they would know who to wake and be able to care for the others. That was the hope, anyway. Peter realized that this plan was a gamble—but his gambles usually paid off. He was here after all, with consortium backing, on a state-of-the-art ship, and all because of gambles.

He placed his finger on the pad and the light in the control panel increased. He heard the power surge into the cryo-pod. Standing over the view plate, he watched the foam encasing inside begin to slowly deflate. If the chemicals were still active after all this time, they were being injected, filling the body with warm fluids, telling the organs to start working again. The lid in front of Peter hissed at the seal and he jumped back. His heart began to race and he realized that he had no clue as to what to do next, and the full reality of what he had just done hit home. He lifted his wrist with the communication device strapped to it. His finger hesitated, lowered, lifted again. Finally, he pressed.

"Donna! Dr Wright! I have a medical emergency!" he shouted.

A moment passed. He shouted again, "Dr Wright!"

"What is it, Peter?" she answered, sleep in her voice. "What is your location?"

"It's waking," Peter stammered. "The lid popped."

"What you are saying is not making sense," she answered. "What is your location?"

"I activated it," Peter said. "It's what we had to do. But something is happening."

"Where are you, Peter?" she asked again. "Are you okay?"

"I'm fine," he said. "But I need you. It's activated. It's waking up."

"Taylor," Olsen cut in. "State your location." Peter's communication had gone ship-wide, not merely to sickbay, as he hoped.

"I'm in the disc," Peter admitted.

"What the hell have you done, Taylor!"

"Not now, Captain," Wright cut in. "I need to speak with Peter." A brief moment of silence followed. "What is happening with the cryo-pod, Peter?" Wright asked.

She was calm and direct, voicing no anger or judgement, now fully alert. "Peter," she said gently. "What are you seeing right now?" She spoke as she walked towards the docking bay, where Kobarev, Olsen, Jensen, Dr Lin, de Werk and Tsuji were also headed.

"It's, ah, the seal of the lid has broken and there's a gap ... a gap of about ten centimeters," he said.

"And the control panel, Peter, what is it reading?"

"Reading?"

"The lights," she tried again. "What color are the lights?"

"Green," he said.

"All of them?"

"Ah, no! One is orange."

Wright muted her comm link to Peter when she entered the docking bay. "If the pods are the same as ours, we have about thirty minutes," she said. "At the most," she added.

She handed her medical bag to Jens, who climbed on board the tori and stowed it near the cockpit. He adjusted the sounder holstered to his hip as he sat down. As soon as he strapped in, he pulled the plasma pistol out of his thigh pocket and examined its clip.

"You won't be needing that," Wright said as she sat down next to him.

Jens slid it back into his pocket. "I hope not," he said.

"Peter, what do you see through the view plate?" she spoke into the comms on her wrist. As soon as she started speaking, the others moved quietly in the craft, strapping into their seats.

"Where are you?" Peter asked.

"We're on our way, Peter," she answered. "Tell me what you see."

"We?" he asked. "Who is with you?"

"What do you see through the view plate, Peter?" she ignored his question and kept her voice calm but firm.

"I ... it's ..." he stammered.

"Peter, stand over the plate and look into it," she instructed. She muted her mic. "He's really scared," she said to Jens. "It sounds like he's about to lose it."

"Oh, he's going to lose it," Jens said. She noticed his hand resting on the knife strapped to his thigh and decided to ignore it. Her job was to deal with whatever medical emergency might be caused by Peter's actions. She turned her mic back on.

"Peter, I need you to do this for me. You called for my help, and now I need your eyes," she said.

"It's all cloudy," he answered.

"Can you clean the surface?"

"No. I mean, I tried," he said. "It's the inside of the view plate. Like it's fogged or frosted over."

"Okay then," she said, trying to sound reassuring. "Tell me what you hear, Peter. Put your ear close to the pod and listen. What do you hear? Leave your mic open so I can maybe hear too. Turn it up to maximum. Hold it next to the pod."

There was a pause as Peter adjusted the volume of his mic. He knelt beside the cryo-pod, everybody in the tori hearing the fabric of his suit as he bent and leaned forward. They next heard the sound from inside the pod, as the protective foam continued to retract away from the body it had encased for so many years.

"Can you hear that?" Peter's voice came through the comms as a shout. Wright winced.

"Yes, Peter," she answered. She knew that as the foam retracted chemicals were circulating, removing those that pre-served the body and injecting others that would revive it. She muted her mic again.

"How long until we can land?" she asked the pilot.

"Another minute," Kobarev replied. "There is the airlock he used."

"How long until it wakes up?" Olsen asked.

"Not long now," she answered. "Can you hand me my bag?"

Olsen unstrapped, reached the bag and handed it to her in one fluid motion. She opened a side pocket, withdrew an injector. She pulled an ampule from the same compartment and inserted it. She held it her palm and showed it to Jens.

"This is the only gun we're going to need," she said, and turned her mic back on, turning away from the man next to her.

"Peter, we're almost there," she said. "Has the lid opened any farther?" she asked.

"Yes!" His shout filled the small craft.

"It's okay, Peter," she said. "Just wait until—"

"It's huge!" he shouted. "I knew they were big, but it's huge!"

"Just turn him off," Olsen growled. "There's nothing he can help with now. Helmets on! Door opening in thirty seconds!"

Jens leaned forward to where Dr Lin sat in front of him. "Did you know he was going to do this?" he whispered.

"Don't be ridiculous!" she hissed back.

"I didn't think so," he said. "I just wanted to make sure."

"That you would even ask—" She was interrupted by the thrusters of the tori flaring as Kobarev brought the craft down by the airlock.

With Jens' help, Wright secured her helmet, unstrapped, and debarked from the tori. Dr Lin took the bag from Wright and carried it alongside her, the two women striding purposefully into the disc and through the airlock door. They waited what seemed an eternity for the air to equalize before they could enter the interior of the disc.

When the inner lock opened, the party jogged forward, following Tsuji as he read the monitor showing the way. They hurried through the chamber holding equipment, descended to the first deck of cryo-pods, then descended into another, a wide room exactly like the one they had left, filled with row upon row of pods. Only in this one, a human figure stood above one of the pods. Tsuji stopped looking at his monitor and pulled out his sounder. Jens had already withdrawn the plasma gun from his pocket and moved around to the right. De Werk moved, gun in hand, to the left. Wright felt herself grabbed and pulled forward as Olsen forced her to keep up with Tsuji.

As they reached the cryo-pod Peter staggered back. He bumped into the cryo-pod behind him, jumped away from it as if it had shocked him with an electric charge, and then continued to back away. As Wright got closer to the pod, Olsen let go of her suit. She leaned over the pod and looked into it. Two black eyes opened and blinked at her. They closed, and then opened again. Wright slowly reached into the cryo-pod, touching the injector against the alien's neck. She pulled the trigger, and the eyes closed again, this time remaining shut.

As she stood, she saw Tsuji pointed his gun into the pod. She pushed his arm out of the way. "Get that away from—" *my patient*, she almost instinctively said. Now that she was here, and it was in need, her ethical duty was to care for it. The first thing she realized she needed to do was to stop thinking of it as an it. She turned back to the Ruan below her, studying the body with Dr Lin.

"Clear," Tsuji announced.

"Clear," de Werk agreed from the left.

Dr Lin looked up and watched Jens cross the space

separating himself and the cryo-pods. She tensed, leaning protectively over the sedated Ruan, but Jens stepped past them, stopping at Peter. She watched Jens' empty right hand ball into a fist, swing upward in a slow arc and connect with Peter's face. Peter staggered under the blow, falling onto his back. She left the cryo-pod and moved over to Jens, grabbing the back of his suit and pulling as hard as her small frame could manage. It was just enough to make him hesitate, his fist suspended in the air; just enough time for de Werk to step in and pull Jens away.

"You son of a bitch!" Jens said to Peter.

"There will be time for that later," Dr Lin said to Jens, her words slapping him, her tone well-practiced in the control of those around her.

"Okay," he said, straightening up and shrugging off their grip.

Dr Lin resumed her place next to Wright, already busy taking vitals. Dr Wright ran her hands down the warm flesh of the torso, ensuring all tubes had been removed when the foam retracted. She palpated the abdomen, poked under the ribs to feel the internal organs protected there. She had studied Dr Lin's notes, had been allocated study time with the cadavers before leaving Earth, but this still felt like guess work.

"I have no idea what a normal pulse should be, let alone blood pressure," She said.

"Nobody does," Dr Lin said.

"We should get her to the *Chōgenbō* sick bay."

"Yes," Dr Lin agreed, running her fingers over the Ruan's face. "Magnificent."

"Patricia?"

Dr Lin flinched at her name, and withdrew her hand from the cryo-pod. She looked at Wright, then at the men in the room.

"Come on!" Donna snapped at the men around her. "Lift her out carefully. We need to get her to sick bay!"

"Her?" de Werk asked.

"Get a move on!"

The men jumped at her command. They holstered their weapons and moved over to the cryo-pod.

"And be careful with her!" Dr Lin added as they lifted the alien up.

22

Donna prepped the injector and placed it against the Ruan's skin. The blood work was fascinating, but it didn't answer all her questions. It kept Patricia focussed. She had never seen the older woman so engrossed, reading and recording new data. Dr Lin may have been the most knowledgeable person on, or off, Earth regarding the Ruan, but even she had never seen a live one, never listened to a beating heart, felt living tissue, studied blood from a system still circulating. They kept the Ruan sedated for twenty-four hours, time the doctors didn't need to fight too hard for. Olsen gladly granted it, merely insisting on armed security at all times. Both women ignored the man in the room, making him stand out of the way by the door, not even noticing when their guard changed.

Donna prepped another injector and placed it on the Ruan's bared arm.

"She's becoming quite a pin cushion," Jens said in a rare interruption.

"Immunizations," Donna said. "We don't want to kill her with our germs."

"It looks like it would take more than that."

Donna smiled at the prone figure below her, almost two

and a half meters tall, muscles well defined despite being at rest. She directed her smile towards Jens. He looked relaxed, but his hand was noticeably close to the sounder holstered on his hip.

"She is much more vulnerable than she looks," Donna said. "Their immune systems are very underdeveloped, at least compared to ours. We can't respond to all the antibodies that are lacking, just the most lethal."

"You could literally kill her with your breath, Jens," Patricia said without turning. Her shoulders shook as she silently laughed at her own joke.

"Why don't you come closer, Jens, and see her better?" Donna invited.

Jens hesitated, before slowly taking a step forward.

"Don't be such a coward, Jens," Patricia said, turning around to watch. "She is helpless, sedated and strapped to an examination chair."

Jens moved closer. The first Ruan he had been near to, he never even saw. Now, the GLR micro dose administered to all of the crew enabled their eyes to ignore the pheromone that caused that earlier blindness. Whether a defensive adaptation in their own evolution, or just a reaction with the human eye that made it hard to visually process, was unknown. Jens didn't care about the what or why of it; he was simply pleased they were no longer invisible.

"We're going to wake her soon," Patricia said. "I'd like you to be here."

"It's my job," Jens said, resting a hand on his sounder.

"Not like that, and you know it," Patricia snapped. "If it

were up to me there would be no weapons at all in this room, but Olsen gives the orders. If you're going to wear that thing, then you'll stand in the back with Tsuji. We need to move on from the past, Jens." Her voice softened, sounding like the old friend she was. "The Ruan in this ship aren't warriors. They're refugees."

Jens nodded, more an acknowledgement of hearing her than of agreement.

"And Peter will need to be here," Patricia added. "It's his job. He's the linguist. Will you be able to behave?"

"I'll refrain from punching him, if that's what you're asking."

"I'm asking if you'd stop being a self-righteous ... never mind. Just don't stop him from working. It's bad enough he's been confined to his quarters."

"He earned it," Jens said. "And I doubt she's going to like those," Jens added, pointing to the restraints.

"She won't care," Donna said. "The GLR in the stimulant will make her feel surprisingly calm."

"Not exactly how I envisioned first contact," Patricia said. "But I'm glad we have these medicines."

"Second contact," Jens corrected, resuming his place near the door.

Olsen entered, followed by Peter and Tsuji. The two Dutchmen, de Werk and Rupert, stood outside the door. Once the door closed, the sickbay was suddenly overcrowded. Tsuji shook his head at Jens. If something went wrong, if their guest didn't want to be restrained and wanted out, it would be virtually impossible to shoot around their crewmates and hit a target. Olsen cleared his throat, which brought everyone's attention to him. Instead of speaking, he simply nodded and stepped back.

Donna hesitated, holding the injector in her hand. Patricia smiled and nodded at the other doctor. Placing the device against the Ruan's neck, she administered the stimulant and stepped back. One second, and then another, passed in what seemed an eternity, as they waited for a reaction. Donna fought the temptation to check the injector, not willing to take her eyes off the alien. She stepped closer, leaning over her patient. The Ruan continued to breathe, but each inhalation seemed longer, deeper. Then her large black eyes slowly opened, looking at Donna. They stared calmly at her for a long moment before closing again.

When they opened a second time they were filled with questions. They moved from Donna to Patricia, and over to Olsen and Peter. Her mouth opened and she spoke, the first words ever spoken between human and Ruan, between human and any other alien race.

"What did she say?" Olsen asked.

"I don't know," Peter said. He held a translator device in his hand, replaying the words to his ear buds. "It's a question. I think."

He stepped closer to the Ruan, held out a hand and showed her an ear bud. It was larger than his, made from moulds of the ears of the Seekers in Dr Lin's laboratory. He gestured to his head and let her see the bud in his ear. He moved carefully and indicated to her ear. Unable to interpret the look in her eyes, he bent down and placed the bud in her ear. She accepted it placidly. He looked at Olsen and then at Donna and Patricia. He shrugged.

"Welcome to the *Chōgenbō*," Olsen said.

"You are safe," Donna added.

They waited and watched. The Ruan spoke again. Their eyes went from the Ruan to Peter. His head was tilted, listening to the words replay. "It's a question," he said. "One of the words is 'why', I think."

"Give us those buds," Patricia demanded.

"Yes, of course," Peter said. He gave out the buds and watched as they put them in their ears. He had planned to have prepared the crew for this moment, prepping and practicing one more time before they actually used them with a Ruan, but being confined to his quarters had prevented that.

"This has only been used on the limited recordings we have of Ruan speech, those from the Artifact, and found on Ruanae. It will improve with more use," Peter said. "It takes training."

Donna was the first to notice the Ruan staring at them, her eyes moving from Olsen to Peter and to Patricia. The others grew quiet as they also saw. For a long moment the humans stood staring at the Ruan gazing back at them.

"Ruanae," the alien said. "Ruanae," she repeated.

"Yes," Donna said. "Human," she said pointing to herself. "Human," she added pointing to the others.

The Ruan tilted her head, pointing the ear bud towards Donna.

"Human," Donna said again.

"Human," the Ruan said after a pause, forming the word with effort. She spoke again, a sentence. The others tilted their ear buds towards the alien. The gesture was unnecessary, a reflex that didn't make understanding or hearing easier. Peter studied the device in his hand as the translator program sifted through all the words on file.

They watched the Ruan's lips move, heard the sound of an unknown language, and almost simultaneously words they recognized. "Why … I here?"

"Why am I here?" Peter said into the device.

The Ruan waited as the humans stared at her, some of their small mouths open. She spoke again. "Why am I here?"

"Dr Lin?" Olsen asked. "Dr Wright?"

Donna breathed in and exhaled slowly. She smiled at her patient, strapped in the chair in front of her. The Ruan's eyes seemed to grow larger. She tilted her head slightly towards the doctor.

"We have found your vessel," Donna tried. "We want to take you home."

"Try different words," Peter offered when the Ruan didn't respond. "Like 'ship' and 'locate'. Simple words."

"We located your ship," Donna said. "Home. Ruanae."

"No Ruanae. Death," they heard from the words spoken by the Ruan, a sentence said slowly, that continued after the translated words were voiced by their ear buds.

"There are no Ruan. There is only death," Peter said into his device.

"Stop that," Olsen said to him out of the corner of his mouth.

"I'm programming it," Peter said, trying to whisper. "Teaching it pronouns, prepositions, articles—"

Patricia glared at them. "Shhh!"

"We can take you home," Donna said. "Take you to Ruanae."

"Death," the Ruan said.

"No more death," Donna said, trying to speak clearly, but not loudly. Enunciate, Peter emphasized in the trainings he held in the weeks of searching. She did not plan to be the spokesperson for her species, but found herself gently nudged to the front by the others' silence. *Speak in normal sentences and enunciate clearly*, Peter said.

"There is no more death on Pema—on Ruanae. It is safe to return," Donna said.

She watched the Ruan's lips move, heard the sounds of that alien language, but in her ear the bud relayed, "There is no more death on Ruanae."

"That was clear!" Peter said. Olsen pushed him towards the back of the room, where de Werk took his arm and pulled him further from the Ruan.

"No, there is no more death," Donna said. "It is long gone."

"Gone," the Ruan repeated. Her narrow face betrayed neither confusion nor understanding. She looked at Donna. "Why am I here?" she asked. She noticed her arms for the first time, the restraints binding them to the examination chair. She tried to raise an arm, giving up when it met resistance.

"Why am I bound?" she asked.

"Where is my ship?" she asked.

"Your ship is here," Donna said. "We are on your ship."

"This is not my ship," the Ruan returned. "Why am I bound?" She looked at her arms again, trying again, without success, to raise them. She closed her large hands to make fists, then relaxed them. She looked at the humans around her, trying to make sense of the scene through a GLR haze.

"What are you?" she asked.

"Captain, I don't think this is working," Donna said. "We should try again later."

"At your discretion, Doc," Olsen said.

The Ruan watched as Donna touched a device to her neck. She felt a pin prick, and then her world went dark.

Donna was well versed in Ruan anatomy and physiology. Her study with the mutilated but preserved remains held by Dr Lin's institute had helped get her shortlisted for this mission. Her reputation within HakKor, especially among its senior captains, assured her the post. But what earned her the esteem those captains held her in was her work with the living, not the dead—even if they were alien. She cared about the crew she was tasked to look after. She made the extra effort to care, not just about their physical wellbeing, but their emotional balance as well. Those with her on the *Chōgenbō* had experienced that for months, and although a couple needed extra persuasion to agree, they all respected her order that they leave her alone with the Ruan in the sickbay.

"Keep your sounder," she told Jens, "but wait outside." She rested her hand on Jens' arm, a gentle gesture that prevented any rebuttal.

His face softened, the worry lines on his forehead still visible yet not as deep. He nodded and left with the others. Donna was certain he, or one of the security men, would be right outside the door, listening and watching the room through a scroll screen in the wall. She knew it would make them feel better, an illusion of control. The only person she allowed to stay was Patricia. She could use the extra hands, and she doubted whether it was even possible to send her away. Some fights are not worth starting.

Peter and his device were sent back to his quarters, watching and listening over a feed, ready to speak corrections or vocabulary into the translator. She touched the bud still in her ear. Stimulants and doses of GLR were useful, but it would be words that reached her patient. She soothed with her bedside manner because she could read people through their eyes, their faces, the language of their bodies, what was spoken and the meaning behind their words. She could communicate the same way. Her hand on Jens' arm, the warmth of her flesh against his, the unhurried length of her touch, the tone of voice, all told him everything she wished to convey: *There is no argument, no protest you can make. This is my area of expertise. I will be okay. You are only in the way. You are not yet ready to be here. You will lead by example, as you always do, and exit my sickbay now.* Jens left, and the others followed.

Donna smiled at Patricia and turned towards the Ruan. Her heart was racing and her hand had a slight shake. But she had no choice. After prepping the injector, she held it against the Ruan's neck. She took a deep breath, triggered the stimulant, and stepped back. Patricia reached forward and took the injector out of Donna's hand. There was a metallic sound as it was placed on a work bench. Both women silently watched the closed eyes of the Ruan.

There was movement under the lids, and then they opened slowly. The dark eyes stared at Donna, moved past her to rest on Patricia, and then surveyed the left and right.

"We are alone," Donna said, trying to sound reassuring. A human might hear it that way, but she had no idea how a Ruan would interpret her tone or expression, or if she could even understand the words. The face of Ruan was unreadable, a stone mask.

The Ruan closed her eyes and opened them again. "Where am I?" she asked.

"You are on the *Chōgenbō*," Donna said.

"That is a word with no context," the Ruan said.

"It is a name. Our ship. It is the name for a type of bird on Earth," Donna tried.

The Ruan tilted her head, a slight and almost imperceptible movement. "You're confusing her," Patricia whispered.

Donna placed a hand on her own chest. "My name is Donna," she said to the Ruan. "My name. Donna," she added, patting the area where her heart was.

"Name," the Ruan said. "Dawn-ah."

"Yes! Donna." She couldn't help smiling when her name was said, but she quickly lost it as she watched the Ruan's eyes grow larger. She moved her hand towards her patient. "Your name?"

"Name," Donna heard in her ear bud. After a minute of silence, she heard a string of sounds. Donna instinctively touched her ear bud, as if that would help in hearing a translation. It played again as Peter made adjustments to the device from his quarters.

"Awwnil," Donna tried.

"Arnil," the Ruan repeated. "My name is Arnil." Clearer now.

Donna smiled again, but noticed a similar reaction from Arnil. She made a mental note to maintain a more neutral expression until she understood more about her patient.

Patricia stepped forward and made the same gesture, hand to chest. "My name is Dr Lin," she said. "Dr Lin."

"Lynn," Arnil repeated. It sounded like a bark. "Dawn-ah. Lynn."

"Where is my ship?" Arnil asked after a moment.

"It is here," Donna answered. "We are on it. The *Chōgenbō* is on your ship." Donna lifted her left hand and pinched her index finger and thumb together to simulate the *Chōgenbō* landing on the massive ship.

"Where are my people?" she asked.

Donna smiled again before remembering to keep her face blank. "Your people are fine. They are well. They sleep in their cryo-pods," she said.

"All those on my ship are alive. They are sleeping?" Arnil asked.

"No, I am sorry. Not all. Those in the cone of the ship were no longer alive," Donna said, noticing Arnil's eyes go wide, and quickly adding, "but we have inventoried the first disc, the disc you were in, and found all systems operational and all those in cryo-pods still in stasis, and very much alive. We have not inventoried the other discs."

"All are sleeping," Arnil said, seeming to relax. She closed her eyes and breathed deeply. Donna watched her chest rise and fall. She waited, standing in front of the Ruan, with no way to know how grief, or relief, were expressed. Arnil remained in her personal darkness, eyes closed, and let the emotion wash over before trying to face the strange beings, and strange situation in which she found herself. When she opened her eyes, she pointed with them to the restraints.

"I am *rrnngtuo*?" she asked.

"I do not know that word," Donna answered. When Arnil did not speak again, and only stared at the restraints, Donna touched her ear bud and spoke to Peter.

"What is that word?" she asked. "She's looking at her wrist straps."

"I'm not sure," Peter said. "There are several translations showing. Undesired. Outcast. Out—"

"Prisoner," Donna said. "She asked if she is our prisoner. Enough of this!" She turned to Arnil. "No," she said. "You are not a prisoner. These were for our safety. I will undo them."

A chorus of objections from all those listening erupted in Donna's ear, as she knelt to unfasten the straps binding the Ruan to the chair. Patricia's voice was heard both in her bud and her ear as the older doctor silenced them. Donna moved from the armrests to the Ruan's legs and ankles. When she was finished, she stepped back next to Patricia, and fought the urge to take the other woman's hand.

"You are not a prisoner," Donna said, to Arnil and all the others listening in. "We are here to help."

Arnil lifted her arms and flexed her large hands. They were easily the size of the human women's heads, and if swung at them would easily kill. But instead of attacking, she opened her fists, put her hands together and rested them on her lap.

"Why do you help us?" Arnil asked finally.

"You have been drifting in space for a long time," Donna tried. "We have found Ruanae. It is safe to return home."

"There is no safety of home," Arnil said.

The translator was processing her words more quickly and the short gap between the words spoken and the words heard became increasingly less noticeable. Donna hesitated before speaking again. Centuries had passed since the seed ship left Ruanae, but for Arnil it was merely a sleep, like that taken prior to a Step or prolonged acceleration. Only the acceleration Arnil slept through was centuries long.

"You have been in cryo-sleep for a very long time, hundreds of years," Donna tried. She waited for her words to be translated into Ruan, for Arnil to start to make sense of them, to realize what had taken place—or at least begin to realize. "We have met Seekers," Donna said. "We learned of Ruanae because of them."

"Where are the Guardians?" Arnil asked. It was more an exclamation than question. She sat up straighter in the examination couch, the most animation Donna had seen in the Ruan so far.

"What is that word?" Donna asked, more to Peter than Arnil.

"I think they're the same thing," Peter answered.

"Where are the Guardians?" Arnil asked again.

"They are not here." Patricia stepped forward. "Guardians attacked a Donut and several ships. They killed many people. But they were also killed. From their records, and from what we located in ruins, we were able to locate you."

It was the most words spoken to the Ruan since the translator bud was placed in her ear. Donna and Patricia thought her silence was due to trying to process the vocabulary. She closed her eyes and breathed deeply. "I do not know this word. Donut." She said it without opening them.

"It is how we travel," Patricia said. "An Einstein-Rosen bridge. A wormhole."

When she did open her eyes, Donna thought she saw sadness, though that was based more on the doctor's intuition than any physical sign. "Ruins," was all Arnil said.

"Many years have passed," Donna said. "Hundreds. Thousands. You are many, many lightyears from Ruanae. We can take you home."

"But we need your help," Patricia added.

"You can meet our captain," Donna said. "He will explain."

"You are not the Controller?" Arnil asked.

"No," Donna said, conscious not to smile. "I am a doctor, like you. Would you like to rest first, maybe sleep?"

"I have slept enough," Arnil said.

"Good," Donna said. She looked at the door, and thought about what Arnil might see outside. She started to speak, stopped and reformed her thoughts, and tried again. "This must all be very overwhelming for you. It is a lot to understand. We can wait until you are ready, and then we can show you the *Chōgenbō*, and your ship.”

Arnil bent forward and moved her legs off the couch. When her feet were flat on the deck, she straightened her body and stood. She looked down at the human women, almost a full meter below her.

“I am ready,” she said.

23

"It started with the *siml*." She spoke softly, her mouth near the rim of her mug.

Moments passed in silence. The woman stared into her drink as if more words were hidden there. Arnil's usual state seemed to be silence. She put up with the antibody tests the ship's doctor wanted to run, allowed her to use the injector to complete another battery of immunizations. She did not need to be told of the importance of the tests prior to returning to her disc, or waking the crew to flip the Seed ship. It was clear she realized that she was now, in a way, contaminated, and that it was unsafe for her to return until this human was certain she was protected, and they knew how to protect the others sleeping. She listened to all of Donna's explanations, absorbing every detail, only asking the rare question for clarification. It had mostly been one-way, but Donna didn't mind. The human couldn't imagine how she would react if the situation were reversed.

"I don't understand that word," Donna spoke calmly. Words were out and she didn't want to scare them away. "Is that a name?" she asked, coaxing, her question like bread-crumbs, attracting a timid bird.

"A name, yes," Arnil answered. "This device is improving, but it is still very lacking." She glanced at the translator badge pinned to her tunic before returning her gaze to her drink. "Not of a place. No," she laughed, or what Donna was beginning to recognize as a show of humor. "*Siml* are small creatures. Were. They are … were … everywhere. Pests. They burrow under gardens, chew into walls. Dirty animals. They multiply if unchecked."

"They sound like mice," Donna offered.

"That is a word with no reference," Arnil said. "What is a mice?"

"Not a mice … mice is more than one, plural," Donna said. "A *mouse* is a small mammal. It can fit into the palm of a hand, covered with short fur, small ears. It can be quite cute. But they breed rapidly, and can infest a home. They can cause damage, even spread disease."

"A *siml* is bigger," Arnil said, setting her mug down on the table. "A *siml* can fit in my palm," she said, opening her hand.

"That sounds more like a rat," Donna said.

"That is a word with no reference."

"A rat is like a mouse," Donna said. "Only bigger and uglier. And dirty. Sharp teeth, carries bugs, germs that infect humans, zoonotic diseases."

"Maybe a *siml* is like a raat then," Arnil said. She took a drink from her mug. "They started to disappear. Nobody knows when it started. Something that isn't liked, that hides and doesn't want to be seen, is hard to notice when it is no longer there."

Donna picked up the flask and indicated to Arnil's cup.

She poured in more coffee after Arnil's cheek twitched. Only through careful observation, and a little experimentation, did she learn that gesture and its meaning.

"The smell," Arnil said. "Dead and rotting *siml*. In wall cavities, under walkways. Most were pleased at the discovery. A disease that eradicates a pest." Arnil shook her head. "Stupid *Fonnen*."

That is word with no reference, Donna thought, but filed it away to ask about later. She smiled at Arnil, letting her continue.

"By that time other mammals were dying," Arnil said. "Mostly small animals, in the bush. Untamed mammals. Again, it was the smell that alerted us. The disease had spread from the *siml*, and was infecting other animals. Only when their precious *merendt* started to die did they begin to think there was a problem. And even then, it took far too long for them to realize what was really happening."

"I am sorry," Donna thought it safe to interject. "But you said a word. *Merendt*. Can you describe that for me?"

"A *merendt* is a mammal that lives inside, where Ruan sleep and eat. It is a disgusting practice." Arnil turned her long, narrow face towards Donna. "Imagine! A mammal treading where you sit, where you eat, even where you sleep! Giving them names! Would you have a mammal walking freely in your sick bay?"

"That would be unsanitary," Donna said.

"Precisely! These *Fonnen* with their *merendt*," she shook her head. "*Merendt* that hunt *siml*, eat them, bring them inside. Idiots!"

Donna turned her head and spoke into the translator pinned to her uniform. "add to dictionary: *merendt*, pet." She faced Arnil. That's close enough for now. Peter can work on the vocabulary later, and hopefully the problem with conjunctions. Words had to remain separate, which was hard to do for English speakers, "*Fonnen*? What is that?"

Donna recognized the glint in Arnil's eyes as the Ruan version of a smile. "It is a name for those living in the north. Not a real name. They don't call themselves that. They don't like it."

"I am learning Ruan slang!" Donna said.

Arnil jolted as Donna laughed. She was still not used to the strange sounds human make when they find amusement.

Donna noticed the flinch and stopped. "I am so sorry," she said. "There is nothing funny about this." Donna looked down briefly, ashamed of her outburst. To Arnil, these events were measured in months, not centuries.

"It is oh-kay," Arnil said, trying out human slang. "There are no more *fonnen* to be offended."

Donna pursed her lips, no doubt another expression that would confuse her guest. The human face had almost four times more muscles than the Ruan. They must look like they are constantly spasming and out of control.

"It started in the north?" Donna asked, attempting to steer the conversation back to its beginning. "With the *siml*, in the north?"

Arnil picked up her mug, took a sip, started to lower it again but stopped, transfixed by the black liquid. "Yes," she said. "It started in the north."

Arnil watched the growing catastrophe, like those around her, not really aware that that was what it was. Not aware at the beginning, anyway. Stories from the northern archipelagos of rodents dying. Mass die-offs. She watched the information feeds, programs reporting happenings, which always finished with clips meant to amuse or reassure the viewer. No matter what was covered—natural disasters, political intrigues, technological developments—these short clips reassured the viewer all was not bad or boring. The *siml* dying off. What could be bad about that?

Arnil didn't know why that particular story burned into her memory. It was just moments long, a few images of emaciated pests. She could vividly bring up the image of the announcer. The humor in his eyes as he joked about the benefit. Maybe on a much deeper level she knew there was nothing good about the news, much as she disliked the creatures. Nothing just dies. There is always a reason. Something to cause it. Her colleagues at the clinic agreed, and they followed the progress of the *siml* disease, as it was called in the beginning. It seemed to be able to jump water, appearing on nearby islands, with no obvious means of transmission. *Siml* do not swim, and they are usually detected when trying to stow away on a sea vessel.

Some argued that the disease might be natural. As if nature were ridding itself of an entire species. There were extinctions in the past, whether caused by climate change, cataclysmic events, or Ruan themselves. If the *siml* could not adapt, then they deserved their fate. They were no longer fit to share the planet.

But Arnil didn't want to believe that. Her training prevented it. And then the disease leapt to other mammals, and that theory was dropped. Bush mammals were found, emaciated and rotting. Some of the larger species even shuffled into settlements, staggering in their weakened state, their muzzles distorted in confusion and pain. Those creatures were dispatched and burned. Some were studied, but little was discovered.

When the *merendt* of the northerners began to die the stories moved up in the information programs. To Arnil, it seemed that the *Fonnen* cared more about their pets than their younglings, which of course was not true. Fear began to infect communities. Although, when island authorities started issuing edicts forbidding the practice of having *merendt* inside their homes, it was surprising how many continued to disobey.

The jump to *merendt* continued to other domesticated mammals. Resource mammals, used for foods, for clothing, for industry. It affected stomachs and livelihoods, so more began to take notice. Exports from affected islands were halted, but the cause didn't stop. It continued to hop from island to island, until the entire archipelago of *Yondrta* was infected.

As with the *siml*, as with every species that the disease touched, the disease was ruthless and efficient. Clinicians like Arnil could not understand a disease that killed all of its hosts, but that is exactly what this one did. Rather than let some of the affected survive for future infections, it chose instead to evolve and consume another species. And then another, and another.

Arnil and her colleagues hung a large map on the wall of the clinic and tracked the epidemic. As the disease spread to other mammals, they used different colors. Lines connected islands. Then they connected archipelagos. The lines became like rainbows of death, multicolor arcs crossing expanses of water. Some communities attempted to cull affected mammals, which was heartbreaking as whole herds were put down, but the spread continued. The colored lines inched their way around the globe, creeping east around the world, and slowly to the south. Towards Arnil's home island.

"It is called *Hestrilx*," Arnil said into her cold coffee. "My home."

"Where was ... *is* it located?" Donna asked, determined to avoid the past tense.

"In the temperate climes," Arnil said. "South of the tropics, away from the heat. We have more than one season, summer tempered by cooler days as the sun rested."

"What did it look like?" Donna asked, trying to place the name on the newer map of Pemako, or Ruanae.

"It is a long island, with a strong backbone of mountains that wear a coat of white in the colder months," Arnil said wistfully. "In the summer they are a blaze of green. As the seasons change it is a joy to watch. The white recedes, retreats, as the green climbs higher and higher, as if the snows are melting in front of a green fire. My favorite time of year."

Arnil closed her eyes and sat silently. Tears slowly ran down the sides of Arnil's face. Donna already knew Ruan cried. She had cried with Arnil, the day she was woken.

"If we had this, it may have been different." Arnil gestured to the sick bay of the *Chōgenbō*. She was impressed with human understanding of their bodies. "You have a much better understanding of medicines," Arnil said.

"Humans are much weaker than Ruan," Donna admitted. "Our bodies … need more care. So, we have devoted a great deal of time studying them. Our fallibility, our frailty, has often given us strength."

"Could you have stopped it?" Arnil asked.

Donna hesitated. The bodies of the Ruan were stronger and generally healthier than humans, which meant they lived longer, with less illness. It also meant their medical sciences were under-developed and far behind that of Earth. Infections didn't manifest when Ruan skin was scratched or cut. Diseases didn't migrate from living near or with animals. The immune system would eradicate the introduced pathogen before the injured Ruan would even notice. They did not experience ailments that humans accepted as normal. Colds, flus, rashes, sexually transmitted disease were all extremely rare. Which led to complacency, rather than the age-old drive of humans to obsessively study their bodies and try to find out why they broke down so easily.

"When you were revived," Donna said, "I gave you an injection to protect you from any illness we may have introduced. Any pathogens that your body did not have immunity to fight. Although your immunity may have defended you against most of them, it would not against all." Samples of seeker flesh had been traded between Consortia and university laboratories. Opportunities to study the two cadavers at Dr Lin's new institute were sought after, and occasionally granted. One of the seekers carried the viral agent that decimated its species, although there were no outward signs. Researchers debated about passive carriers, dormant germs, transmission periods, and a host of other theories. Regardless of view, they had obtained a sample of what killed the alien species. It was also accurate to say that human scientists had a better understanding of Ruan physiology than the Ruan themselves did. Donna didn't say it, but she suspected Arnil knew.

"We would have used an anti-viral treatment," she said instead. "One similar to antidotes developed during the pandemics of the Decline, prior to the Great Awakening on Earth. Unfortunately, we have had a great deal of experience with disease." *A simple anti-viral that would have protected your people,* she thought.

Arnil looked around the sick bay, at the clean work surfaces and instrumentations she was only just becoming familiar with. The human taught her how to use the electron microscope that allowed her to see the individual atoms within cells. No foreign invader could hide from the eyes of these aliens, no matter how small or how buried in the flesh it might be. *Yes, this technology could have saved the Ruan,* Arnil thought. *But you were not here when we needed it.*

"It doesn't matter," she said.

"It does matter," Donna said. "It means your people will be protected when they return to Ruanae."

"My people," Arnil repeated. "We don't even know exactly when the first began to die," she said after a pause. "It was only when … this is very difficult."

Something began to itch at the back of Arnil's mind as she and her colleagues drew the colored lines on the map. As yet more species of mammals were added to the list of infected, lines became dashes or dots, or shapes, to differentiate from the other lines as they ran out of colors to separate them. But even that practice stopped when the collection of lines grew too crowded. Nothing stopped the relentless progress. All shipping on the sea, all transport through the air, was halted. Archipelagos isolated themselves, and the islands within locked down, quarantined. Yet islands without contact of any sort still watched their mammals die.

And then the first Ruan grew ill. It was near the epicenter of the outbreak. A Guardian masked his sore muscles as long as he could, but the eating pain grew too much, consumed his pride and courage until he broke down. The disease grew throughout his musculature, wasting what was once pure strength into soft weak flesh. Others complained of pain—their arms, thighs, abdomen. Soon, like the first, they died as wasted shadows of their former selves, jaws slack and open as even their masticatory muscles degenerated. The Guardians were the strongest among the Ruan, and they were the first to fall. A wasting disease taking the pride of the species, laying waste to an entire caste.

But they were soon followed by others. A disease that took the strongest first inevitably turned to the weaker. Elders began to succumb. Younglings woke crying in pain, and by day's end were silent in death. Where ever the plague touched, no one survived.

"It is unimaginable," Donna said. "A one hundred percent death rate."

"It was a nightmare, a dream that had no waking," Arnil said. "We could only helplessly and impotently watch it progress, from land to land. We watched our mammals intently. We watched each other. We worried about every ache."

Tears ran down her long face. She let out a shuddering breath and held her head in her hands. Donna reached over and touched Arnil's shoulder, an act of sympathy and comfort, but a human act, alien to the Ruan. Arnil moved her shoulder away from the unwanted touch. She rubbed the tears from her face.

"It took time to see it," Arnil said. "We weren't the first to notice, but there was a pattern in the spread." She turned and looked at Donna. "By that time the populations of whole Archipelagos were gone. Millions dead. More were dying elsewhere. For some ... it did not bring out their best. No one wants to die. They tried to flee the onslaught of the disease by leaving their homelands. They took to the sky and the sea. But none would have them. These refugees were sunk, or they were shot out of the air. Many were killed. Our Guardians were weakened, dying, so others took their place. Those who were common, weaker in mind and body. It was ugly, and it was brutal. It was a time that tested our character, and we were found wanting."

"The Guardians are better than you?" Donna asked. "What do you mean?"

"Guardians do not only protect our homes and communities," Arnil said. "They protect our essence, our *xentoldt*—"

"I am sorry," Donna interrupted. "That is one of those words the translator cannot process."

"Guardians are chosen when they are younglings," Arnil said. "They are brought up in strict discipline, in special, holy places. They are taught how to fight, how to be protectors. They learn all types of combat, the use of weapons, including their hands and feet. Their physical form is very beautiful."

Again, Donna recognized the Ruan form of a smile. "But they are untouchable. They live apart, where they study the old ways. The Guardians sit in silence for hours, sometimes days, contemplating why they might fight, and when they might use their strength. I will say a word that this device may translate."

Donna heard two words, *deep* and *reflection*.

"I understand, I think," Donna said. "They are warrior monks."

Arnil bent her head forward, as she had learned was a non-verbal human way to indicate the affirmative. "Your words translate to something close. There are many conceptual words that can be used to describe what a Guardian is." Arnil had grappled with several conceptual words the aliens that woke her used. She decided that it wasn't the fault of the translation device, but that some words were layered with meaning and used in many different situations. She deactivated the device on occasion to hear some. The muscles in her tongue didn't allow her to repeat some. Like the word 'love'.

"Your word," Arnil said. "I will try to write it. This device will not offer an adequate alternative."

Donna produced a pad of paper and a pen. Arnil took the small writing implement in her long fingers and made a downward mark, followed by a circle, and then two short lines converging to form an angle. She was determined to learn the alien script, as the translator only worked with sound.

"Love?" Donna asked.

Arnil turned off her translator, had Donna repeat it, and then bent her head forward.

"Yes," she said. "The Guardians learn this and apply this in all aspects of their waking. They strive to feel this and express it in everything they do, and everything they think. It is why they are apart from the common. They take it upon themselves to maintain all that is good about the Ruan. What makes us Ruan. Our *xentoldt*. They would willingly sacrifice themselves to protect what is good in us, if that is what was required, even when, out of our weakness or hatred or greed, we do not want protection."

Arnil breathed deeply. A sigh, one of the few gestures that, like tears, both species used. "When the Guardians became ill ... when they succumbed ... it was an unimaginable loss. There was nobody there to protect us, and we were truly lost."

"And yet they did protect you," Donna said. "They saved you. It was because of the seekers, the Guardians, that we found Ruanae, and that we learned of you."

"We both know that is not what happened," Arnil said.

"Although their intentions were pure, they killed your people. And they were too late."

Arnil studied the map on the wall, with its colored lines blurred into a thickening smear that covered whole swaths of the northern hemisphere. She took her earlier suspicion and married it to current speculation. Wild theories sprouted like fungi, but one made more sense than the others. Arnil searched through databases until she found what she wanted. She printed it off and took it to the wall. She held it up and studied both the large map and the smaller sheet of data. On an ocean world the winds seem to roam free, when and where they like.

But they do not. Like the ocean itself, the wind follows currents, moving across the globe in patterns. The currents flow in a circular motion over the north, until the seasons change and they wind their way south, circulating over the entire globe. Circulating the disease. The southern temperate zone was currently untouched. It wouldn't be for long.

Arnil and other clinicians rushed to sound a warning, as Elders rushed to calm panic. They were both too late. The decision to leave was made in the midst of chaos. Society was collapsing even faster than the disease spread. As panic ensued, Guardians removed those in civil authority and tried to restore order themselves. But as they too sickened, order died with them. Islands were deserted, all their inhabitants dead, or desperately trying to flee. The seas filled with boats large and small, all heading south. Many disappeared under the waves, as their vessels took on water, or as fights broke out, or as they were deliberately sunk for straying too close to other boats. The rare islands that took them in were soon infected—by the refugees, or by the winds, none knew.

Before long, no refugee was welcome. Strangers were shot on sight. Broods locked in their dwellings fought any trying to enter, but they were still not safe, because there was no safety. Many who realized this took their own lives the moment symptoms began to manifest. Fatigue. Pain deep within the muscles. Headache. Blurring vision. They did anything to avoid the inevitable and horrendous death that waited. Early information feeds showed the victims, but that was before the producers realized that they were looking at all of their fates. Shaking limbs. Hands contracting into bird-like claws. Faces contorted and twisted until too weak to even hold in the tongue. The drooling. And towards the end, merely wasted shells lying limply on a sleeping mat. Those feeds ceased when it became clear there would be no survivors to interview. However, the fear and hopelessness could not be shut off. It spread faster than death.

Arnil was among the lucky, at the right time and place, and with a priority skill. She and her younglings boarded a transport and left Ruanae behind forever. Only then were they safe, rising above the planet and into the vacuum of space, leaving behind the invisible virus and the atmosphere that carried it.

Debarking on the half-constructed orbital city, she, her colleagues and their broods made their way through the anxious corridors and into the Seed ship. The clinicians spread out over the discs on which they were stationed, prepping cryo-pods not meant to be used for another five cycles. That was when the Seed ship had intended to begin its original mission, taking select and trained Ruan to courageously venture into the unknown, to seed other planets and perpetuate their species. Instead, the pods were now readied for the panicked and frightened islanders lucky enough to leave before the winds brought infection and death.

The *Anarokt* had been designed as an act of hubris, a display of greatness and superiority. The Ruan were to reach out and seed a star. But on the planet of Ruanae there was no more hubris or greatness. Their superior race was being eliminated by an unseen and unknown enemy. And the *Anarokt* was reduced to nothing more than a lifeboat.

Elsewhere, reactors flared, accelerating ships at magnificent speeds, with teams of Guardians turned Seekers, already asleep to the past and to their future, in a desperate and doomed attempt to find help among the stars.

24

Arnil uncurled from the tori. Her tall frame sat hunched over during the flight from the *Chōgenbō* to the *Anarokt*. Jens felt her presence, more than saw it, on the short trip over, choosing to stare forward at the back of Kobarev's head rather than glance over at the Ruan. He heard her head rub against the roof as she turned to look down at the pilot, sitting motionless and controlling the craft with his eyes, as well at Jens. She saw him relaxed, so became more so herself.

"She is in awe of you," Donna tried to explain. "To her you are a Guardian, a human Guardian. In Ruan society Guardians are the most respected members. They're like, I don't know, a Samurai warrior, philosopher monk, aristocrat, and judge all rolled into one. And you defended your people by killing two Ruan Guardians."

"She doesn't have to do that every time she sees me," Jens said.

"What, that small bow?"

Jens clasped his forearm in front of his chest and bent slightly in imitation of Arnil's gesture.

"Yes, she does," Donna said.

"Just accept it, Jens," Patricia added. "Deep down you'd like us all to do that."

Donna stifled a laugh. She had initiated the first interaction between Jens and Arnil, though Jens felt coerced more than invited. In doing this, the ship's doctor was looking after two patients at the same time, easing Arnil into normal interactions with the human crew, and applying salve to Jens' emotional wounds. If all Ruan were mindless killers, a belief she suspected Jens harbored someplace deep within his psyche, then they might as well detach from the *Anarokt* and let it disappear into the depths of space.

But she knew that they weren't, and after some desensitizing sessions, Jens came to fully accept that truth as well. She had sent Patricia to collect him and bring him to sickbay, where she and Arnil waited. It took longer than she expected, but the door finally opened and he walked in, followed by Patricia. Donna half expected to see the other woman holding a sounder to his back and was pleased to see her hands empty. Jens stopped two meters from Arnil, as far away as possible in the confined space. The last time he had seen her, she was fully restrained and drugged. He glanced at the unoccupied examination chair, then towards Arnil. The Ruan stood, towering over the humans. She placed a hand on her forearm, formed a pentagon with her arms in front of her chest and bowed her large head.

"I am honored to be in the presence of a Guardian," she had said, eyes focused on a spot of floor in front of Jens feet.

Jens made a small movement forward, caused by Patricia's finger poking his back.

"It is a pleasure to meet you," he said, wondering how that phrase might translate into her language.

"Lynn and Dawn-ah have told me of the saving of your people," Arnil said.

Jens felt another prod to his back. "That was a long time ago," he said.

"I am secure in your presence," Arnil said, lifting her face. Peter's device could translate the words, but not the depth of meaning they carried in Ruan culture. She stared into Jens' eyes for a long moment, and bowed again. The simple phrase, *I am secure in your presence*, offered many things—trust, respect, and a faith that the person it is said to will always make the right decision.

"Arnil," Jens said, after being prodded again, "I would be honored if you would accompany me on a tour of the *Chōgenbō*." It sounded to Donna like words Patricia had instructed him to say—which they were.

Arnil raised her face and smiled, a subtle ocular gesture lost on the humans.

"Come," Jens had said, indicating to the door. He led her into the corridor, and the two walked beside each other, followed by Donna and Patricia. They listened to Jens' stilted tour, and heard his speech loosen up in response to Arnil's questions. By the time they reached the bridge he appeared almost relaxed. She bowed her head to Olsen and Mori, and then to Tsuji, standing against the bulkhead with his sounder unseen in his back pocket. Jens pointed to the viewing monitor, which Mori activated, and the Ruan stood silent and still as the image of the *Anarokt* filled the screen.

Jens gave her the time she needed to take in the picture. Donna and Patricia tried to prepare Arnil for what would be asked of her, and Olsen readily agreed to let Jens explain. The Ruan could grasp the idea of a Donut, just not the reality. The names of the scientists who first conceptualized a worm hole, Einstein and Rosen, could not quite translate, and were irrelevant to the explanation. They tried with a piece of paper, then with a cloth, making a mark on one side, then doing the same on the other side.

"This is what we will do," Patricia demonstrated. "With the Donut, we create a gravity well, that bends space, that warps it, so that you can travel from this mark, to this mark, quickly. By putting them in the same place. Then we Step from point to point. It is called Stepping."

When Arnil continued to stare without comment, Patricia illustrated with the cloth, making marks and putting a weight in the middle of it to make it sag.

"Folding space," Arnil observed. If Ruan shook their heads, she would have at that moment.

"It takes an incredible amount of energy, vast amounts," Patricia added. "We harness the power of the sun, charging the Donuts, and then we Step across space. Lightyears across space."

They drew pictures, and showed Arnil images and video feeds. She was almost ready by the time Jens spoke.

"The *Anarokt* is a beautiful ship," he began, "a very large ship."

"It is home to many," Arnil said.

"But we need to stop it, so that our Donut can be used. As Lynn and Dawn-ah have explained."

"They have spoken of your Stepping," Arnil said. "But stopping *Anarokt* does not help us reach the stars, nor return us to Ruanae."

"What you say is true," Jens said. "But we have another way. A faster way to go home." He thought he saw her mouth a word, and guessed it was the Ruan word for home.

"We need the *Anarokt* to flip, and then to decelerate," Jens continued. "We need you to wake those who can do that. Who can control the ship."

"The controllers are dead," Arnil said. "Lynn and Controller Olsen have told me. I have seen the images."

"Yes, they are. But there are others on the disc, the disc where we found you. Some that could do what is needed?" It was half statement, half question.

"I am a clinician. I am not crew," she said.

"Yes, but you can identify crew. You can safely wake them." Jens smiled inwardly. Not too long ago, the last thing he wanted was to wake Ruan, to have them not only walking among them but controlling the massive ship. Now he was actually encouraging it. He glanced at his hand, and thought of the one moment of satisfaction he had had when he punched Peter Taylor. A stupid and childish reaction, Patricia called it, and Jens didn't argue her point.

"The disc has a reactor, which means it has engineers," Jens continued. "And it appears to have a bridge. You can wake the crew who work there, and we can explain the situation. We can give them the technical data they will need to rendezvous with the Donut."

Arnil stepped closer to the primary view screen on the bridge and stood silently. She reached out a hand and touched the image of the disc with a finger, a motion obvious to those watching as being filled with affection. Finally, she turned to the humans.

"Yes," she said. "I can wake controllers who can stop the ship."

Arnil slowly followed Jens out of the tori, stepping onto the surface of the disc. She reached out a hand towards the green energy field keeping out the vacuum of space. Jens put his hand on her arm, stopping her. The field was hybrid technology, part stolen from the airlocks of the Artifact, part human ingenuity.

"We need to stay inside without suits," he told her, gesturing to the door leading into the disc. "The energy creates a field to keep us safe."

She lowered her hand to her side and walked towards the airlock of the disc, an entrance she had used only once before —what seemed to her as mere weeks ago, and yet also a lifetime. She stepped through, Jens by her side, and proceeded down the corridor. She took the ramp to the upper levels, striding past the cargo in the level below the cryo-pods. Her gaze took in the labels affixed to each container, words in the human script, written and catalogued by Okada and Yasuda. Jens noticed the slight pause by the Ruan as she scanned the room. Jens knew the techs had been busy, and still were, inventorying the third disc at that very moment, but he was only now realizing how thorough the two were.

Arnil didn't stop, didn't ask any questions, but continued up the ramp to the first cryo-pod level. She paused at the entrance to the area, her eyes moving from right to left. Her own cryo-pod was to the left. She took a step in that direction, lifted a hand, and opened her arm until it pointed to the right. She turned and strode purposefully in that direction, past dozens of cryo-pods. Jens kept pace, followed by the remainder of the party—Wright and Lin shouldering their medical kits, Tsuji and de Werk with weapons holstered but ready, Olsen, and finally Taylor with a satchel of customized translators.

Arnil walked for hundreds of meters, past row after row of cryo-pods, not even pausing momentarily to read names or positions. Tsuji and de Werk closed the distance between themselves and the Ruan, suspicious as their role required, but Arnil suddenly stopped. She touched a cryo-pod, letting her large hand run over the surface. The figure within was obscured by foam and frost. She bent down and closely examined the lights indicating the condition of the Ruan inside. Satisfied, she stepped to the next cryo-pod, ran her hand over the surface and studied the display.

Jens felt a tug on his sleeve and turned his ear in the direction of the pull. "Her brood," Donna whispered. Jens looked at her, uncomprehending.

"Her children," Donna explained.

Jens nodded, looked at Tsuji and de Werk, and patted the air with an open palm. The tension in their shoulders eased.

Arnil spoke softly, the murmur too low for Taylor's translator to pick up. Jens rightly imagined they were words of comfort, of reassurance.

After several minutes he interrupted the reunion. "You will be with them soon," he said. "When we return home."

Arnil faced him and nodded in a gesture he couldn't read, then walked away in large strides. The party hustled to keep up, almost bumping into each other when she suddenly stopped beside a cryo-pod.

"This is the lead control officer, the controller of the disc," she said.

"The Captain," Jens confirmed.

"Yes, the Olsen. The Controller. His team is in these cryo-pods." She indicated to four nearby pods before walking to another cryo-pod. "This is an engineer," she said. "He can work the reactor, and will know who else he requires to assist."

"Thank you, Arnil," Donna said. "Lynn and I will assist you with revivification. We can start with the captain, if you agree."

"Yes," Arnil answered. "The word is Controller." She moved to the cryo-pod as Donna and Patricia placed their bags on the floor beside it. They both began removing the prepared injectors; immunizations to protect against the infections carried by the humans, and any remnant of the plague that destroyed their species. They waited silently as Arnil studied the control panel, moved around the lid examining the seam, and returned to the panel. She pressed a sequence of buttons.

Arnil stepped back and watched the cryo-pod. Green

lights turned to orange. The inner foam began to retract from around the Ruan inside. The lid made a faint sucking sound before lifting several centimetres. The human doctors flinched at the sound, but Arnil stood unmoving, arms at her side. The lid slowly lifted further, its hydraulic arms sliding it back, tilting it up and manoeuvring it beside the pod.

"Well," Olsen said. "Let's do this properly. Form a line."

Jens straightened his green jacket, touched the knife strapped to his thigh, and stood beside Olsen, feet shoulder width apart and hands clasped behind his back. Arnil had insisted on the weapon. A Guardian is always armed, ready to defend. Jens thought he would feel better wearing it, but looking at the cryo-pods around him and the vulnerable Ruan within, it felt more like a costume prop. Tsuji, de Werk and Taylor completed the line. Jens felt Olsen's hand on his shoulder.

"I think you're expected to be in front of us, Mr Guardian," he said.

Jens shook his head and took a step forward. "Taylor, are you ready with that device?" he asked, without turning.

"It's all set," Taylor answered.

"Now might be a good time," Jens said.

Taylor left the line of men and stood next to Patricia. He wiped his hands on his legs and tried to calm his breathing. Donna reached into the cryo-pod and placed the injector against the neck of the Ruan inside. She withdrew her hand and reached back. Patricia took the empty injector from her and put another in its place. Donna reached in and repeated the process, selecting another exposed piece of skin for more immunisations. The third injector was waiting as soon as she reached back again. She stepped back and dropped it into her medical bag as soon as she finished.

She glanced at Peter and tilted her head in the direction of the pod. "Now," she said.

Peter fumbled in his bag and withdrew the ear bud and translator. He stepped to the cryo-pod, reached in with a shaking hand and attached the device to the Ruan's uniform. He placed the bud in the Ruan's large ear and backed away, taking his place in line. He closed his eyes, trying again to calm himself, and largely not succeeding. He felt Patricia and Donna take their places beside him. When his breathing took on a semblance of normality, he opened his eyes and watched as Arnil once again checked the panel, pressing a control instructing the pod to administer a stimulant.

Arnil leaned over the pod, reached in and touched the face of the waking Ruan. To the humans it looked affectionate, a stroke with the back of her hand. For Arnil it was diagnostic, checking both body temperature and circulation. She saw the desired flush. The Ruan's eyes opened, grasping onto Arnil's face for focus. When they showed recognition within, Arnil stood straighter.

"Controller," she said. "Welcome back." She bowed so that the Ruan inside could see the gesture. She knew she had much to explain, in as few words as possible; she needed to summarize what she herself had found overwhelming and disorientating when she was revived. She swallowed before starting.

"Many ages have passed. Our ship has been found. The

Primary Controllers have not survived. I have woken you to meet the strangers. They wish to help us return."

Her Controller remained lying in the cryo-pod, shifting his gaze from her to the ceiling.

"The ship?"

"The *Anarokt* continues to voyage. You are now Primary Controller."

"Help me out, Clinician," he said slowly.

Arnil took his arm and he sat up. He looked at the waiting humans, then returned his attention to Arnil and the edge of the cryo-pod. She helped him lift a leg over the side, and he followed with the other until his feet reached the deck. His hand remained gripping the frame of the pod, and he leaned against it for support as sensation slowly returned to his legs. He touched his ear where Peter had inserted the bud.

"It is for communication," Arnil explained. "It brings meaning to their words."

He stood straighter as his strength returned and stared at the humans lined up before him. Jens breathed in slowly through his nose and stared back.

"This is Awn-Drew Jensen," Arnil said. "The Guardian of the Humans."

The commander clasped his forearm in front of his chest and bowed. "I am secure in your presence," he said, straightening up.

Jens made a fist with his right hand and tapped his left shoulder as Arnil had instructed the previous evening, politely explaining that the human practice of touching hands would be perceived as entirely inappropriate between Guardian and civilian.

"As is my duty," Jens said.

The controller touched the bud in his ear and tilted his head.

"Are my words translated into your language?" Jens asked.

"Yes," he answered. "It is a magnificent device."

Jens could almost hear the grin forming on Peter's face. "Controller," he said, before the linguist might interrupt. "We have travelled a great distance to find the *Anarokt,* to help you return to Ruanae." Jens searched the Ruan's face for reaction but could not read anything. "You have travelled deep into space, where there is no sanctuary. But it is safe to return home. However, this we cannot do without your assistance."

Arnil had helped him shape the speech. She assured him that the words were appropriate.

The controller once again clasped his forearm in front of his chest and bowed. Arnil caught Jens' eye and he watched her tilt her head towards her captain. *A name is not given to a Guardian unless asked by a Guardian*, Arnil had explained.

"Controller, may I have your name?" he asked.

The Ruan straightened. "I am known as Gruajunt," he said.

"Gruajunt," he repeated firmly, as Arnil has said should be done; a valued acknowledgement. "Let me introduce the crew of the *Chōgenbō*. There will be much to learn of each other, and much work to complete, but let us begin with names." Jens cleared his throat, reminding himself that only

Guardians had two names. He made a small motion with his hand and the Ruan stepped forward.

"This is the Controller of the *Chōgenbō*, Olsen, of the planet Earth," Jens said.

25

"Any sign of Ruan waking in other discs?" Middleton stood beside the captain's chair, watching the disc on the view screen. It took up the entire field of vision, even with the lens angled as far up as it could go. Lights showed on several decks. He activated a lens on the hull of the *Chōgenbō* and scanned down the length of the cone they were anchored to. Olsen and Kobarev were checking and strengthening the ship's grip on the massive Ruan vessel. Middleton scanned along the shaft of the first leg and saw the charge. He smiled. Olsen and his redundancies—should the legs grip too well and not release, or should the *Chōgenbō* need to leave in a hurry, there was another way. Power had been restored to the cone and the bridge made operational. Light showed through the small window in the airlock they had first used to enter the seed ship. He turned away from the screens.

"I'm still reading only twelve Ruan," Mori reported. "Eight are in the cone. Three are at the main reactor. I mean *reactors*. Doi is with them. He's rather impressed."

"I'll bet," Middleton said. The engineer had never seen reactors as large or as powerful, simply because nothing like them had ever been built. At least by humans.

"Yasuda and Okada are in Disc Five," Mori added.

"Counting their treasure." Middleton noticed his tone as it came out, wondering if it was contempt or distrust. Or both.

"They've been very thorough," Mori said, better at concealing her personal opinion. "It is why they are here."

"Indeed," Middleton agreed.

"Doctors Lin and Taylor are also in the cone," she added.

"Of course. They are the reason we're here, after all. Every scientific theory and fantasy they've ever had has just come true. And the last Ruan?" he asked.

"Still in Disc One," Mori said. "Jens said she spends her time at the cryo-pods of her brood, and checking all the others. There's twenty thousand of them. It keeps her occupied."

Mori swivelled in her chair to face the First Mate. "She examined Olsen's pod with Wright," Mori said, "because of the trouble with it opening. The Ruan said properly designed cryo-pods don't malfunction that way."

"Is that all she said?"

"Essentially," Mori said. "She made it clear that if the pod was engineered correctly, it would operate smoothly, even after two thousand years. All twelve of their pods opened without a glitch, and ours are the same design. But the Ruan didn't build ours, so she couldn't be certain. If a Ruan built it, it wouldn't malfunction, was her basic diagnosis."

"Worrying," Middleton said. "One more sleep in those damn things."

"Protocols are in place," Mori said. "Wright will be the last one in, and she'll check all pods before she goes under." Mori swivelled back to her panel.

"The Donut sends their hellos," she added.

"That took a while."

"Five days and a bit now," Mori said. "But they said when final numbers are sent, they'll compute an ETA and Step to rendezvous to meet us. They sent some personal messages. I've forwarded those to crew feeds."

"Has Jens spoken to the Ruan about the fourth disc yet?" Middleton asked.

"I don't know," Mori said. "Now that the cone is functioning, they must see the lack of power in the disc."

"That's a hell of a piece of news to deliver," Middleton said.

The Ruan moved his hand over the screen and an overlay appeared. To Jens it looked like the illustrations of the vascular system he was made to study in high school biology. In a way it was similar—the veins and arteries of the ship. It all came down to flow and blockages. One clot in the system can cause a crash, a temporary disruption of blood flow to the brain and the damage can be lasting. Or fatal. While they all slept the ship had suffered a stroke and nobody was awake to respond. They slept through the crisis, and many would never wake. In the cone, there was a weak link, a faulty line in a series of parts that finally gave way hundreds of years past their expected lifespan. A clot that blocked the flow of power to the cone. The brain of the ship.

The Ruan technician spoke as he traced the lines with a finger. He pointed to the weakness and traced back the chain of faults that had caused the death of the crew. He had repaired and replaced what was needed, respectfully declining Jens' offer to help. It was unseemly for a Guardian to get his hands greasy. He was yet to find the fault that had cut power to the entire fourth disc, resulting in twenty thousand deaths. Gruajunt had reacted with a stoicism Jens had never witnessed. The Ruan leader simply placed one hand over his forearm and bowed, thanking Jens for the notification, informing him that they had become aware of the fault when running diagnostics in the cone.

"We have forgotten how to mourn," he said, declining Jens' inquiry about a break in their work, a chance to pause and remember. "Perhaps we will one day learn again," he added, before turning back to his console.

Jens walked across the bridge to where Patricia stood surveying the action. Each Ruan that noticed his passing stopped their work, saluting him with a hand on their forearm and a bow. She grinned at him as he neared.

"Gruajunt says they should be ready to Flip in a matter of days," he said, before she could add the sarcasm that usually followed the look.

"Has he requested your presence for the event, Mr Ambassador?" she asked.

"Yes, as a matter of fact, he has."

"Don't pretend you don't like it, Jens," she said.

"This is why you invited me, isn't it?"

"There were a lot of reasons why I invited you," she replied. "But, yes. This is one of them. You did it before, and you can do it again."

"That was between humans," Jens said.

"Same job."

Patricia pointed to a Ruan at the navigation station, glancing towards them. "I helped him find Sol," she said. "Helped convince them that Stepping is a real thing. He kept checking his data, and it kept showing Sol at over ten thousand light years away. Go talk to him and make his day."

The navigator turned back to his monitors when Jens continued to stare.

"Go on," Patricia said. "It's hard to tell what they're thinking, but they're probably just as shook up and frightened as any crew would be. As you would be. But you're the grown-up here. So do your job."

Jens smiled at her, reached over and in a rare display of physical affection gently squeezed her arm. The navigator turned as he approached. He let the Ruan finish bowing before speaking.

"Navigator, what is your name?" he asked.

Jens thought he saw a smile, of sorts, hidden in the eyes. "I am honored, Guardian. My name is Mrtangl."

"Mertangle," Jens tried. "Navigator Mertangle, I am told you have located the star of my birth."

"Yes, Guardian," he said. "And the star of Ruanae. If I may?"

"Please," Jens said.

The navigator waved his hand at the screen and a new schematic appeared. He pointed to a small dot of light near the far corner. "It is here," he said. "So far."

"Very far," Jens agreed.

"Is it from that place, your home world?" the navigator asked, looking at the knife strapped to Jens' leg.

"Yes, it is," Jens answered. He removed it from the sheath and cradled it in his hands. "It is from an island known as Japan, which is an archipelago much like those on Ruanae. It was made by a master swordsmith. You see the pattern, in the steel? That is his signature. This was a gift from my mentor." Jens remembered Wan, the captain of the *Sunrise Blossom*, who currently lived in comfortable retirement on an equatorial island on Pemako. Jens sheathed the blade.

"But I live on Ruanae now," Jens said. "And all I want to do is go home. And that's what we're going to do."

"Yes, Guardian," the navigator said.

Again, Jens noticed the Ruan's eyes; a tell, albeit discreet. "Believe it, Mertangle," Jens said. "We are going to stop the *Anarokt*, and then we are going to Step across space and go home. What are we going to do?" Jens asked again, as the image of the young crew of his first command flashed through his mind. Patricia was right. The tall Ruan standing before him was not so different.

"We are going home," Mrtangl answered.

"Good," Jens said. "Now I will let you resume your work."

The navigator clasped his forearm and bowed. "I am secure in your presence," he said.

Jens caught Patricia smiling at him, and he nodded to her before walking across the bridge to a Ruan at another station.

Powerful thrusters fired from the side of the third and fifth discs, and the tail of the *Anarokt* began to tilt. The only way Jens could tell something was happening to the ship was the image on the view screen. The Ruan around him stared intently at their monitors, some making slight movements with their hands as they scrolled through data. As he watched the ship lift, he felt himself tilt slightly to his left as his mind tried to balance what he saw and what he felt. He felt nothing. The artificial gravity of the disc maintained an up and down regardless of where the ship might be pointing.

A burst of light fired out of a single thruster on the third disc, making a correction to an unfelt error. Jens placed a hand on a nearby console to give his mind the illusion of stability. After an hour the ship was midway through its Flip, looking to the drone sending pictures from outside as if it was balancing on the tip of the cone. The *Chōgenbō* stuck to the ship like a tick on a dog. Olsen would have to turn off the gravity on his ship or they would be standing on a wall. Their technology was far behind the Ruan's in many areas. Thrusters from the opposite side of the two discs fired, slowing the turn. The precision and power were awe inspiring. Small corrections were made with thrusts from other parts of the discs, but after another hour the *Anarokt* was on the same plane as when the flip started, only facing the opposite direction.

The Ruan began to step back from their consoles. Screens flickered and disappeared. Jens stood, hands behind his back, waiting. The Controller would come to him.

"The manoeuvre is complete," he said. "Reactors report readiness for thrust."

Jens breathed slowly several times, wondering about the cause of his sudden anxiety. All that was left was cocooning in the cryo-pods and initiating a thrust of fourteen g's from reactors that had not fired in hundreds of years. He placed a hand gently against his chest and felt his breath go in, and then out, forcing a calmness to return.

"I am impressed," he said with absolute sincerity.

"With your permission, Guardian," Gruajunt said. "May we speak?"

Jens studied the Ruan's face but gave up trying to read it. He looked him in the eye when he answered, but still drew a blank. "Certainly."

"The female, Lynn, has told me you live on Ruanae."

"Yes," Jens answered, "only we call it Pemako. The name of a mythical land on Earth. A promised land."

"She has told me you live on a southern island."

"That's right. I live on a long island with a mountain range running down its spine," Jens agreed. "But it isn't islands you wish to speak to me about." And there it was, in the Ruan's eyes, an emotion Jens thought he understood.

"May we use the ready room?"

Jens nodded, adding, "Yes," when he remembered that the Ruan found human faces equally mysterious and unreadable. He followed Gruajunt to a room off the bridge, chairs around a central table, all fixed to the deck. Jens sat in one, feeling like a child on a grown-up's chair, his feet not reaching the floor. The Ruan sat opposite. He ran a hand over the table top in front of him and a screen materialized. He turned his hand and the screen swivelled so both could see the image, the *Anarokt* seemingly at rest, but still moving at incredible speed, readying for Decel.

"You did not have to come," Gruajunt said. "And yet you did."

"I didn't think so at first," Jens admitted. "But no, we had to. Once we knew you were out here." He tried to maintain eye contact, but the Ruan turned to the screen.

"She is a magnificent vessel," he said.

"She is magnificent."

"A tremendous prize," Gruajunt added.

Jens didn't answer, his silence making the Ruan turn his face towards him.

"I have been watching your people. They appear very interested in what we carry," Gruajunt said. Jens waited. What the Ruan wanted to say or ask wasn't coming easy. He wasn't going to make it easier.

"Counting," Gruajunt added. "I do not know how this word should translate."

"Inventory," Jens said. "That is the word. They are taking inventory of the technology you possess. For Dr Lin, Dr Taylor, and myself, we came for you. The others, and even the *Chōgenbō* itself, was built on the promise of what your ship might contain."

"The *Anarokt* contains my people," Gruajunt said.

"And they will be going home," Jens said.

"Where they will die without your medicines."

"We will manufacture the immunizations they will need," Jens said.

"You have everything," Gruajunt said. "Our planet. Our lives."

"Your people will be safe," Jens said. "They will return to

their home islands, and we will live together. That is my word. As you expect from a Guardian, and my people expect from a promise."

"Your engineers have no doubt told you that the *Anarokt* is designed for one purpose," Gruajunt said. He stared at Jens, unblinking. "To find a habitable planet, and to decelerate at that planet. The reactors then become something else. A power source for a new colony. They are not designed to fly again."

He waved a hand over the table and a schematic hologram appeared. It showed empty space.

"This is where Decel will bring us," he said towards the image. His hand glowed as it entered the light of the projection. He snapped his fingers and the image disappeared.

"There is nothing there," he said.

"There will be," Jens said. "The Donut will rendezvous, and it will take us all home."

Gruajunt studied Jens' face, but the Ruan did not know how to read human expressions. What he saw was enough. "I am secure in your presence," he finally said.

Jens sensed the 'but' that the Ruan would not say.

"You will be secure," Jens said. "We can make sure of that together."

Donna's eyes snapped open as the stimulant streamed into her blood stream. She wanted to react quickly, so she had upped the dose she received upon waking. The protective foam retracted excruciatingly slowly to her amped-up mind. She saw the lid of her cryo-pod emerging, exhaled as she saw it was opening, first a crack, and then fully. As soon as her arm could, she reached up into the empty space, as if crawling out of a grave. In a very real way, she was. Sixteen months of chemically induced hibernation and a nagging fear in the back of her mind that she never would wake.

She breathed in a lungful of processed air and lifted herself to a sitting position. The cryo-pods around her were still closed, just as she had programmed them. She leaned over the edge of the pod and swung a leg over, followed by the other. She looked at the vision on the screen on the chamber wall for balance. The disc filled the image, the view up the massive structure making her feel like she was falling. She shifted her gaze to a cryo-pod to maintain balance. Olsen's pod was set to open in minutes and she could see the timer counting down. Stumbling forward, she slapped at her thighs, trying to encourage some feeling. She reached for her med bag, encased in its own protective foam container.

By the time she grabbed it, the lid on Olsen's cryo-pod popped its seal with an audible hiss. She stood on shaky legs, ready to help it open, but it slid effortlessly to the side and folded out of the way. His vitals read fine, and as soon as flesh appeared from beneath the retracting foam, she injected stimulants. His eyes opened, pupils dilating as he focused on her face. He struggled in the remaining foam.

"It will finish retracting in a moment," she said.

"Report," he responded.

"We're still on the *Anarokt*," she said.

"Are we stopped?"

"That's all I know, sir," she answered. "I can contact the Ruan."

"Tend to your own people first," Olsen said. "Why can't I move my arm? Help me get out of this coffin."

Donna lifted him by the arm he offered. The other hung limply from the shoulder. He grabbed her roughly as his legs threatened to buckle, but he managed to stand. The grimace on his face told her he was angrier at his own unsteadiness, rather than in any real pain, and he shook his head when she reached for some meds.

"Just pin this thing to me so it won't get in the way," he said, lifting his shoulder to her and making the arm swing forward. She took his sleeve at the cuff and pinned it to his shirt at a right angle. As soon as she finished, he walked to the control panel below the view screen and pulled up data.

"Kobarev and Mori," he said without turning. "Then Anders, Jens and Tsuji. The rest can wait for now."

She was already at the pilot's cryo-pod, the order of revival agreed before going under. Both Kobarev's and Mori's vitals read normal as their lids opened and slid to the side. While the foam encasing them retracted, she turned to the First Mate's cryo-pod and studied the panel. His heart rate was elevated and blood pressure high. She adjusted the pace of his waking, adding a GLR sedative to the mix. His vitals stopped climbing into hazardous territory. Returning to Kobarev and Mori, she administered stimulants.

Kobarev made a sound that was either groan or growl, or a combination of both, and pulled himself out his pod. He stood beside it, flexing his hands into fists before nodding to Donna and walking over to Olsen. Mori accepted the doctor's assistance, allowing her to check her limbs and ask questions, and administer pain meds. When the comms officer joined Olsen, he turned quickly and took the others to the bridge.

Donna administered stimulants to Jens and Tsuji, not essential to waking, but speeding the process. Once Olsen was satisfied the ship was where it was supposed to be, he ordered that the crew be awake and alert as soon as possible. She left the two men, once satisfied with their fitness, and returned to Middleton's pod. His heartbeat raced across the monitor, a quick succession of blips. She administered more sedative, not enough to put him back under, but enough to let him wake without sensation. A touch to the pod's monitor continued the process of revivification. The foam withdrew into the pod and she immediately saw the problem. Reaching into her bag she withdrew a tourniquet, wrapped it around his leg just above the knee and pulled it tight.

Jens came over at her shout. She had already shouldered her bag by the time he reached her.

"Pick him up and follow me," she said.

Jens looked at the man's leg, that was no more than a band of exposed meat, scooped him up and followed the doctor to the sickbay. After laying him gently on the examination couch Jens was gently pushed back by Donna. She picked at the fabric on Middleton's crushed leg with a pair of tweezers, but set the implement down when it took the flesh with it. She injected the area around his knee with antibiotics and anaesthetics, then placed an intravenous catheter against his arm, letting the needle seek the nearest vein and insert itself. Sedative immediately flooded the man's system while Donna wielded a surgical laser, cutting through flesh and bone and cauterizing his leg as she amputated.

"Grab that tray," she told Jens.

He held the platter while Donna laid the pulp of Middleton's lower leg on the clean surface. Aside from the toes at the end, it was unrecognizable as a human appendage.

"What the hell happened?" Jens asked.

"A foam malfunction," she said. "A small portion of it, lucky for him. But I have no idea why. Too long under too many g's, maybe. He'll be sleeping comfortably for a while now. Let's go check the others so I can get back here." She placed a hand on Middleton's forehead like a mother checking her child's temperature, then scanned his vitals again.

"Doc?" Jens said.

Donna turned and led Jens out of the sickbay, back to the cryo-pods, using the hand holds on the bulkhead to steady herself on her numb feet. At Tsuji's pod she checked the readings and confirmed all were normal before activating the waking sequence. Once initiated, she turned to the rest of the security team. She paused at Koos Rupert's pod.

"What do those colors mean?" Jens asked.

"Nothing good," Donna answered. "We leave this one closed," she added, turning to de Werk's and starting the procedure to revive the man. She then moved to Patricia's pod, whose medical background was sorely needed, before turning to the xeno-linguist, the engineer and the technicians.

Mori interrupted the two men on the bridge as they stared at the disc looming above them, Jens with his hands clasped behind his back and Olsen looking like a disheveled Napoleon Bonaparte with his numbed hand pinned to his chest.

"Captain, I'm reading a lot of action in the disc. In all the discs."

"What kind of action?" Olsen asked.

"Power surges," she answered. "And a lot of movement."

"What does that mean?"

"Life forms," Mori said. "Lots of life forms. And increased power in all areas of the discs."

"All?'

"Sorry. Discs One, Two, Three and Five," she said. "Disc Four is still inert."

"They're waking all the Ruan," Jens said.

"Did you know about this?"

"Not at all," Jens said. "We worked through the plan for Step, as well as the dangers of infection."

"They don't seem too worried about that," Olsen said. "Get me Gruajunt, please, Ms Mori. On the screen."

The view of the disc turned dark, quickly replaced by the Seed ship Controller. Ruan could be seen moving behind him, faces Jens was unfamiliar with. Olsen nodded to the controller, and then turned to look at Jens.

"Controller Gruajunt," Jens said. "I am happy to see you. Our position is exactly as computed by navigator Mertangl. Please pass on my compliments."

"I will, Guardian," Gruanjunt replied. "He will be honored by your words."

"We have processed the messages received from the Donut once Decel was completed," Jens said. "They have confirmed that they received the coordinates plotted by navigator Mertangl and they will arrive in a short time."

The Ruan stared into the screen, waiting for Jens to continue. Jens watched his eyes but learned nothing.

"We have had one cryo-pod failure during Decel," Jens said. Olsen shot him a glance, which he ignored. "Are your people recovering well from the maneuver?"

"We have had no mishaps, and all are responding well to revivification."

"I am relieved to hear that," Jens responded. "May I join you on board the *Anarokt* to advise during the coming Step?" he asked.

The Ruan clasped a hand over his forearm and bowed

slightly. "Certainly, Guardian," he said. "We will be secure in your presence."

"Thank you, Controller," Jens said, and Mori cut the link.

"What the hell was that about?" Olsen asked.

"I'm not sure."

"Why didn't you ask about the revivifications?"

"It didn't seem ambassadorial," Jens said. "I'll tell you what's happening when I get over there. I'll take Drs Lin and Taylor with me. Extra eyes and insight."

"They've chosen to trust us, but they have very little to base that trust on," he added after a moment's reflection. "I am aware that is a two-way process."

"The *Chōgenbō* is like a fly on a horse with that ship fully activated," Olsen murmured. "I wonder if it has a tail that can just flick us away."

"My thought exactly," Jens agreed.

The three sat in silence as Taylor piloted the tori to the disc. As the energy field was deploying Jens felt like some words were needed. He looked over at his old friend sitting next to him, picturing Patricia as a younger woman, secluding herself in the Artifact that sat in a docking bay on the Donut during the voyage back to Earth from Pemako. She didn't seem to care about the planet, or the settlers who claimed it. Her focus was singularly on the Artifact and the Ruan corpses preserved in the alien cryo-pods. As the months passed, she had come to see Jens as an ally, as well as a friend, and Jens had come to see her less as his most obdurate crew member, and biggest pain in his ass, to much the same.

He had also come to see her growing obsession as her way out of the life she thought she was condemned to. She had guarded her past, but all colonists had records, and as the captain of the *General Xing* he had access to relevant data files. Her file was limited but told her story. A doctor in the southeast China economic zone controlled by a powerful consortium, she had been charged with malpractice, had her medical license revoked and was sentenced to twenty years hard labor. The way the 'option' of transport to a distant mining colony had been offered as an alternative was enough to tell Jens more was at play. By the time they returned to Earth she was the leading expert on the only known sentient life form discovered by humanity, feted and fought over by every major university. She had basked in the role, but also found time to settle old scores. Several Consortium executives disappeared from the record after information had been leaked regarding the use of illegal chemicals in production factories near Lin's practice.

Jens smiled at her. She never blew a whistle after being sent off Earth, but she whispered powerfully. He opened his mouth, then closed it, at a loss as to what to say. They stepped out of the craft, through the deployed forcefield and through the airlock leading into the disc. The noise that greeted them was followed by a cascading silence as Ruan nearby stopped what they were doing and watched the three humans. Many clasped a hand to a forearm and bowed as they acknowledged Jens. He touched the bud in his ear.

"Looks like they're unpacking," he said.

"Not everything," Patricia answered. "That's a manufacturing printer there. Medical supplies. Clothes and food."

They walked up the ramp to the cryo-pod deck, each Ruan they passed stopping and showing their respect to the human Guardian. Jens paused at the entrance to the deck and scanned the hundreds of Ruan filling the space. The noise diminished as more and more noticed the humans and stopped what they were doing, moving aside to form a pathway across the deck.

"Let me hear you too, Peter," Jens said. "Check your comms."

Peter touched his ear bud. "How's this?"

"Good. Report what you see. This is for Olsen, too."

"Will do," Peter said. "I'd like to try communicating with the Ruan without the device."

"It looks like you'll get lots of opportunity," Jens said. "Just leave this link on."

They were interrupted by a tall, familiar, Ruan accompanied by two shorter ones. They stopped in front of the humans; the taller of them placed a hand on her forearm and bowed. The two shorter ones watched and copied their mother. She tilted her head at her brood.

"I am secure in your presence," they said together, staring at the knife strapped to his leg.

"As is my duty," Jens replied to them. "Tell me, young ones, what are your names?"

"Tell the Guardian your names," Arnil translated.

Their eyes were easy to read: surprise and awe.

"Rentg," said one, timidly raising her eyes to Jens' face.

"Rengt," Jens repeated. "I am pleased to meet you. And what is your name, my young crewmate?"

Jens let Arnil translate and thought he saw the youngling blush, if it was possible to do so with eyes. "Kol," she whispered.

"Kol. A fine name," Jens said to her, as well as to the audience forming around them. "I am glad you have joined us. That so many of your crewmates have joined us," he added, looking at Arnil.

"Cryo-sleep ceases when the ship ceases, Guardian," Arnil said.

"And this was known before we decelerated?" he asked. Jens felt a light touch on his arm and let Patricia move forward.

"Arnil, it is good to see you," she said. "But is it safe? They are not immune."

"Greetings, Lynn. We are replicating the anti-virals you have given me," Arnil said. "They will be distributed to the other discs when there is enough."

"Arnil," Jens said. "I must speak with the Controller to prepare for Step."

"Certainly, Guardian," she said. "I will summon a guide."

Jens bent to the young ones. "I have a crewmate who would like to speak your language," he said, pausing to let Arnil translate. "His name is Peter. Can you say that?"

"Pee-tair," they repeated.

"Good. Very good." Jens turned to Taylor and grinned. "Play nice," he said.

"I'd like to stay also," Patricia said. "To look at their replicators."

"Yes," Jens said, tapping his ear bud. "I'd love to hear about it," he said.

A Ruan approached and stopped in front of Jens, standing a half meter over him. He wore a belt around his waist, from which hung what he guessed was a weapon. He clenched his jaw and felt his knees soften for balance. His arms slowly went to side, his right hand closer to his blade. The Ruan placed a hand on his forearm, made a pentagon in front of his chest and slightly bowed.

"I am secure in your presence," he said.

Jens copied the movements and the speed, slowly placing his hand on his forearm and bowing without losing eye contact. "And I am secure in your presence," he said. Arnil translated, and the Ruan lowered his hands.

"If you will," he said, turning and walking away.

Jens stepped into the bridge of the cone and the crew momentarily stopped what they were doing, to clasp their forearms and bow at the two Guardians, before turning back to their consoles. He watched Gruajunt say something to a crewman nearby before walking to where Jens waited. Jens couldn't recall waiting on his last visit. There was a difference on board, not just in numbers, but in the feel of the place, a tangible sense of purpose and confidence. Gruajunt covered his forearm and bowed quickly.

"Guardian, welcome to the bridge," he said.

Jens saw he was wearing the translator device Taylor had

fitted for him. "Thank you, Gruajunt. The *Anarokt* has performed admirably," he said.

"Yes," the controller agreed. "The ship has ceased motion."

Jens waited for any mention of Rupert, or his death, a human show of etiquette, but death was all the Ruan knew before fleeing their planet, and they had much to learn about each other. Did one death merit mention in Ruan culture?

"If you will," Gruajunt indicated his panel and the large screen in front of it. It was filled with a splash of stars and the inky black of space.

"Olsen has notified me that the device will appear soon," Gruajunt said. "Out of thin space," he added, with a hint of disbelief. "What are we to expect of this appearance?"

"I don't know," Jens admitted. "I've never seen it happen. I have always been on one."

"Would you like refreshment while we wait?" Gruajunt asked.

"Yes, please," Jens answered.

Gruajunt raised a hand and moments later a Ruan Jens had not seen before Decel brought a tray with cups on it. Jens took the large vessel in both hands and sniffed.

"It is from a leaf on Ruanae," Gruajunt said. "A popular drink."

"Tea," Jens said, nodding. "Thank you. You will have to show me the plant from which it is brewed."

The Ruan looked at Jens, but did not reply. He took a sip of his tea, holding the cup comfortably in one hand.

"It will happen," Jens said. "We will all be home soon.

The Donut will arrive at the coordinates Mertangl has transmitted."

The wait wasn't long. As soon as sensors detected an anomaly, the Ruan with the tray appeared to take the half-empty cups, and the crew became more transfixed on their panels. The image of deep space on the view screen became blurred from the center out to the edges, a spreading haze growing until the stars were indistinguishable from the black around them. A dark pinch formed in the middle and seemed to pull away, as if two fingers gripped a fold of space. Suddenly, it stretched away violently and jerked back.

And then the Donut was there, blotting out all else. The massive disc filled the entire screen. The Ruan on the bridge gasped.

Jens shouted and pumped his fist. "Hah! There she is! There she is!" He lifted a hand to slap Gruajunt on the back but caught himself and tried to act in the Guardian role he was assigned. He grinned and shook his head.

"Mertangl!" he called. "Your calculations were spectacular!"

The Ruan navigator tilted his head as he looked at Jens, unsure of the proper way to respond to the outburst.

"And our astrogator, oh our astrogator," Jens said. "Unbelievable!" He cupped his ear to hear a message from Mori and smiled.

Most of the crew on the bridge ignored his outburst, standing mesmerized by the apparition before them, but Gruajunt turned away from the screen to face him. "This is the device that will take us across space?"

"Yes," Jens said. "Would you like to see it? To visit? You have been invited. It is a rare privilege. Perhaps Mertangl would like to join us?"

After a minute of silence, Gruajunt bowed slightly, his earlier distrust or disbelief seeming to evaporate. He motioned to Mrtangl and the two followed Jens back to the disc. As they walked, Jens turned off his translator and spoke to Taylor and Lin. "Our long-lost friends have arrived. They would like you to visit and meet our newest crewmate."

"What does that mean?" Lin responded.

"I think it means they didn't sleep through the long wait," Jens answered. "We're heading your way. Report back to Olsen if you haven't done so yet."

As the tori covered the distance to the Donut, Peter spoke to Michael over the comms, leaving the translator on so the Ruan could understand. He doubted that they were able to follow much of the story. Rather than sleep in cryo-pods programmed to revive them when a message carrying coordinates arrived, they decided to make the most of their time. That made sense—two people in love. The last thing they would want to do is go bed to sleep. There were ample supplies on board, enough to last the fifteen months it took for the *Anarokt* to Decel. The result of that, though, was a bouncing baby girl.

Peter landed his tori next to the airlock, pleased to see the other tori already there. Tsuji waited by the elevator to escort them to the Hole, where de Werk already waited. Their weapons were worn discreetly, unseen by the untrained eye.

Although their guests were unarmed, Jens noted Olsen's precautions, suspecting they were, at least partly, for him. Olsen was aware that the last Ruan to enter a Donut were also unarmed, and that had not prevented a great deal of violence. Jens examined himself and realized a feeling was missing. Absent was the anxiety he felt around both Donuts and Ruan. He wondered if he would feel the same had the Ruan Guardian felt it proper to accompany them.

Anna and Michael stood mutely in greeting as the lift doors opened and the party stepped out. They both stared up at Gruajunt and Mrtangl, mouths open. Dr Lin broke the silence.

"Don't just stand there," she said, in her typical impatient tone. "Let me see this baby!"

Anna handed her daughter to the older woman, as Jens managed introductions and Peter gave the new parents translator devices. Michael led the tour of the Hole, discussed the quantum computer, the physics of warping time and space, and the giant talons Kobarev would use to fix the *Anarokt* to the Donut so that they could make their home.

There was no way to prepare the Ruan for Step. Before he left the Seed ship, Jens tried to explain, and left them with the assurance that any unpleasant sensation would pass.

"You will feel yourselves stretching and warping," he tried. "As if your head and stomach want to remain in different parts of the galaxy." He stopped, remembering his first Step. He shrugged, smiling inwardly.

"You will be secure," he said.

Back on the *Chōgenbō*, Jens checked in on Middleton on his way to the bridge, and took the First Mate's chair when he arrived. Numbers counted down. The crew looked relaxed. Step after Step after Step in pursuit of the *Anarokt* had, if not immunized them to the sensation, at least numbed them. The Step home took on a feel of its own, just like returning to port after weeks at sea when he was a young man working on the scow. Soon he would feel the sun, enjoy a beer, sit next to Fran in old chairs and watch the sea from the front porch.

The numbers continued to get smaller. He looked at those around him. Kobarev and Peter at the helm with nothing to do as long as the ship was fixed to the *Anarokt*. As soon as Step was successful, though, they had to coordinate the

Donut's release of the Ruan ship with the detachment of the *Chōgenbō*. They would wait for the large disc to move away then blow the charges on the legs, leaving the fixed feet of the *Kestrel* on the cone where they had become fused during Decel. Mori had her eyes closed, listening to any communication within or between the ships. If she sent a message to Pemako now it would arrive over four hundred years after they arrived. Olsen nodded when Jens caught his eye.

The numbers continued their downward count. As they neared zero, Jens stopped any pretence of nonchalance. He clenched his jaw, gripped the arm rests, and waited. When the count ended, the view screen seemed to pull away from him, taking a part of his eyes with it. Black formed around the edges, a darkness that crept to the center of his vision. He felt his waist grow heavy until it began to sink into his chair. His head moved in the opposite direction; the darkness spread until it was all Jens could experience.

Gruajunt magnified the view screen and gazed at the blue planet speckled with green. His head still ached and his stomach continued to feel like it wanted to empty itself. He ignored the feelings and focussed on the world below. He increased magnification until an archipelago filled the screen. There, in the top corner, was home. Or what used to be home. The humans told him almost two thousand years had passed while the *Anarokt* fled through space in search of a sanctuary. If what they said was true, and their own data confirmed it, there was nothing left of what he had known on the island below—the ancestral dwelling, comfort of the hearth, the warm welcome from brood and mate.

Ruins, the one with the hairy face said, with no apparent understanding of the magnitude of that word, or of the pain it inflicted. The human was excited about his research in those ruins, places he described while explaining the route of these strange beings to the location of the *Anarokt*. Gruajunt couldn't tell him the Ruan names for the great cities the human described. He spoke about diggings, about ... Gruajunt pushed the conversation from his mind. They were the names of ghosts. They were dying when the ship was leaving. Why was it so hard to face now, looking at them from on high? He had assumed control of a disc with the hope of starting over on a new planet. Now he faced starting over on his home world and the task seemed even more daunting. Perhaps he could restart the family trade in cetaceans, hunting the behemoths in the open seas. The humans told him they are plentiful once again. Or he could develop a land empire, investigate this mammal the Guardian called cat-tal. A four-legged animal producing meat, with skin one could wear or even make a chair of. Gruajunt smiled at the idea. It was appealing. But he pushed these thoughts aside. There was no place for them in the now. And he strongly suspected them fanciful in their thinking. He doubted he would ever be able to cast aside this new role.

Everything was happening quickly.

He returned the screen to actual view and the planet returned to the size of a *ftintl*. There was work to do. The human ship detached from the cone, a part of the *Anarokt* now rendered superfluous. It had unified the five discs into one massive ship for a journey to the stars. The journey was over, exactly where it started.

He watched as the distance between the *Chōgenbō* and the *Anarokt* increased. The humans appeared proud of their ship. The one called Olsen seemed pleased to have the opportunity to show it off during his one visit to the craft. To the Ruan's eye it was another example of technology adapted from a superior source, and inferior because of it. But looking at the planet below, there was nothing superior on display for the humans to see. Only ruins. The human technology seemed lacking in many areas, rudimentary and practically primitive, but folding space and time in order to travel was ingenious, if uncomfortable. Whatever Gruajunt might have thought of the frail species leading his people back home, they had managed to not only travel great distances through space, they had vanquished the foe that reduced a once-mighty race to a handful of refugees.

The human Guardian was due to visit soon, to play his role of intermediary between peoples. Such is the business of Guardians, although Gruajunt suspected most of what this human did was play acting. So be it. They were all acting in some capacity. Gruajunt was a mere controller, tasked with managing a single disc in a desperate exodus. Now he was the leader of his people, asking permission—yes, that is what it felt like—to reside in their own homes. He did not know what to make of that feeling, so he filed it away for later processing. The human, Jensen, described the island he called home, the name he gave it, Pou-nah-moo. Gruajunt knew of the place, and its actual name. But he did not inform the human, as such behavior was unbecoming in the parts they were playing.

It was time for another act, a display of ... Gruajunt wasn't sure, he would decide later. The world was watching, and as Jensen informed him that a feed of the event would Step to their home planet, two worlds would be watching. Pride. It was a display of pride, Gruajunt thought, but added to it: it was politic. They were still a proud people, yes, but they had little with which to negotiate with these strange beings. He was aware that two of the humans had recorded as much data as they could. He had a good list of everything they accessed, as well as everything they could not. There was still a lot they did not know about the ship, its operating capacity, and what was within it. Let them see something of Ruan prowess, feed for both worlds.

"Initiate separation," he ordered.

"Yes, Controller," he was answered. "Separation is initiated."

Gruajunt felt nothing as the maneuver took place, just as it was designed. The cone slowly detached from the first disc. as each disc simultaneously detached from each other. Thrusters rotated the discs until they all lay parallel. The movement was smooth and graceful. Only the fourth disc remained in the vertical, its power source still inert. As expected, the human Guardian tried to make contact as soon as separation commenced. Gruajunt fought the reflex to respond immediately. If a Guardian requested response, response was given, not withheld. But there were no Guardians in this world. Those that travelled on the *Anarokt* were in disc four. The crewman who greeted Jensen after the awakening of all Ruan was just like he felt right now—an actor playing a part. The last Guardians he had seen were long gone, a rear guard on a dying world, trying to maintain some semblance of order among the panic and death. At the time that he and the *Anarokt* had departed Ruanae, chaos was taking the upper hand.

Jens stepped onto the bridge of the disc with Drs Lin, Taylor and Hollis. Olsen handed Jens the envelope before leaving, the cryptic secret turning out to be merely instructions by HakKor headquarters, a script for such an event. There were several scenarios pre-prepared, each with their particular spin—failure to find anything (a brilliant display of HakKor ingenuity and altruism), finding a derelict ship with long dead aliens on board (a brilliant display of HakKor ingenuity and altruism). Both were thinly veiled marketing exercises, ready to exploit either the technology they had already created, or what they had just found. The script he was to follow was the scenario few outside the three with him actually expected—first contact between sentient species. It was actually a second contact, but Jens didn't belabor the point.

His role was brief—announce their arrival, introduce the scientists so they can describe their part in the journey up to the present, and then introduce the representative of the surviving Ruan. He saw that in each scenario his name was beside Lin's, Taylor's and Hollis's—and he was certain that the scripts were written well before he was approached by Taylor, or Patricia, about coming. He was meant to be a part of it, expected from the moment HakKor agreed to finance it, from the moment he had asked his godfather for one more favor.

Jens straightened his uniform, a jacket Olsen had kept stowed, with crisp edges and epaulets on the shoulder. An image of a kestrel represented the *Chōgenbō,* with the name, as well as that of the consortium, proudly displayed. Gruajunt waited by the view screen, in a uniform obviously designed for the occasion. Its wide shoulders tapered to sharp points, and were Jens a taller man, could potentially put an eye out. Gruajunt placed a hand on his forearm, forming a pentagon at chest height, and bowed slightly.

"I am secure in your presence," he greeted Jens.

"Thank you, Controller," Jens replied. "Are we ready to begin?"

"The communications links have been joined," Gruajunt said.

"Great," Jens said. "A bit of a ceremony, and then we can breathe some fresh sea air."

"I look forward to it," Gruajunt said.

"Well, let's get this done," Jens said. "Time to talk to a planet. Let me know when we're live."

Gruajunt tilted his head to the screen and it filled with the scene outside, a blue world speckled with green islands. Jens took a deep breath before beginning. He would stay on script for the occasion, except for the first line, and a wink for his granddaughter, Jiao.

"Greetings, people of Pemako," he began, pausing for the wink. "My name," he continued, "is Andrew Jensen, and I stand before you as Ambassador at the behest of HakKor consortium, to represent the Originals, the Ruan of the planet Ruanae, who have returned to their homeworld from the depths of space …"

Epilogue: Second Seed

Laant watched the planet below, the blue of the wide oceans speckled with greens and browns of the many archipelagos. A gossamer veil of white clouds passed over the scene. He studied the southern hemisphere. Home. It looked peaceful from the bridge of the orbiting ship; an idyllic scene painted on the viewscreen. The warm blue waters brought back memories of morning swims, of sails with his older brother before being chosen. Those early times etched so strongly into the synapses of memory. He could not lose them even if he wanted. He should forget, he knew, but he kept the memories safe, like a prisoner with a hidden jewel that the guards would never find.

Soft sand between his toes. He was not supposed to crave pleasure. But soft sand between his toes, a warm sun on his naked flesh ... Laant breathed out a laugh, a mere snort of air from his nostrils that nobody noticed. He was the guard now. Guarding secret memories, guarding his people. What was left of them. Maybe if he was able to fully complete his training, he could purge such thoughts, such cravings or aversions. To be a Guardian was to be above the common concerns of the people. It was to be responsible for the people, for the continuance of culture, to guard against threats both external and internal. His training was cut short by circumstance, which meant he had to continue by training himself.

Laant knew that the planet below was only peaceful, or *idyllic*, from a distance. Part of the northern hemisphere lay in shadow. The islands below absorbed the darkness, becoming an inseparable part of the blackness. All the cities slept so deeply that no dawn would ever waken them. No light escaped the night that would soon spread over the entire world. Laant pursed his lips. There was no place for hyperbole in his thinking. Not anymore. He must practice precision of thought and action.

He closed his eyes and heard the panicked shouting, the desperate pleas, the gunfire that he so recently left below. He was meant to feel compassion for the people, to show only strength, to *be* only strength. They were supposed to feel secure in his presence. He was ashamed that he felt fear instead. He wanted to run as far away from them as he could. In the end they all did, those of his cohort that survived.

"Ensign!"

He was drifting, his mind wandering, and he was on duty. He could not afford distraction. Laant blinked and sat up in his chair. It took a moment for him to realise that the Controller was addressing him. He was not yet used to the new rank. Only recently he was a mere cadet. Promotions happened quickly these days. There were many vacancies to fill, many that would never be filled. The controller himself was new to the role, never meant to lead this ship. These ships were designed to seed the Ruan seed in the far stars. The Seed

Ship *Anarokt* had already departed, not taking the chosen few to find and build a new world as originally designed, but evacuating refugees from a dying a planet, the grand ship nothing but a lifeboat.

Laant looked at the other crew on the bridge, Guardians he just met. Were they hiding inner turmoil like himself? The astrogator, sitting in front of his terminal, avoiding eye contact as he finalised the course. The second controller, looking too young for the role he was thrust into, his chin firmly jutting outward in a false display of confidence. Systems specialists, checking life support and cryo-chamber efficacy. Communications with the five discs making up the body of the massive ship. The engineer, operating the reactors that would take the ship to another star, and another planet they could call home. Was the moistness from his eye emotion escaping down the side of his face?

He tried not to speculate too deeply on where the original crew were. Were they *merendt*? Laant corrected his thought, to show respect for the dead and dying in the northern hemisphere. They were all Ruan, like himself, and deserved his honour and service, wherever they may have originated. A *merendt* was an animal, domesticated to bring pleasure and comfort, kept in the houses of the northers, treated almost as Ruan. What else did they call their northern ken? *Fonnen*. Soft. Southers thought the northers soft. Domesticated, like their pets. They used the term derogatorily. Now, there were no longer northers or southers, there were only survivors. The disease that began in the north spread throughout the entire planet. None were safe where it touched. None survived the pandemic. Whoever it infected died. They could find no cure, no origin, no pattern. All that was certain was the death in its wake as it travelled in the winds that swirled and followed the great currents of the oceans.

Maybe the original crew were still alive, locked down in the Sky City. Laant had a momentary glimpse of what it might be like in the once glorious structure. He pushed the image out of his mind and repeated a mantra for those trapped inside, sealed remotely from the surface when the contagion arrived. All escape pods deactivated, all shuttles disabled, all docking bays sealed. Those on the city were no doubt trying to override the safety measure and escape without triggering fail safes. There had been no explosions from the complex, nor exiting craft. They may still be trying. Or they may all be dead.

Laant looked at the structure. Next to the ship he was in, it was considered the greatest triumph of Ruan technology. Except what he saw was an empty and dead shell. Once they leave, how long will it continue to orbit the dead planet below? He could do the mathematics. Laant enjoyed calculations. The life of the power cells, the absence of replenishment or maintenance, the speed and height of orbit. A quick assessment gave him a figure of four hundred to five hundred years before it fell into the atmosphere, a fiery comet that would be seen by none, finally disappearing beneath the waves. His people might leave ruins behind, for a time, at least, but not their greatest achievement.

"Ensign!" His mind was wandering again, seeking shelter from reality.

"Yes, Controller!" he responded.

"Identify that ship," the Controller said.

Laant passed a hand over the monitor in front of him and examined the readings. A ship had just left the atmosphere. He opened his hand and the image grew larger. He could faintly see the thrust of the approaching ship. He opened his hand again and it grew still larger. He computed its flight from a southern island and on a course directly towards their ship. As soon as his sensor targeted the ship, its identification beacon grew dark.

"It has ghosted, Controller," Laant reported.

"Establish contact, Ensign."

Laant opened radio contact. "You are approaching the Seed Ship *Knrarokt* on an unauthorised flight plan," he said. "Identify yourself and state your intention."

In response, the light from the ship's reactor increased.

"They are increasing thrust, Controller," Laant said without turning away from the monitor.

"Establish contact, Ensign," he responded. "Let them know what will happen if they fail."

Laant swallowed. "Unidentified ship, state your intention or we will be forced to fire upon you." He looked at the controller, who nodded and gestured at the monitor, an order to repeat the message.

"I repeat, we will be forced to fire upon you if you fail to reply."

"Now target weapons, Ensign," the controller said. "Ready the plasma canon."

Laant did as he was told. As soon as weapons were locked on the approaching target, their identification beacon flickered briefly, only to go dark and remain that way. He locked the plasma canon on the target once the weapon signalled its preparedness. The Controller nodded, issuing a silent order that Laant understood. He raised his first finger in front of the computer monitor and bent the middle knuckle, making it point downward. The plasma canon shot a flash of molten light that crossed in front of it's nose cone.

The other ship's radio came to life, and Laant and all those on the bridge with him listened to a struggle playing out on the approaching ship. Muffled shouts, the crash of equipment, finally the report of a weapon, and a voice emerging from the sudden silence.

"*Knrarokt*! *Knrarokt*! Our identifying beacon is disabled. Please do not shoot! Guardian, we are secure in your presence!"

"Identify yourself, reduce acceleration, and alter your course," Laant said. His eyes went to the controller, who nodded approvingly.

"This is the transport freighter *Strade*. We have a cargo of two hundred passengers from the uninfected island of Ruboaen. We seek refuge, please, Guardian." The speaker was cut short by the sound of glass shattering. Another report from a weapon brought silence.

The light from the ship's reactor dimmed, but its course did not falter.

"What is happening, *Strade*?" Laant asked.

A voice different from the first responded. "We have subdued a disturbance on the bridge, but are now in control. We ask for refuge, Guardian. We are in need."

If asked for refuge, a Guardian was to provide it, even if it led to their death. This every Guardian was taught, from their first days as cadet. But the *Knrarokt* was sealed, as was the fate of all those left behind.

"We can offer no succour," the controller said, to himself, to Laant, to all those on the bridge.

"*Strade*, deviate your present course as requested," Laant said.

"We cannot do that," the voice said. "There is nowhere for us to go. We need your assistance! We seek refuge! Our arrival time is—"

"Deviate your present course as requested," Laant repeated. "We are a closed destination." The controller's face was stone, devoid of emotion. Laant tried to copy it, to bury his fear.

"We cannot do that!" the voice responded. "There is no place to deviate to! Please, do not let us die! We are broods, only broods, children, women. Please, Guardian, we seek refuge."

"There can be no refuge on the *Knrarokt*," the controller said, looking at his crew. "We can risk no infection. Our purity must remain unthreatened."

"*Strade*, alter your course immediately," Laant said, the pleading in his voice unmissable.

"My name is Treelek," the voice said. "I have a wife. Her name is Sunil. We have a brood of four younglings. They are all here. Please, help us."

"Ensign, eliminate this threat to the *Knrarokt*," the controller ordered.

"Please," Laant said, opening begging this time. "Alter your course!"

"Ensign!" the controller shouted.

"Guardian! My name is Treelek! I request refuge for myself and my brood, for all the broods on board, for—"

Please, Laant shouted in his mind. *Please deviate!* But the *Strade* did not alter its course, approaching what it thought was its last chance for safety. Laant watched as his hand moved of its own accord. It passed lightly over the monitor and took control of weapons.

"—the sake of us all! We are secure in your presence! We are—"

The index finger of Laant's hand twitched, activating the plasma canon. A molten slug shot across the vacuum. The *Strade* exploded in a flash of light. The bridge of the *Knrarokt* was as silent as the space outside. Laant could feel the liquid emotion escape his eyes and run freely down his cheeks.

"Return to your duties," the controller said, each word forced, each word prying the crew from the moment that held them.

"Engineer," he said, louder. "Prepare reactors for acceleration."

"Yes, Controller," the engineer answered. The engineer manipulated his hands over his monitor, beginning activation sequences in the massive reactors located over two kilometres away at the stern of the vessel. In between were the five discs, each half a kilometre in diameter, filled with equipment and supplies for building a new world, and thousands of Ruan suspended in cryogenic sleep, for a voyage designed to take centuries. Acceleration would increase until the ship eventually travelled at fourteen gravities, enough force to turn any Ruan outside of a cryo-pod into a liquid mess.

"Secure your stations and report to cry-pods for acceleration," the controller said to the bridge crew.

"Ensign," he added. "Power down weapons."

"Yes, Controller," Laant heard himself answer.

One by one, bridge crew left their stations. Laant was among the last. He powered off his monitor, leaving ship's defenses to the AI that would be responsible for all of their lives as the ship crossed the great expanse. He stood and straightened his tunic. His eyes met the controllers, but they were unreadable. He could feel the gravity slowly increase as he lay in his cryo-pod. The ship was underway, leaving its orbit of their home world, the birthplace they would never see again. He felt a needle slide into his arm, and another probe between ribs until finding his liver. Chemicals were injected. He welcomed the darkness and oblivion that rushed upon him, felt comfort in the coldness spreading throughout his body, turning him into unfeeling ice.

There are no dreams in cryosleep, a small blessing. But the time taken to sink into the icy oblivion was enough. Laant knew dreams did not operate in linear time. A moment, no matter how brief, could contain a lifetime of image and story. As he felt his consciousness fade, he was also aware of others around him. His elder brother, guiding the small vessel across the waves, his eyes communicating joy and love. His mother sat nearby. That was not a true image. Despite being a youngling, he never remembered his mother joining them. And yet here she was. He smelled the sea, the freshly caught fish at the bottom of the boat, even the scent of his mother. That was how he knew, on some level, that he was dreaming. That awareness should have added control to his dreaming, but he was a helpless spectator, watching himself from someplace outside, and yet also from within. He looked at his hand, in this dream that felt so real. He watched as one finger was raised, his fore finger. He watched as he bent his finger at the knuckle. And he watched his brother and his mother burst into flames, the fire from their bodies spreading to the boat, running up the mast and sails, and covering his own body.

Laant wanted to scream, but no noise escaped his mouth. Instead, he sat in front of the Selector, in another dream, tasked with finding adept younglings to become future Guardians. The Selector held a prize in his palm, and it was Laant's task to grab and claim it. The Selector held the shiny bauble in his hand, palm up. Laant reached for it and had his grasping fingers slapped by the Selector's other hand. Laant tried again and received another slap. He tried to reach out quicker, only to receive a stronger slap. His finger's tingled and his hand throbbed. For the briefest of moments, or ages of eternity in the time measured in dreams, Laant the ensign sat before the Selector. Then, he was a mere youngling again, unaware that he would soon leave his brood and never see them again. He reached for the bauble, slowly this time, giggling, aware of the futility of trying. But this time the Selector did not strike. He held his open palm still and allowed Laant to take what he held. It was a finger. The Selector smiled.

Laant tried to feel warmth in the Selector's smile, but could only feel a creeping cold that originated form deep within, until nothing but darkness and ice remained.

Where the journey begins: *MisStep*

Jens needed to get off the planet in a hurry so he took the first job on an interstellar freighter he found—part of a convoy to a far-flung mining colony, three Steps and almost three thousand lightyears away. Only the desperate went so far—colonists willing to trade a life on Earth for a new start on a rock somewhere across the galaxy, or spacers one step ahead of the law.

But as each Step takes him farther from home, Jens learns that the job isn't exactly what he was told, the cargo not as legitimate, and his situation even more precarious. Jens finds himself being groomed for a role in an interplanetary drug racket, with no way out.

Then the convoy mis-Steps, emerging lightyears off course, and the miscalculation might not be their fault!

Climate fiction meets science fiction in this high-seas adventure:

Pirates Come Down
A Southern Ocean Saga

Fishing in the near future takes more than a net!

Rickets is a PAC-Man, his patrol and attack craft the first line of defence against encroaching vessels. Moss is a Fisheries Observer, tasked with ensuring companies abide by the quotas set on target species. Together they play a part in ensuring the waters are not fished to extinction.

But as fisheries elsewhere play out, New Zealand waters start to look more attractive until every ship protects itself with PAC boats, missiles that skim the surface, and kamikaze drones equipped with explosives.

Only there is a bigger shadow on the horizon, one that deflects all radar, is lethally armed, and takes what it wants!

To learn more about Christopher's books, visit him at:

www.christophermcmaster.com